LAST
ONE
TO
LIE

OTHER TITLES BY J.M. WINCHESTER

All the Lovely Pieces

LAST
ONE
TO
LIE

J.M. WINCHESTER

 THOMAS & MERCER

Published by Thomas & Mercer, Seattle

www.apub.com

Amazon, the Amazon logo, and Thomas & Mercer are trademarks of Amazon.com, Inc., or its affiliates.

ISBN-13: 9781542005838
ISBN-10: 1542005833

Cover design by Shasti O'Leary Soudant

Printed in the United States of America

To my son, Jacob:
thank you for wanting to read my "scary books"—
someday

And to my husband:
thank you for allowing me to steal your last name
for my thrillers

PART ONE

PART ONE

September 6—11:45 a.m.

Sixty minutes of yoga have only made me more anxious. Maybe I'm just not the type of person who can relax in a roomful of strangers.

"Let me guess—you're a new mom."

After punching in my locker's four-digit code, I glance at the tiny woman sporting a matching Lululemon outfit next to me. The coral trim along the sports bra and waistband of the leggings makes her tanned skin pop. She's obviously been on vacation. We haven't seen sun in Maryland in weeks—the summer consisted of several scattered days in July; then fall arrived early. "How'd you know?"

"The instructor barely had *Namaste* out of her mouth when you had your mat rolled up. No long Savasana for you." The woman takes a set of car keys from her own locker and shuts the door. "So either you only have limited time for the search for inner peace, which is *my* thing, or you're nervous about being out of touch for too long."

I laugh as I reach inside the locker for my phone.

No missed calls or messages. "It's silly, right? Class is an hour. I just wish they'd allow phones in the room. On silent."

"Expecting an emergency?"

Am I? "No. I just . . . we just moved here a few weeks ago. My husband and I and our two-year-old daughter. She's at a new day care." I tuck the cell phone into the pocket of my yoga pants and close the locker door.

"Ah . . . that explains it. There's nothing scarier than leaving your child with a stranger for the first time. See you next class," she says to me; then she waves to the girl at the check-in desk as she leaves the studio.

I gather my things and quickly shove my feet into my shoes. I walk the two blocks to the car and climb in after tossing the yoga mat into the back seat.

The empty car seat makes my chest tighten. A few hours is long enough. I'm going to go pick her up early.

I hit the phone feature on the console and reach for my seat belt. "Call Malcolm."

"Dialing Malcolm," the Bluetooth connection says.

I pull out into traffic and head south. "Shit. Wrong direction."

Four rings, then his voice mail.

"This is Malcolm Jennings. Leave me a message."

"Hey, honey . . . I'm just leaving yoga; thought I'd call to see how your day was going. I'm picking Mikayla up now. Let me know what time you'll be home for dinner." I pull a U-turn at the light. The next words stick in my throat. "I love you. See you soon."

After disconnecting the call, I turn up the volume on a high-tempo country music song and realize I do feel a little better after taking the yoga class. My chakras have definitely benefitted from the alignment. The move to Ellicott City has been a lot more stressful than I expected. Moving somewhere new is always challenging, but it's been a good challenge. I have to believe that. I am here now; my new path has been set in motion; I have to see it through and give it my best shot.

Malcolm's parents are here, so there's more family support, and it's important for Mikayla to get to know her grandparents. They are the only other family she has—my parents have been gone a long time now.

This new job of Malcolm's is definitely the right step for the family. In Florida, the opportunities for him were slim. Here, he will be principal of the high school in three years. Small towns like to support and promote their own, and Malcolm's family has done a lot for the community here . . . not that he needs his family name to get ahead.

I stop at the light and take in the quiet neighborhood. It's nice in this area of town. So different from the surroundings I grew up in. A family could live a peaceful, quiet life in a neighborhood like this. Build a real future and be happy.

Five minutes later, I pull into a parking spot on the street in front of Paradise Day Care. It's a two-story house that's been converted into a business, which makes it feel warm and inviting, unlike day cares located in schools or church basements. I like that it's only three blocks from the house and has great reviews on Yelp. After getting out, I jog toward the front door and try the handle.

Locked.

Good. Safe. That makes me feel better.

The babies might be napping, so I don't ring the doorbell. Instead, I knock and wait.

From inside, I hear children's music playing softly and the sound of little voices and tiny feet. This is good for Mikayla. She's an only child. Will forever be an only child. Socialization is important.

I knock again when no one answers and then peer through the window next to the door.

Finally, a young girl I've never seen before opens it. "Can I help you?"

"Hi . . . I'm here to pick up Mikayla. I know I'm early, but I wanted to see her, take her home," I say with a laugh. I can't be the only parent with separation anxiety.

The young girl frowns. "I'm sorry . . . who are you?"

"I'm Kelsey Jennings. My daughter, Mikayla, is here. There was another woman here this morning when I dropped her off." I look past her into the house. A row of toddlers sit in high chairs in the kitchen. Small, colorful plastic bowls on the trays in front of them. Tiny hands shove food into their mouths, and messy faces turn to look my way.

"And you say your daughter's name is Mikayla?" the girl asks. She looks confused, and my pulse quickens.

"Yes. Mikayla Jennings." I don't see her in one of the high chairs.

"I think you might be in the wrong place," she says.

"Can I come in?"

"Um . . . we have a strict policy not to let anyone inside . . ."

She tries to close the door, but I push against it. "My daughter's in there," I say, feeling the hair on the back of my neck stand up. A shiver makes me cold despite the lingering body heat from my workout.

"I'm sorry, ma'am, but we don't have a child named Mikayla here. No one new has started recently," the young girl says.

My knees wobble, and I push hard against the door, causing her to stumble backward. I hurry past her into the house before she can stop me.

"Ma'am . . . you can't come in."

I ignore her. "Mikayla!" I call out as I go into the kitchen. Six unfamiliar faces stare back at me. "Mikayla! Mommy's here." The main room is empty. Mats lie on the floor. Pillows and blankets and stuffed animals set up for nap time. I run down the hall, but the bathroom is empty . . . the Lego room is occupied by several older children. "Hi . . . have any of you kids seen a little girl? Blonde hair. Blue eyes." What was she wearing this morning? I realize I don't know. "She's two."

The kids all shake their heads.

"Ma'am, you can't be in here. I have to ask you to leave, or I'm calling the police," the young girl says as she follows me through the house.

"Where's the other woman who was here? Fran, her name was." She gave Mikayla a tour of the day care and registered her. She'd recognize me. She'd know where Mikayla is.

"There's no Fran that works here. Just Rebecca and myself."

No Fran. What the hell is she talking about? I have a business card with Fran's name on it as a childcare provider at this day care. Her photo is on their website. I left the card in my purse in the car, but there's no way I'm leaving to go get it. I refuse to leave here without Mikayla. "Where's the other woman, then? Rebecca, did you say?"

She attempts to guide me toward the front door. "At the playground with the older kids. Ma'am, you can't be here."

I don't budge, and my five-foot-eight frame is no match for her. I reach for my phone, my hand shaking.

"You need to leave now," she says.

"I'm calling my husband." One ring, then voice mail. "This is Malcolm Jennings. Leave me a message."

"Malcolm, call me right away. Did you pick up Mikayla from the day care? Call me. It's an emergency." I disconnect the call and turn back to the girl. "Where is Mikayla?"

"She's not here. No one came to pick her up because she was *never* here. Are you sure you have the right day care?"

"Are you fucking kidding?" My raised voice makes her retreat slightly. "Do you think a mother would forget where she left her child?" The room spins, and my knees are all but useless.

"Okay, ma'am—calm down. Take a breath." She places a hand on my shoulder, and I pull away, heading back toward the kitchen.

This is a cruel mistake. She has to be here. Maybe Rebecca took her to the playground with the older kids. Maybe she went outside in the backyard when no one was looking. I glance through the kitchen window, but the yard is empty.

The front door opens, and excited-sounding voices enter. I hurry toward them. The older kids and another woman, presumably Rebecca. I scan the faces. No Mikayla.

"Where is my little girl?" The trembling of my body is uncontrollable as I walk toward them.

Rebecca's eyes widen as she steps in front of the children, putting herself between them and me. As if I'd hurt them. *I'm* not the one who's lost a child. I force a breath, but it sticks in my throat. "I'm looking for my daughter." I need to stay calm. There's an explanation. "Her name is Mikayla. She's two. She was dropped off here this morning with a woman named Fran."

Rebecca frowns. "I'm sorry, ma'am, but there's no one who works here by that name."

My heart pumps so hard and fast I swear it's about to explode from my chest. I grip the doorframe as the kids hurry past me into the kitchen. "I need to call my husband again," I say, sliding down the wall to the floor. I hit redial. His voice mail comes on.

Why isn't he answering? Several calls within minutes obviously indicates an emergency.

My hand shakes as I open a search engine. I'm unable to type. "Please . . . type in Saint Bishop's High School on Maple Street . . ." I extend my cell phone to Rebecca. I need to speak with Malcolm. He will know what to do. He will know where Mikayla is.

Rebecca hesitates and looks at the other woman, but she reluctantly takes the phone.

A moment later, she hands the phone back to me. It's ringing.

A cheery receptionist answers. "Saint Bishop's High School. How may I—"

"I need to speak to Malcolm Jennings. He's a tenth-grade teacher there. It's an emergency." My mouth is dry, and the words barely form. My hand shakes so violently I grip the phone tighter to keep from dropping it.

"Malcolm . . . Jennings, you said?"

"Yes!"

"He's a teacher here? At this school?" More confused tones.

"Yes! Please hurry. I need to talk to him."

"Um . . . I'm sorry, ma'am, but I don't see that name listed in the teacher directory . . ."

"He just started there this year. At the beginning of the semester. He's new."

Rebecca and the other woman are silent. They watch. They listen. They judge.

"Hold the line, please," the receptionist says.

"Please hurry," I whisper. Something is wrong. I can feel it in every fiber of my body. Something terrible is happening.

Rebecca and the other girl whisper in the hall, watching me.

Come on, Malcolm! Maybe he got through his lesson planning early and picked Mikayla up. He has to know where she is.

My stomach turns, and I swallow the saliva gathering in my mouth.

"Hello, ma'am, you still here?" The school receptionist is back.

"Yes. Where's Malcolm?"

She hesitates. "I just confirmed that there's no teacher here by that name."

"I told you he's new. He just started this year." Why is no one listening to me?

"I'm sorry, ma'am. There is a record of a Malcolm Jennings here for an interview . . . but that was last year. He was offered a position, but he never came in at the start of the school year."

The phone slips from my hand and I can't find a breath. My vision blurs and my body trembles.

"Ma'am . . . we're calling the police."

I don't know who said it . . . the voice seems far away. But police. Yes. We need the police.

September 6—12:56 p.m.

The woman is clearly nuts.

"Aren't you going to write any of this down?"

I turn to the officer who was first on the scene. A fairly new recruit, by the look of him. His uniform still has the original creases. He's clean shaven, and his teenage good looks have yet to fade. His eyes still hold the optimism of a cop who thinks he can make a difference. It's like a mirror reflection of myself . . . fifteen years ago. "I don't need to. It's all up here," I say, tapping my temple.

I'll steal his pages of notes later if I need them.

I scan the rooms of the day care, but it's exactly what I'd expect. Multiple cribs for the babies, mats on the floor for the toddlers, high chairs, lots of toys . . . the faint lingering smell of baby shit.

"The staff say they've never seen her before, but she's adamant that she left her child here. Husband can't be reached." He lowers his voice. "Apparently, Mrs. Jennings didn't know her husband wasn't working at the local high school, the way he claimed."

"Yeah, I've been briefed."

And I argued, back at the station, that what they needed was a crisp white straitjacket, not a crime-division detective. Missing kids aren't my department. Everyone knows that. Damn Mike for taking a vacation and leaving me with a case I'd never touch, given a choice.

"Kids don't just vanish into thin air," Rookie Cop says.

If he stays on the job long enough, he'll start to believe otherwise. Loud voices in the entrance have us heading that way.

A woman ducks under the single strand of crime scene tape across the open front door. "Rebecca . . . Jacqueline!"

"Ma'am . . . you can't enter. The day care is closed." Rookie Cop blocks the woman's path.

All the parents were called immediately to pick up their children once this . . . Kelsey Jennings refused to leave without her imaginary child.

I glance at Mrs. Jennings, now sitting on the floor in the hall. Carla, a department crisis therapist, sits next to her. Mrs. Jennings might be pretty, if I could see her face beneath the streaks of mascara and smeared lipstick. Yoga outfit suggests she's just come from a workout. Meaning she's most likely upper middle class. Suburban housewives are the only reason for midmorning group fitness classes.

Carla glances at me. "Hi, Paul," she says, her expression confirming my gut.

Yep. Nuts.

I nod in greeting.

"This is my day care," the woman who entered says.

"You're Alisha Bennett?" Rookie Cop says.

I glance over his shoulder at his notes. He has been thorough in his questioning. He's made notes of all the key players and the time-lines of events. Even provided his own assessments along the margins. Hopefully it will make for a quick day.

"Yes, and someone needs to tell me what the hell is going on," Alisha Bennett demands. Business suit, three-inch heels, dyed blonde hair, and medically enhanced lips. Dollar signs probably appear in her eyes when she looks at children.

Admittedly, I was hoping for a short, cute old lady who smells like chocolate chip cookies. You know, the *definitely not guilty* type.

"We're in the process of figuring that out," Rookie Cop tells her.

"I'm getting a lot of calls from angry parents threatening to remove their children from my facility," she says.

Yeah, business might not be so shit hot for Paradise Day Care after this.

"We're keeping this as low key as possible."

Rookie Cop must have a background in customer service. His reassuring tone helps to deflate Ms. Bennett a notch.

"Ms. Bennett, I'm so sorry!" One of the young staff looks wrecked as she approaches. "We tried calling you before we called the police."

"I was in appointments all morning," Ms. Bennett says, holding up unfinished nails.

Obviously, we've interrupted her spa day.

"That her?" The day care owner nods toward Kelsey Jennings, who now looks like she's been sedated. Her head is slumped forward, blonde hair falling into her face, and her eyes are closed.

I nod, then hold Ms. Bennett back as she advances toward Kelsey Jennings. "Don't worry—she's not going anywhere." Turning to Rookie Cop, I ask, "Did they give her something?"

"I think so. A mild sedative. She was losing it pretty hard when I first got here. Had to cuff her at first until she calmed down. Yelling and demanding that they hand over the child . . . kids and parents were terrified."

"Right. Okay . . ." I turn to the day care owner. "Ms. Bennett, we'll need to ask you a few questions."

"And who are you?"

"Detective Ryan."

"In my office," she says, leading us down the hall into a locked room in the back. She tosses her purse onto the desk and opens the window blinds. The sun shining through illuminates a cloud of dust that she's stirred up. It's been a while since anyone has been in here.

I'm sure she's just the type of owner who doesn't like her competent staff to feel micromanaged by being on site too much.

"So, Ms. Bennett . . ."

She holds up one of the manicured fingers. "I'm going to need caffeine first."

Rookie Cop shoots me a look, but I nod. "Absolutely. There's just a child missing; no rush."

While she's busy putting a Keurig pod into the expensive machine on her desk, I look around.

This office doesn't look like it belongs with the rest of the house. Painted a dark navy with white trim accents, furnished with expensive mahogany furniture and impressive oil paintings on the wall, it looks like a lawyer's office. A few thank-you cards and several horribly drawn pictures of families and animals hanging on a pegboard are the only indication that this woman might have any interest in children.

Her coffee is ready, and she rips open several sugar packets and motions for me to proceed with my questioning.

"How long have you owned this day care?" I ask.

"I opened this location in 2010. I have several others . . . and before you ask, there's no Mikayla Jennings there either."

Shit. More work. "Unfortunately, we will have to send someone out . . ." I look at Rookie Cop, and he's on it. More notes in his book.

Ms. Bennett throws her hands up as she collapses dramatically into her chair. "I'm trying to run a business here—one that relies heavily on trust, Detective. Parents are already emailing their notifications to terminate our childcare services." She places her cell phone on the desk and leans forward. "Is it really necessary to disrupt the other locations? Do you seriously believe there's any validity to this woman's insane story?"

Nope. "We treat every missing person case seriously. But we will wait until end of day to send officers over to the other locations."

Rookie Cop coughs.

That's against protocol. Yes, I know. I don't care. Ms. Bennett has rights as well—ones I'm sure she's fully aware of. Piss her off too much, and the department could get sued or slapped with a fine for the inconvenience this will cause the business once it's proven that the mother is in the wrong.

"Mrs. Jennings is adamant that she dropped her daughter off *here* . . ." I reach for Rookie's notes and flip through. "She claims it was just before eight a.m."

"We don't even open until eight thirty." Ms. Bennett sits back as though that should solve everything.

"That's tough for most working parents, isn't it?" The nine-to-five workday is a thing of the past. Most offices and businesses open earlier and close later these days. What do double-income households do with their kids before operating hours?

Ms. Bennett takes a deep breath. "Our day care caters to a slightly different . . . upscale demographic, where usually only one parent works outside the home."

Rich snobs. Got it.

"Put the judgy face away," she says.

I look at Rookie Cop; he nods. I guess I have a judgy face.

"A lot of the moms are stay at home, and they bring the kids here for a break . . . and for the child's socialization and early-education benefits, of course," she continues.

"Of course. So no one was here early today?"

Ms. Bennett stands and walks toward the door. She reaches for the time cards of the employees hanging on the wall outside the office. She reenters and hands them to me. "These girls barely log in on time."

I scan the date and times. Eight thirty-four and nine forty-eight that morning. "No one else was scheduled to work today?"

"We limit the number of admissions to our programs each year. We comply with the standard ratio of five toddlers to one worker, eight older children to one staff member. Therefore, our employee list is also small. Rebecca and Jacqueline are the primary caregivers in this location, with one rotating employee in case of illness or vacation."

"I assume employee records will confirm that?"

"They will."

So no one was there before eight besides Kelsey Jennings. "Are there any video cameras on the premises?"

She points to the one in the corner of her office. "That one . . . I have confidential information in here . . . and there's one in the babies' nap room so they can be monitored without anyone having to enter the room and wake them. A third one overlooks the front door. Otherwise, no. I trust my staff and respect their privacy."

"You just don't trust them enough around the confidential information in here?" I nod toward the safe under her desk.

"Do you have any other questions, Detective?"

I flip through Rookie's notes, but it seems he's gotten all the required information from the other staff . . . and some of the parents. Damn, he's thorough. Might make a good detective in ten years, once his optimism dies.

I turn to leave. A quick look at the camera footage from above the door should prove Ms. Jennings was never there this morning. "No, I think . . ." I stop, seeing another note. "Oh, one thing—she said she dropped her daughter off with a woman named Fran?" I scan the row of punch cards, not seeing the name.

"Fran? She quit a while ago. An older lady in her sixties. She was wonderful with the kids, but she was having some medical issues . . ."

"But there was a Fran?"

"Yes. But as I said, she no longer works here."

"Can I see the footage of the camera above the door from this morning?"

Annoyed unfinished fingernails fly across her computer keyboard, and a second later, she turns the monitor toward us.

I squint at the black-and-white images. Unfortunately, the camera is pointed toward the street, not the front steps, and it's angled in an odd way. But I can see enough of a vehicle parked on the street to have my attention now fully on this case. A few minutes later, the car drives away.

"What happened?" I glance at the timer. The footage was from 8:03. "Can we back it up?"

Ms. Bennett shakes her head. "The cameras are on timers. They start at eight. We have a local security company that monitors all three properties on rotation every night. Just to make sure the outside play equipment is safe. Other than that, we typically don't have a need for high-level security in this neighborhood."

Security cameras don't start recording until eight. Something Fran would know.

"Does Fran still visit the day care?" I ask, knowing things are about to get complicated.

"She used to," Ms. Bennett says carefully, "but not in recent months."

"Would she still have access? A key?"

"The front doors are keyless entry. Each employee has their own code."

"I assume the codes are voided once an employee is terminated?"

She nods, but her teeth catch the inside edge of her lip.

"Always?"

Ms. Bennett blows out an annoyed breath. "Fran was like family. She'd never hurt anyone or abduct a child. This is ridiculous."

If I had a dollar for every time someone's believed that. "I'm going to need Fran's contact information—a phone number, address . . ."

Ms. Bennett folds her arms across her chest as she stands. "Absolutely, Detective. As soon as you get a warrant."

September 6—2:04 p.m.

My legs wobble and my thoughts are fuzzy as I climb the stairs to the house. Whatever sedative they gave me at the day care hasn't helped to calm my anxiety; it's just made it impossible to show it. My limbs can't react to the intense adrenaline coursing through me, and my mind has trouble comprehending what's real and what isn't. I want to scream. I want to hit something. I want to demand Mikayla back. But I'm trapped inside my own body.

I still can't reach Malcolm. An unanswered call to his parents only made me look crazier. They're away on another mission trip, with limited cell service, which I already knew. The authorities are doubting everything I say, since there's no one available to confirm my story. Seems awfully convenient to them.

But I'm not crazy or making any of this up. Mikayla exists. She's out there somewhere . . .

I'd be running down the streets banging on doors if my body and mind were cooperating, but that pill the police department therapist insisted I take is hitting me harder than any drug I've ever tried. I shouldn't have taken it, but complying with the police seemed like the best option at the time. I need them on my side.

Detective Ryan is so close as we walk up to the front door that I can smell his cheap aftershave. A combination of fusty bergamot and fresh mint. It's making me nauseated. I want to be alone, but I know that's not an option. This is just the beginning.

"Is that your car?" he asks, pointing to a vehicle parked on the street in front of the house.

I turn to look at it. "It's been around the neighborhood a lot lately."

He jots the vehicle's description and license plate down in the notebook he stole from the younger cop—the nice one, with kind eyes and a sympathetic demeanor, who questioned me first at the day care. He seemed as though he at least *wanted* to believe me, and he took the situation seriously.

I wish *he* were still here.

At the door, I fumble with the keys in my hands, flicking through the tarnished gold and silver. I try one in the lock, but it sticks.

Detective Ryan's intent gaze makes me drop them. The loud clang of metal hitting the threshold makes me jump.

"Here, allow me," he says, picking them up. "Which key?"

I move back from the door, staring at the key ring. I need to pull it together. "One of the silver ones."

He tries one. It works. He opens the door and steps back to let me enter first.

I walk inside on numb legs. The strong sedative from the crisis therapist was definitely a mistake. I'm walking through a dream. Nothing around me feels familiar or safe. Cool air blows around me, and there seems to be an echo of my breath when I exhale. This isn't how a home is supposed to feel.

I hear other vehicles approach from outside. A search crew. They've already combed through the day care. Now they'll search the house. They don't believe that Mikayla was ever at the day care. They don't even believe she exists, despite the photos in my wallet and my careful, detailed account of the day. One I've repeated the exact same way over and over.

This search is a waste of time to them. Detective Ryan didn't even try to hide his disdain when he'd ordered it over the radio in his car on the drive here.

I swing around to face him. "What about my vehicle at the day care?" I was in no shape to drive, and I haven't even given the car a second thought till now.

"We'll have it towed here for you, if you'd like, or you can go pick it up . . . when you feel better," he says.

Feel better. As if I'm ill. I'm a victim of a crime.

He doesn't wait for my preference as he continues. "My crew will need to comb through the house. Every inch. The child could be hiding anywhere."

The child. So cold. So unfeeling.

Hiding. Why would my little girl hide? How could she even get home from the day care on her own? He's not making any sense. My heart thunders in my chest . . .

They think she never left the house.

Uniformed officers wearing rubber gloves enter through the open front door. Detective Ryan leaves me to speak to them, and I scan the house. In an hour, these strangers will know every inch of it. They will see all the personal things, rifle through the memories, turn everything upside down, tear everything apart, and leave it all for me to put back together again.

A dog barks, and I jump and swing around. Two German shepherds wearing police smocks at the end of a handler's leash demonstrate their understanding of their orders.

Detective Ryan turns to look at me. "It's just standard protocol," he says.

"Search dogs? What could they possibly find that these three officers in their rubber gloves can't?"

"That's not exactly the kind of dog this is . . . ," Detective Ryan says.

The dogs come closer, and I know what they are. Cadaver dogs. "You think she's dead?"

He clears his throat. "We don't know anything for sure right now."

A wave of nausea hits, and I bolt for the open powder room door in the hallway. I slam the door and sink to the floor, sitting against it with my knees against my chest, my forehead pressed to them, forcing deep breaths.

I can't be out there while those people are looking through the house. While those dogs search for a body.

Mikayla isn't here. She isn't dead. She's missing, and they are wasting their time searching here. They should be searching Fran's house. The other day care locations. The workers' homes. They should be trying to find Malcolm. My gut twists at the thought of him. He lied. He never accepted the position at the high school. Why would he lie about that? Where has he been all this time if not at the school?

Where is he now? What else is he lying about? And why the hell isn't he answering the phone when his daughter is missing?

I try his number again, and the call goes straight to voice mail.

"This is Malcolm Jennings. Leave me a message."

I hit the disconnect button and slam the cell phone onto the floor. I've called his number every five minutes for the last three hours. I've left sixteen voice mails. Each one more desperate, more pleading . . .

Where. The. Hell. Is. He?

I stay on the floor a long time, until I've gathered enough strength to stand. As I push myself up off the floor, I try to drown out the sound of footsteps upstairs while I strain, desperately praying I don't hear the sound of dogs barking.

Just footsteps and silence.

I wash my face. The cold water splashing against my skin helps to wake me from the medicated trance. I open the medicine cabinet, moving aside bottles of prescription pills until I find a small tube of light concealer.

It works its magic, covering the dark circles beneath my eyes, but the bloodshot look of desperation will take a miracle to diminish. Reality of the situation sinks deep into my chest as the sedatives start to wear off.

Mikayla is gone.

September 6—2:17 p.m.

While the team searches the house and Kelsey Jennings tries to pull herself together in the powder room, I look around on my own. A lot can be learned about people by looking into the places they don't want anyone to see.

The Jenningses' home is impressive. All the homes in this neighborhood are big and expensive—normally outside a teacher's salary—and this house has obviously been recently renovated. It has a modern feel, with upgraded appliances and real hardwood flooring throughout, but the structure of the old house hasn't been destroyed; the curved archways and colonial moldings help to maintain its character as a home built in the early 1900s. It sits on several acres of land, the nearest neighbors far enough away not to get into one another's business but close enough to form a quiet elitist group.

How can the Jenningses afford this place? Wise investments? An inheritance? Wealthy families?

This is a safe part of town. Rarely are there police cruisers lining the streets around here. The neighbors are less intrigued at the possibility of a crime and more annoyed at the disturbance this investigation is causing.

We will question them if needed, but the unpacked moving boxes and the FOR SALE sign in the front yard confirm Kelsey Jennings's story that they've just recently moved into the home and back to Ellicott

City . . . for her husband's job, one apparently he hasn't actually gone to every morning.

I start in the kitchen, since it's the only room that seems to be completely unpacked already, and it's the one that search crews tend to gloss over in preference of more interesting spaces—like attics, crawl spaces, and lingerie drawers. Other than the breakfast dishes still in the sink, it's immaculate. Either they have a house cleaner, or someone in the home is a neat freak. Everything has a place. Countertops are clutter-free, and there's not even a trace of a fingerprint on the stainless steel fridge. Odd, with a child in the house.

Besides a photo of Mikayla on the counter, the room is absent of any usual sign of a family living there. Even the "Busy Moms Calendar" hanging on the wall has yet to be filled in with appointments or obligations or events. I flip back through various months, but there's nothing. I flip forward, and it's completely blank.

I open the fridge and look inside. Milk, juice, vegetables, fruit . . . nothing unhealthy. No wine or beer . . . health freaks?

I open the pantry and dismiss that idea. Three different types of cookies, sugary cereal and boxes of rice, pasta and crackers reveal that the family likes their sugar and carbs. I'm not judging. My pantry is stocked with ramen noodles, and my fridge is an oversize beer cooler. Full stop.

I open the kitchen drawers. Cutlery in one. Spatulas, ladles, and other utensils I couldn't name if my life depended on it in another. Dish towels in a third.

Where's the drawer I'm looking for?

The junk drawer. The one that hides all manner of sins. The one that reveals more secrets than anyone realizes. We all have one. A drawer that catches all the odds and ends that don't have their own place—a roll of tape, pens that don't work anymore but never get thrown out, an old postcard from a friend on vacation, a hair elastic . . . paper clips . . .

This family doesn't have that drawer.

The last one I open contains only a stack of cookbooks, splattered and stained, recipes stuffed in between the pages.

The living room is equally boring. New furniture that still hasn't fully adopted the family's scents, the lingering smell of the furniture warehouse to the fabrics. A few open boxes reveal photo albums and dust-collecting ornaments and trinkets that haven't been unpacked yet. The hardwood floor is shiny and clean—again, an unusual occurrence in a home with a child. So far, it's impossible to tell that a toddler lives in this home. Not a toy or book to be found.

Then I know why.

I open the door to what I assume is a playroom. There's no bed, so it's not Mikayla Jennings's bedroom. This room is full of toys. Toys everywhere. Unlike the rest of the house, it's messy and chaotic. There's no organization or sorting bins for different items. Just lots of different kinds of toys.

Suspicion that Kelsey Jennings has fabricated a child fades. The photos and toys are proof that one existed at one time . . . but it's not unthinkable that maybe the child has died and a mother's grief is at play. Until Malcolm Jennings or his parents are located, there's no way of knowing what the hell is really going on.

I close the door and head into the master bedroom.

Here is where most of the secrets hide.

Having done countless home searches, I've learned never to leave my house in a way that, if it is searched, I will be embarrassed or my secrets will be discovered.

It's in the master bedroom where we find sex toys and lubricants for experimental play among couples. We find hemorrhoid cream and night guards . . . we find hair dye and Rogaine for Men. Push-up bras and Spanx. Everyone has secrets they keep to themselves. Things they'd rather no one discovered.

In the center of the room, a large, king-size four-poster bed is neatly made. No throw pillows. I don't know why that strikes me as odd, but an unwanted memory of another bed and dozens of useless fucking throw pillows that had to be taken off every night and put back on the next morning flashes in my mind, and I wonder how Malcolm Jennings won the battle against throw pillows.

Crisp, new, white blinds at the window are closed, and I open them and peer down into the backyard, where the crew is searching under the deck and in a small storage shed near the back. The grass is overgrown. How long was this house on the market? Might be worth a look into the previous owners. I make a note to call the Realtor listed on the FOR SALE sign out front.

I move away from the window and look in the large walk-in closet. Nothing's been hung on the racks or placed on the shelves yet. Packed boxes—one labeled "Kelsey's Clothing," the other labeled "Malcolm's Things"—sit open on the floor.

They are still living out of boxes. Odd. Clothes would be one of the first things I'd unpack.

I keep searching. There's nothing under the bed or in the dresser drawers. There's nothing hidden under a mattress.

A writing desk in the corner of the room contains paper, pens, stationery, and an old fountain pen sitting in an inkwell. A laptop sits on the desk. I open the lid. Password protected of course. If needed, I'll have to get a warrant to access it.

In the bathroom, everything is spotless. Not even toothpaste or water spots on the mirror.

I open the drawers and find deodorants, makeup, perfumes, a nose-hair trimmer, razors . . . nothing out of the ordinary.

It's almost as though the Jennings knew someday their home would be searched.

I open the medicine cabinet, and it's a whole new story. Dozens of prescription bottles are lined up inside. I scan the labels—they all belong to Kelsey Jennings. They are all from a medical clinic in Florida.

I google the names of the drugs.

Memory impairment. Painkillers. Sedatives. Muscle relaxants. Depression and anxiety medication.

Jesus, Kelsey, you really are a mess, aren't you?

"Hey, Detective, we're done." Tom, the lead search crew member, appears in the bathroom doorway.

"Find anything?"

He nods to the medicine cabinet. "Only that Mrs. Jennings seems to require her own pharmacy in order to function."

Right.

September 6—3:01 p.m.

A loud knock on the bathroom door means my hiding reprieve is over. I grip the edge of the counter as the floor ripples beneath my bare feet. I've lost all hope that this is just one big nightmare. That I'll wake up and my life won't be collapsing around me.

"Mrs. Jennings? You okay in there?" Detective Ryan's voice, coming from the other side of the door, contains a sharpness.

No. Nothing is okay. Nothing may be okay ever again.

And the fact that they've assigned a detective to the case who believes I'm crazy, that I've made all of this up, doesn't help.

"Ma'am . . . whenever you're ready, I'll need to ask you some questions."

To determine I'm lying.

I open the door, and he's too close. In my space. I can smell his poorly masked body odor and twenty-year disdain for his job. The younger cop questioned me at the day care, the crisis worker asked a dozen questions of her own . . . but I'll keep answering them. I know the drill, how this all works. So many questions, over and over again, in slightly different variations. The goal is to trip me up, catch me in a lie . . .

"I'm ready," I say. I need to do this now. I need to hold it together. For Mikayla's sake. The best-case scenario is that she is with Malcolm. The worst . . . I shake my head. "In the living room." The other officers are done combing through the house, digging into places that are none of their business.

I never expected to have someone here, scrutinizing every aspect of this new life I was about to start living. Have they found anything interesting? Incriminating? Any secrets even *I* don't know about?

I swallow my nerves and sit on the edge of the chair near the window. The cushion is stiff. Not at all comfortable. Definitely not a relaxing cuddle chair. The pale-beige fabric a horrible choice for a house with a toddler in it—it'll have dirty handprint stains in no time. I'd never have selected this chair had the furniture choice been mine to make.

Detective Ryan continues to stand. He studies me. "How are you feeling?"

Is he seriously asking me that? "How do you think I feel?"

"I know the officer at the day care asked you a series of questions already, but I have a few more."

I nod, bringing back the details of the day to the forefront of my mind. The sedatives have completely worn off by now, and I find myself craving a little of the numbness back. My chest is tight, and air struggles to make it to my lungs. My hands clench and unclench involuntarily, and I shove them beneath quivering legs.

The detective refers to his notes, but before he can ask his first question, the two dogs appear in the living room entryway.

"Detective Ryan . . . we are just about done here."

Just about.

The handler's gaze shifts to me. I can tell that this is the part of his job he likes the least. He looks as uncomfortable and apprehensive about this as I am.

But Detective Ryan simply nods as though he witnesses dogs sniffing out potential murderers every Tuesday morning, and the handler leads the dogs into the living room.

I hold my breath. Two large, menacing-looking snouts and dark, piercing eyes approach. Thick, muscular bodies under soft-looking fur.

"It's okay—they just need to smell you."

To try to pick up the scent of a murderer. How the hell can he say it's okay?

I stare straight ahead as they sniff my knees, my toes, my hands gripping the seat cushion. One walks around the back of the chair, and the other sits, staring at me, as though waiting for me to break under its intimidating gaze.

Silence.

Seconds pass torturously slow.

I didn't hurt Mikayla! I want to scream at the dogs. But I clamp my lips together tight and await their verdict.

The second dog rejoins the first one, who stands. They both turn to walk away from me; then one pauses. One reapproaches.

Detective Ryan and the handler stare at the animal.

Everyone waits. Everyone stares.

Silence.

"Okay, let's go," the dog handler says from the hallway, and both dogs accept their treats and leave the house.

I'm shaking. What if they'd barked?

Detective Ryan clears his throat, and I jump. I'd almost forgotten he was still here. He is now surveying the pictures on the mantel. "There's quite a few of your husband and daughter, but not many of you."

My hands clench tight together on my lap. "I'm sure you'll find that true of any family. Moms tend to shy away from cameras. Too fat. Bad hair day. One day we'll look back, and there won't be a trace of ourselves in our children's lives."

He nods, pointing to the only family photo in the group. Malcolm holds a baby Mikayla in his arms. Waves crash up on the sandy beach. "Hawaii?"

"Yes. Our first real family vacation." Hopefully not our last. This move was supposed to make things better. This was supposed to be a fresh start. So where is Malcolm, and why has he been lying? I want to believe it's everyone else who is lying. That Malcolm is in danger too. As bad as that sounds, it would be easier to live with.

Detective Ryan picks up a photo of Malcolm with his parents on his college graduation day. "These are the Jenningses? Malcolm's parents?"

"Yes. Meredith and Walter."

"They're on a mission now?"

"Yes."

"Have you reached out to them?"

I nod. "I tried once, but they didn't answer." I was actually relieved. What would I tell them? I lost their grandchild, and I can't find their son? Do they already know? Admittedly, I don't really know my in-laws. Maybe they have a part in all this. It wouldn't make sense, but nothing does right now.

No sign of Mikayla. No word from Malcolm.

The walls around me start to sway, and my mouth fills with saliva.

"What about your family? Friends?"

"My parents are dead." All of them. I haven't had anyone looking out for me, or being there for me, for a long time. Part of the reason I'm doing this—this move, this new life—is for Malcolm's parents.

My stomach twists, and I feel light headed.

Detective Ryan appears in front of my blurry vision. Dark-navy pants . . . badge on his belt. A gun. "Hey . . . you okay?"

Why does he keep asking me that? How could I possibly be okay? I wonder if he realizes how obtuse the question sounds. If I wasn't on the verge of a mental break right now, I wouldn't be a normal mother, would I?

I force a steadying breath. I need to hold it together. "When are you going to go talk to Fran?" Mikayla might be with her. This woman could have her. She may have hurt her. Why wasn't there more of a sense of urgency? If I weren't being supervised every second, I'd be knocking on every last door in this neighborhood and beyond until I found her.

Why weren't the police doing more?

"We should have a warrant in a few hours, and I'll contact Ms. Bennett right away to get Fran's contact information." He sits and picks up the photo of Mikayla. A recent one. "Can I take this with me?"

No. The idea that he's taking the photo to open a missing-child file down at the station makes me nauseated. The thought that Mikayla's picture will soon be blasted out across media and online sources with a big "Missing" caption makes my blood run icy cold. This is not supposed to be happening to me. "Yes."

He tucks it into his pocket. He checks his notepad and squints. "Your husband's vehicle—it's a Toyota Prius . . . license plate . . ." He pauses. "Sorry, I can't read the other officer's writing."

Maybe he should have taken his own notes then. "It says 'T3ACH3R.' It's a custom plate . . . his parents gave it to him when he graduated with his teaching degree. Are you going to go to the school? Talk to someone over there? Maybe they made a mistake . . ." Maybe the receptionist had the wrong information. Maybe Malcolm's been there all along. I'm grasping. I'm hopeful.

"I'll be heading there next," he says. "We'll soon have a unit tracking your husband's phone, and we'll contact border-crossing officials. Everyone is on high alert in these crucial first hours."

"Except you."

"Excuse me?"

"You're not on high alert, because you don't believe me."

"I believe something is going on here. But I think you're not telling me everything."

My pulse races under the scrutinizing gaze of his dark-brown eyes. Every family has secrets. Skeletons they'd rather keep buried.

"Until the pieces start lining up, I need to look at the evidence in front of me and not draw premature conclusions," he says.

"You've drawn premature conclusions about me."

"I assure you that won't affect my ability to do my job . . ." He checks through the curtain as a marked squad car pulls up in front of the house.

"Who's that?"

"Officer Ray. He's going to stay outside tonight." He releases the curtain and turns back toward me.

"You think I'm a flight risk?" First they assume I'm lying, that I've made this up; now I'm a suspect? They think I'm going to leave? Without my family? Never.

"We have no idea where your daughter and husband are. They could both be in danger. You could be in danger. Protocol at this stage is to keep you safe."

Safe. Under surveillance.

"If you need anything, don't hesitate to call him." He places Officer Ray's business card on the table in front of me. "I think I have everything I need for the moment. Sit tight. Try to rest. I'll be in touch as soon as I know more or have more questions."

Sit tight. Try to rest. Impossible, when I don't know how much more Detective Ryan will have to uncover in order to bring Mikayla back.

September 6—4:10 p.m.

It's weird walking the halls of my former high school. It still looks the same—gray concrete walls, lined with dark-blue lockers, thick with new coats of paint applied every year to hide the previous year's graffiti. Shapes of old stickers show beneath. The building smells the same too. Musty, old, and damp, despite a new heating and air-conditioning unit the school installed a few years ago. Seems it was a futile attempt to reverse the signs of rotting within these walls, just like it's impossible to reverse the damage four years spent here can inflict on a person.

The school is empty—the kids gone for the day. Only teachers remain, sitting behind their desks in the classrooms. They glance up as I pass. Already they look exhausted, and school's only been in session a few days.

In the school's glass case, the dust-collecting trophies from decades of achievement are displayed. New ones added each year. I don't stop to look at the photos of the school's victorious football team or the generations of Bishop's Queens—the cheerleading squad, appropriately nicknamed Bishop's Bitches by competing schools.

I pick up my pace as I pass the case but still shiver, knowing those familiar dark eyes of my sister's follow me down the hall. Her smiling face in her cheerleader's pose asking me why I haven't found her yet. Or at least laid her corpse to rest.

Ellicott City is haunted. It's been that way for centuries. A historic town with too much past, stories of ghosts that kept us kids up at night, especially in the fall months, when the wind howled at night and the trees cast shadows in our peripheral vision, playing with our minds. Taunted us with images of things that weren't really there.

I didn't believe in ghosts until I had my own haunting me at every turn.

In the school's office, the receptionist is already gone for the day, so I knock on the principal's door and enter at her invitation.

"Paul! How nice to see you."

The same principal since my time there, Mrs. Delores Hannaford. One of those women who is never young but never seems to age either. Always wrinkled, always white haired, always the same purple-rimmed glasses. "Hello, Mrs. Hannaford. Thank you for agreeing to see me."

"A Saint Bishop's High alumnus is always welcome."

This is the first time I've been inside the school since graduation day. I didn't even return the following fall for the certificate ceremony, opting to have mine mailed.

"Would you like to take a tour of the school? Some things have changed since you attended," she says with a bright smile. Pride in her school, her accomplishments, her winning athletic teams . . .

All I remember are her failings. "No. I'm just here on a case."

Her smile is slightly forced as she nods. "Yes. Right. You want to know about a potential employee—a Malcolm Jennings?"

"Yes. His wife insists he was starting a job here. That's why they moved here from Florida just a few weeks ago, before the start of the school year."

She shakes her head. "When you called, I pulled the file. As we told Mrs. Jennings on the phone, her husband doesn't work here." She hands me a file with a job application inside.

I scan it quickly.

"We interviewed him for the position, and we did offer him the job, which he accepted, but then he didn't show up the first teaching week before classes were scheduled to start. We tried reaching him, with no luck. I hadn't even known he was here in town. We assumed he changed his mind. Luckily, Ms. Lorette was ready to return to work after her maternity leave. She and her husband decided to share the leave. Three months each. Never knew you could do that. It wasn't an option in my day."

As if I give a rat's ass about Ms. Lorette's maternity situation. I have a missing child and an apparent lying husband. "So when was the last contact with Malcolm Jennings?"

"As I said, we offered him the position—just after the Christmas break, I believe."

"And that was the last time anyone spoke to him?"

"Yes. As far as we understood, he was moving his family back here in the summer and getting settled before the start of classes."

"Back here?"

"Oh yes. He was originally from Ellicott City. His parents—lovely people—lived here for years. They travel a lot now, but they still have a home here . . ."

"Have you seen them around?"

"Not for a while . . . no. I'm sorry, that's really all I know."

"And you never met Mr. Jennings's wife or daughter?"

"Unfortunately not, no. I . . ." She pauses, looks unsure.

"What is it?"

"I don't know if it means anything or not, so I probably shouldn't comment on it . . . but I got the impression that his wife wasn't thrilled about the move. About him accepting the position."

Interesting. Kelsey Jennings reiterated several times that this move had been the right choice for their family. Change of heart? "Why would you say that?"

"I saw him in the parking lot after the interview . . . he was on the phone, arguing with her over it. He was annoyed that she couldn't be happy for him . . . that the interview had gone well, I assume."

"But you don't know for sure that's what they were arguing about?"

"I'm not certain. No."

So, Kelsey Jennings wasn't thrilled about this move at first. Who would be excited about leaving Florida and living here? But somehow, she'd agreed to it. Then Malcolm Jennings tells his wife he's going to work at the school every day, but he never shows up? Where was he instead? How long did he think he could deceive his wife? Unless his plan to skip town with their daughter was one he'd been ready to carry out. What made today the day? Was he working with someone at the day care? Fran?

I feel a tinge of sympathy for Kelsey Jennings. Betrayed by her husband. Whether he's abducted the child or not, he's been lying to his wife and he's nowhere to be found. Makes him the most likely suspect.

I stand and nod. "Thank you. I appreciate you taking the time. If I have any other questions, I can call you?"

"Of course, honey. You know anything I can do to help."

Years before, she'd made the same promise to my father when my sister didn't show up at home after cheerleading practice. Apparently, it was just something she said, because she hadn't helped. In fact, the school had taken the stance that after-hours extracurricular activities on the property were at a student's own risk, and once Julia had left school grounds, they were no longer liable for her safety.

I leave the office before I can place the blame and guilt I live with on her shoulders. She may not have helped, but it's my fault my sister went missing in the first place.

As I reach the front doors, I hear her voice calling me from down the hall.

I stop and turn as she hurries up to me. Her expression is full of sympathy, concern as she places a gentle hand on my shoulder. "I just wanted to say that it's time you stop blaming yourself for what happened."

I move away from her and nod as I leave the school. She may be able to move on, to forget, to forgive herself in whatever part the school might have played in my sister's disappearance, but that day will never come for me.

❖ ❖ ❖

Julia was always afraid of the dark. When we were kids, she rarely spent a night in her own room. I got used to getting up in the middle of the night to sleep in a sleeping bag on my bedroom floor, letting Julia have my bed.

She believed in the stories about our hometown. The myth about the teenage ghost that haunted the halls of the old girls' school, despite the lack of record of that girl ever attending. She'd take the long way to school every day, often making us late, so she wouldn't need to pass the old historic building that served as part of the town's haunted hike for tourists. She was terrified of seeing something no one actually ever had through the windows in the upstairs rooms.

She hated to be downstairs in our basement alone, where the old woodstove creaked and spooked her, its flickering flame casting dark shadows on the wall. She kept the bathroom door ajar in the hallway and would call out a conversation to anyone nearby while she did her business.

She didn't like to be alone. She had this fear that something bad was always about to happen. She felt like someone was watching her, following her. She had nightmares about drowning, so she avoided the water. She feared heights, so she refused to fly, which meant family vacations were done by road trips, where we would spend hours arguing until the vacation was ruined.

I resented all her fears. I told her she was crazy. That nothing bad happened in our small town.

I always wished something would.

There were no murders here in Ellicott City. No abductions.

Not until that fall.

Fall evenings meant the darkness came sooner. Trees cast ominous-looking shadows along the woodsy trails, and the crisp leaves blowing across the ground in the wind sounded as though someone was creeping close by.

Turns out there *was* someone creeping in those woods near the river that flowed from our town into the next.

One by one, teenage girls started to go missing. No clues left behind. No trace of them. Always girls. Never boys. The community was filled with fear. Parents begged for justice, pleaded for their daughters to be returned. The police searched but came up with no answers. They urged everyone to stay safe. To not walk alone at night. To travel in groups and to report all suspicious activity.

My homicide-detective father worked long hours, around the clock. The growing stack of missing person files quickly meant all hands on deck for the investigation. He grew more and more agitated and on edge with each new disappearance and not one case solved.

My mother was paranoid and didn't want Julia or me going out at night. Julia was fine with that. I wasn't. Whatever psycho was snatching teens was only interested in girls. I was safe. But my father insisted I needed to be at home when he was working overnight. No one had disappeared from their homes, but that didn't mean it wouldn't happen. Suddenly, I was in charge of Julia's safety, and it irritated me that the burden had been placed on my shoulders. I had friends, a social life, a girl I made out with when her parents weren't home. Unlike Julia, I was popular and not afraid of what might happen.

As more girls disappeared, the halls of the high school started to adopt a quiet, zombified atmosphere. Our classmates, our friends were disappearing. School counselors offered support to those who needed it, but even they were freaked out. What was happening in our quiet, uneventful town? Who'd be the next one to be taken? Who'd be next to disappear?

At the same time after school on Thursdays that I had football practice, Julia had cheerleading practice. We walked home together. But a week before Christmas, I'd been injured in a game, so I was ditching the last practice before Christmas break.

Julia begged me to wait for her anyway. No one else was going in our direction. The boys on the football team always went out for wings and beer at Ellie's Diner, where the waitress didn't give a shit about serving minors, and Julia refused to date jocks.

The other cheerleaders weren't exactly friendly to Julia.

I never understood why she'd wanted to be on the squad. They always treated her badly. They refused to include her in activities that weren't directly related to practice or competitions, though they all hung out together on the weekends. The more she impressed their cheerleading coach, the worse the treatment became. Cheerleader hazing was one of the most brutal I'd ever witnessed. Julia had been put through the demeaning, often dangerous tasks worse than most, but she'd endured it. She'd been hoping for a cheerleading scholarship for college. It would be the only way our family would be able to afford to send her.

Then the cheerleaders started to go missing. One disappeared after leaving her job at the ice cream shop. One vanished while walking the two blocks to her home after a night of babysitting. The third after a date with a college boy she wasn't supposed to be with.

With them gone, Julia had been promoted to captain of the squad, which helped her scholarship chances, but the treatment from the other girls only got worse. Still, she refused to miss a practice.

She'd be walking home alone that day if I didn't stay.

I didn't stay.

She didn't come home.

September 6—8:23 p.m.

Every light in the house is on. I've always been afraid of the dark. This new neighborhood, these new walls around me, haven't sunk into my bones yet. Every little noise makes me jump. And now I'm here alone.

I stare at my silent, unringing phone. Hours without a call or text from Malcom can only mean one thing. Malcolm and Mikayla are gone.

I want to hate him, but I'm still numb.

Emotions take the longest to sink in, to take hold. So much of my life has changed, been altered in the last few days. Emotions take time.

At first, my body was acting on impulse—scared, angry, confused—but now those involuntary reactions, spurred by the unexpected, have subsided, and I'm calm, clearheaded, as I wait for answers, for clarity.

Detective Ryan's update didn't reveal anything. The school confirmed what the receptionist had told me on the phone. Next, he's going to talk to Fran. All I can do is wait. Wait and hope that Mikayla is okay. Wait and hope that Mikayla is safe. That Malcolm will walk through the door, safe, unharmed . . . not a liar.

Truth rocks my core.

I don't know Malcolm.

I don't even know myself.

Right now, nothing makes sense. Puzzle pieces are missing, and I need to put the whole picture together before Detective Ryan does.

Time passes as though I'm trudging through quicksand. Has it really only been nine hours? This nightmare feels like days.

I can't sit still, but there's so little to do. The house appears clean as I wander through it now for the first time since walking in the door with the detective. I felt safer being confined to the living room, but I can't just sit on the sofa forever. My shadow follows me, and I feel as though I'm being watched. The secrets in this house threaten my sanity.

I pass the laundry room and see that the dryer is full. I open it, and the sight of Mikayla's tiny clothing makes my chest tighten.

Can I do this?

I reach in and take out a white-and-yellow sundress. Soft, delicate lace trims the edges, and buttons shaped like little baby ducks adorn the front. So small. Hard to believe a real live child fits in it. I hug the fabric against my chest and breathe in the scent, wishing it were still dirty so that it would smell like Mikayla instead of fabric softener. Sweet, baby powdery innocence instead of this chemical, floral, sickly smell.

My fingers grip the fabric as my jaw tightens.

Where is she?

I force several calming breaths, and my fingers relax.

She's with Malcolm. She's fine.

The words provide no comfort.

I fold the laundry, ignoring the tears that fall and dry on my cheeks. Sadness and despair are the emotions rising to the forefront now. I don't know why this is happening. I don't know what I could have done to prevent it or what I can do to fix it.

I pick up the tiny stack of clothes and slowly climb the stairs. I haven't been up here yet today, but I can't avoid these rooms forever. The hardwood floor is cold beneath my bare feet, and a shiver runs down my spine at the eerie, empty silence. The feel of a house not fully lived in yet surrounds me. It's cold and hollow upstairs. No happy memories have been made here yet, no lingering permanency of a loving family inhabiting the home.

I walk slowly down the hall and enter Mikayla's room.

Unlike other parts of the house, there's nothing left to unpack in here. The convertible crib has been set up near the window, transformed into a toddler bed. She's so big already . . . pink ballerina-themed bedsheets and comforter neatly wrapped around the tiny mattress.

The small white dresser in the corner is princess themed, with girly pink accents, and I walk toward it with the clothes. I carefully place everything in the proper drawers.

On top of the dresser are several framed baby photos, and a lump strangles me as I stare at them. I need to find her. I need to get her back.

In the center is an old jewelry box. An item from my own childhood. My hand shakes as I open the lid. A tiny ballerina rises up into the center, and the familiar music from the *Nutcracker Suite* starts to fill the air around me.

I stare at the pink tutu as it spins around and around . . . the music getting slower . . . then broken, choppy as the wind-up key reaches the end of its rotations. The ballerina stops.

I shut the lid quickly and put it down. I scan the bookcase along the wall. Dozens of children's books line the shelves. All of Mikayla's favorites.

Seeing her baby album, I take it down, sit on the floor, and open it.

Her birth announcement on the first page is starting to fade slightly, the blue ink smeared a little. April 3, 2018: five pounds, two ounces.

She was early. By almost six weeks.

I stare at the announcement, memories clouding in my mind . . .

I knew the moment I felt pain shooting across my stomach that something was wrong. My last doctor's appointment and ultrasound had revealed everything to be okay, but things had changed in those last few days.

The baby had been so active before, but I'd felt little movement in weeks, and my anxiety levels had been difficult to control. Things had been challenging. Life had been difficult. The pregnancy had been meant to make things better, but that hadn't been the case.

Stress was bad for the baby.

I still blame myself.

Things were a blur at the hospital. Nurses, doctors, IVs, and machines monitoring my heart rate. The baby's heart rate.

Under duress. Not much time.

I was in too much pain to focus on the words, to try to understand what was happening. Sharp, intense, shooting cramps raged across my stomach, my legs, my back. Too late for medication.

After forty-six minutes of pushing, feeling exhausted and weak, I saw my baby.

But everything was wrong. There was silence. No crying. No movement.

No breathing.

Every mother's worst nightmare.

Then the doctor taking her away . . .

I touch the picture of Mikayla next to the announcement. Alive and healthy. Beautiful and precious.

Not all babies are beautiful. We say they are. We tell sleep-deprived moms that their babies with odd features or misshapen heads are beautiful, but they aren't all, truly.

Mikayla was. She was perfect. *Is* perfect.

It's a miracle that I have her. I have to believe Detective Ryan will find her. I have to believe she will come home. I need her.

I flip through the album, watching Mikayla go from a tiny preemie to the two-year-old she is now. Her life captured in the stills that are all I have. May ever have again.

Photos of her sleeping. Photos of her playing. Along the side, the details of the moments are captured in neat writing—words that ooze love and affection.

How could Malcolm take her away? Hasn't he read these words? Beautiful descriptions of Mikayla's early adventures. Couldn't he feel a mother's love coming through the pages?

My grip tightens on the book, and the pointed plastic edges dig into my palms. I close the album and stand and then put it back on the shelf.

I can't be in here anymore.

I head toward the door, but something catches my eye, sticking out from under the bed.

Mikayla's favorite stuffed animal—a pink-and-purple unicorn, wearing a sparkly blue ballet costume and crystal tiara. I pick it up, and my hand tightens around it, squishing the soft fabric. She can't sleep without him. How can Malcolm be this selfish? He knows she needs him.

That baby girl is somewhere tonight without her favorite toy—the one that provides security and comfort.

She's somewhere without her mother.

Malcolm is no longer someone I can trust. Not someone I need to remain loyal to. Not someone who deserves my forgiveness.

So for his sake, he'd better not hurt his daughter.

September 6—8:48 p.m.

I run a hand through my hair as I enter the criminal investigative unit. As far as pain in the ass cases go, this one tops the list. People go missing all the time, vanish into thin air, leaving no trace behind. There's no shortage of psychos and pedophiles lurking about . . . waiting for their next victim, their next opportunity.

But parental-abduction cases are the worst. So many levels of deceit. As time passes with no word from Malcolm Jennings, the investigation is leaning in that almost certain direction.

I push through the door and walk down the hall to Parsons's office. The tracer is barely out of high school . . . and always just barely out of jail. She can break into any secure system, hack any account.

We are happy she's on our side. For now.

"Hey, got anything for me on that cell number I gave you for a Malcolm Jennings?" I ask as I enter the crammed six-by-six space we've given her as an office. Dozens of computers have been set up, and shelves are covered with technical equipment that I couldn't even name, let alone explain the use of.

Her fingers go a million miles an hour over two separate keyboards. One hand plays a violent video game on one computer screen while the other types crazy code I'd never be able to decipher on the other machine. She utters a string of profanity to an online opponent and removes her headset. "Oh, hey, Ryan . . . no, not yet. It has a pretty sweet ghost app."

"Ghost app?" Am I supposed to know what that is? "So, untraceable?"

"Nothing's untraceable. I'll just need more time." She turns in the chair. "If the phone's turned off, it doesn't connect to any surrounding networks, making it harder to trace."

Chances are, Malcolm Jennings would have ditched his cell phone by now, but if we can at least find where the phone was at last point of contact, then we'll have somewhere to start. It's been almost ten hours since Kelsey saw her daughter . . . ten hours is a hell of a long time when getting far away, as fast as possible, is a priority. Malcolm Jennings could be anywhere by now.

"So, you think the kid is with the father?" Parsons asks.

"Most likely. We're still looking into a few other possibilities, but the guy hasn't exactly been the most forthcoming with his wife these days, so chances are, we're dealing with a parental abduction."

"Well, then, she's probably safe, right?" Parsons grew up on the streets, ditching every foster family she was placed with. She was a victim of abuse and was serving a juvenile sentence for theft when we discovered her hacking skills, so she's a hard-ass. Still, she has a soft spot for missing-children cases. Always cautiously optimistic.

"That's not an assumption I'm willing to make." I don't know Malcolm Jennings, and his motivation for abducting his daughter is unclear. In most cases, it's a woman leaving an abusive relationship or a violent domestic dispute regarding custody that leads to these kinds of cases. A man taking off with his child outside of those situations is something we don't see often. "Let me know as soon as you get anything."

Parsons nods and returns her attention to her monitors.

After going into my office, I open a new file and put in the picture of the missing child. She's cute. Blonde hair, blue eyes, big dimples. She looks just like Kelsey Jennings, but unlike her mother, this child looks happy, carefree . . . not the face of an abused or abandoned child. I take out Rookie's notes and read them again, more carefully this time, but there's nothing of use in there. Nothing I've missed.

Mom says she dropped the kid off. Day care says they've never seen the kid before. She's not registered. But there's evidence of Mom being there and the existence of a woman named Fran.

So, Mom may be crazy, or she's a victim as well.

I believe Ms. Bennett and her day care have nothing to do with this. Fran, on the other hand . . . accomplice? I'll know soon enough.

Rookie Cop enters and places my warrant on the desk. "This just got approved at the courthouse. Want me to come along?"

He's eager to get his nose wet. He still sees this job as exciting, challenging . . . that will change. And I don't need his pesky optimism interfering with my practical mind-set. "No. I got it. Thanks." I tap his shoulder as I leave the office.

I get back in my squad car and call the day care as I head in that direction.

Ms. Bennett is standing on the step with Fran's employee file in hand as I pull up and then get out of the car.

"Was that so hard?" I ask as I take it.

"Fran has nothing to do with this. You're wasting your time," she says before going back into the day care and closing the door.

"It's always the ones you least expect," I call out.

September 6—9:46 p.m.

Thank God I own a gun, because I will swallow a bullet before anyone can commit my old ass to a place like this.

I can't decide what's worse—the sound of screaming coming from some of the rooms, as if someone is being tortured, or the musty, rancid smell of piss and body odor that seeps from every square inch of the stained, peeling wallpaper and the seventies shag carpeting.

Prison visits are better than this. Those guys just spit and cuss, and at least the smells are identifiable.

This particular seniors' home was opened in the late fifties, and they've made no significant upgrades since they hosted their first round of near-death occupants. Despite protests from family members and the community to have the place either restored to livable condition or condemned and demolished, the local government continues to allow the elder abuse that is this place.

I stop outside the "entertainment room" and look inside. Old people sit around a small flat screen, watching some old black-and-white movie that probably brings back nostalgic emotions. I bet some of them don't even know what year it is.

Near the window, a few men sit around a card table, each playing his own game.

"Pick up two," one says.

"Gin!" the other replies.

Jesus.

In the corner is Fran.

I was told at the check-in desk she'd be the one knitting in the rocking chair. Thin knitting needles move at a crazy speed, two long lengths of wool stretched out in front of her. An oversize pale-pink sweater hangs loose on her, and she wears matching knitted slippers on her feet.

No one even looks my way as I walk toward her.

"Fran Gallant?" I ask.

She looks up. "Yes?"

"I'm Detective Ryan from the Ellicott City Police Department . . . I was hoping to ask you a few questions."

"If it's about the extra bread roll I took at dinner, I admit it, but it wasn't for me. I feed the birds by the lake," she says.

"That's not it . . ." What kind of place is this if the woman thinks she could get arrested for something like that?

Her face clouds. "Is this about my son?"

Her son. Maybe . . .

Now we've caught the attention of several others in the room. "Can we go somewhere private to talk?"

"Of course." She gathers her wool and hands it to me as she stands. "Keep those from tangling."

Right. I keep the two strands of colors as untangled as possible as I follow her out of the room, down the hall . . . out the back door . . . down a dark trail to a collection of duplexes with brick exteriors. Old and poorly maintained structures, overgrown grass and weeds make up the small yard in the front, and the concrete steps leading to the door are chipped and crumbling. The lights above the doors must all be burned out, because none of them are on. This entire residence is a hazard.

I squint in the dark to scan the area. Eight sets of duplexes crammed together at the back of the property, surrounded by areas of forest and walking trails that I assume lead to the lake I passed as I drove in earlier this evening. If Fran does have the child, I'd hate to think that she may have hidden her somewhere. "You live out here?" I ask.

"Yes. It costs a little more than the rooms inside the main building, but at least I have more privacy."

No shit. She could probably die out here, and it would take weeks for any of the staff to notice.

"The rooms inside are mainly for old folk who need extra assistance. I'm quite capable of taking care of myself."

Still, I offer an arm to her as she climbs the steps to her unit.

With rock-steady hands, she unlocks her front door. If she's nervous about me being there, or if she's hiding something, it doesn't show.

I follow her inside, and she hits a light switch. A low buzzing sounds before the place lights up in a yellow-orange glow.

There's very little inside. A tiny kitchen with a hot plate and micro-wave, a small two-seater table in the corner under a window. Beige blinds that used to be white are closed, and I can hear the buzzing of a fly trapped behind them. Light-gray laminate flooring has peeled back from the edges of the room and near the counter, curling in to reveal dirty yellow floorboards beneath.

Beyond the kitchen is a seating area with a love seat and a television that I'm surprised to see is a flat screen. On the other side of the kitchen is a three-foot-long hallway—bathroom on one side, bedroom on the other.

"Do you want to look around?" Fran asks.

I can see everything from where I'm standing. "Um . . . is this the entire space?" I peek into the bedroom—the small closet door is open. More knitted sweaters hang haphazardly off metal hangers, and a pair of new winter boots with the price tag still left on sits beneath them. Other than that, just a rolled-up sleeping bag and large duffel bag inside.

"This is it," she says, going into the seating area. "You can put the wool down there in that basket. Careful not to tangle . . ."

I place the wool in the basket next to an old rocking chair.

"Would you like tea? I don't drink coffee. Keeps me awake," Fran says, heading back into the kitchen.

"No, thank you, Mrs. Gallant. As I said, I'm here to ask you a few questions."

She fills an old teakettle with water and sets it on the hot plate, then sits at the kitchen table. "What can I do for you?"

"This living facility . . . it's not guarded. You're free to come and go?"

She nods. "Those of us who live out here in the duplexes are allowed to leave the property whenever we want. The main house has a security gate and a nasty old security guard who yells at everyone. They even have bars on the windows to prevent the adventurous ones from breaking out, I guess. The really old folks, or ones who are losing their marbles, are only allowed to leave with family signing them out." She shakes her head. "Not that that happens often. I swear, most of them have been ditched here to relieve the family of the burden of taking care of them. Some haven't seen a visitor . . . since I moved in. Sad, really."

"When did you move in?"

"Nine months ago. I used to have a house in Springview, but the upkeep got too much for me to handle on my own. My husband died two years ago . . . heart failure."

"Sorry for your loss."

She nods. "I hated to leave. We'd been in that house since we got married. Raised a son . . ." Her voice trails off, and I again make a note to ask about this son of hers.

"Anyway, after I stopped working, I decided to sell it and move in here. Well, living here wasn't my first choice, but it's what I can afford on my pension."

"You mentioned work. You mean at Paradise Day Care?"

She looks surprised. "Yes. I worked there for ten years after I retired from teaching. How did you know?"

"That's actually what I'm here about. The staff there say you still visit sometimes."

She nods, and her smile is sad. "I miss the children."

Enough to help abduct one of them? My gaze drifts through the window to the woodsy trails. I need to speed this up. "Were you there this morning?"

She stares at her hands. Silent.

"Please answer the question, Mrs. Gallant."

The door opens behind me, and I turn to see a thin man about forty enter. "Who the hell are you?" he asks, dropping a bag of groceries on the counter.

"Detective Ryan from Ellicott City PD. You?"

"None of your business," the man says, moving closer to Fran.

I see the resemblance. Same fair complexion; thin, straight nose; light-colored eyes—though the man's are bloodshot, with dilated pupils.

"This is my son, George," Fran says.

"What's going on, Mom?" George asks.

"I'm here to ask your mom a few questions regarding a missing child," I say.

Fran's eyes widen. "What? Who? Is everyone okay?"

Her response seems genuine. Still, I ask, "As I said, a child's been reported missing. So I need to know if you were at Paradise Day Care this morning."

She hesitates. "Yes. But it was early. No one was there yet." She glances at her son.

"Should we have a lawyer present?" George asks.

I get the feeling he's asked that question before. "Not yet." Maybe soon, though. "Why were you there?" I ask Fran.

The son stands even closer and places a hand on Fran's shoulder. "Don't answer, Mom."

The older woman looks back and forth between her son and me. She takes a long, deep breath. "I was trying to contact Ms. Bennett . . . Alisha . . . I'd called a few times but didn't have any luck reaching her. I thought maybe I'd just stop by. She doesn't spend a lot of time at the centers, but she used to go in early on paydays to leave checks in our time card slots, so I thought she might be there this morning."

"Was she?"

"No."

"What did you want to speak to her about?"

Fran looks at George again. "I was wanting to go back to work. Not full time. Just a few hours a week. Money has been tight, and my pension only goes so far."

She was helping her son. The sleeping bag . . . the duffel bag in the bedroom closet. I study George more closely. Ripped and dirty jeans, worn T-shirt, and holes in his running shoes. "You're staying here?" That has to be against the rules of the seniors' complex.

"Just temporarily," he says quickly. "Until I get my own place."

Close to forty years old and still living off his mother, expecting her to go back to work to support him and his habits. Sometimes I wish I could arrest people for being a waste of space.

"Please don't tell the facilitators," Fran pleads. "They could kick me out if they knew I was letting him stay here. I told them he was visiting for a few weeks."

"Your living situation isn't why I'm here." We're getting off track. I need to know whether Fran saw Kelsey Jennings with her daughter that morning. One person to confirm that the child was there and whether she knows anything about where she might be now.

"Well, we're not answering any more questions without a lawyer present," George says, moving to stand between me and his mother. He glares at me, and I'd love an excuse to arrest his ass, so I stare back.

"Am I in trouble?" Fran asks from behind him.

I return my attention to her. "Did you see a woman dropping off a little girl? Two years old . . ." I retrieve the photocopy of the picture of Mikayla.

She takes it despite her son's attempt to block her. "George, stop. A child is missing. I want to help if I can," she tells him. She studies the photo but shakes her head. "Like I said, there was no one there while I was there this morning. The day care wasn't open yet."

But she was there, which puts her at the scene of the crime and further confirms Kelsey Jennings's claims.

I reach for the photo, but she holds on to it. "I have seen this little girl before, though. She was a little younger when I met her and her mother. They came to check out the day care a while ago . . . planning to move to the neighborhood, they said. The mom was really nervous about the idea, but all mothers are. I got the feeling that it was her husband who wanted to move here . . . something about being close to family."

Not much wrong with the woman's memory.

The kettle whistle blows, and George turns it off. He pours his mother a cup of tea in a dirty mug that's been sitting on the counter for who knows how long and sets it in front of her on the table.

Fran cradles the cup between wrinkled, age spot–covered hands and continues. "She didn't seem thrilled to return to work either. She would have stayed home with the child, given the choice, I think. But these days it's hard to support a family on one income. Anyway, I left the day care shortly after that, so I didn't see them again. Is this the child that's missing?"

"Yes. So, you met Kelsey Jennings and her daughter, Mikayla, a while ago, but you say you didn't see them this morning?"

"No, sir . . . Detective."

Her hands start to tremble.

"Are you sure? Kelsey Jennings said she left her little girl with you. This morning."

Fran looks nervous . . . then slightly confused, as though maybe that's a possibility. But then she shakes her head. "No. I didn't see them."

"Have you ever met Malcolm Jennings? The child's father."

Fran shakes her head slowly. Less confidently.

"We aren't saying any more without a lawyer," George says again. "Mom, do not answer any more questions."

I look at Fran.

She nods, obviously realizing she may have incriminated herself already.

"Okay. Well, since you admit to being there, I'll have to have an officer come out to do a search of the premises."

George is visibly distraught at that idea. Fran may or may not be hiding something, but her son sure is. "A search for what? My mother isn't a kidnapper."

"I have a mother who says she left her child with your mother at the day care this morning, and your mom just admitted to being there. No one else saw this child. Unfortunately, that makes your mother a person of interest." Our only possible suspect, other than Malcolm Jennings. I won't tell them there is a real possibility that the child's been abducted by her father. If Fran is an accomplice, I want to see if she turns on Malcolm Jennings on her own. She's admitted to needing cash . . . was money involved? Did Malcolm Jennings hire her to take the child from her mother and then give her to him so that Kelsey wouldn't be suspicious until they were well out of Ellicott City?

"Person of interest?" George says. "This is crazy." He takes a step toward me. His shoulders are tense, his jaw locked, his hands clenched tight at his sides.

I don't back away an inch. Strung-out drug addicts are the least of my daily concerns.

"George! Don't make it worse," Fran says, getting to her feet. "If it can help find this child, of course it's fine."

"Mom . . ."

"I said it's fine, George," she says.

George storms out, the front door clattering as it slams shut, causing the entire house to vibrate. I expect it to crumble down all around me.

"Sorry about him," Fran says.

Funny, I feel like I'm the one who should be offering condolences to her.

September 6—10:04 p.m.

Beginning a new life is always hard. Moving from one place to another has a jarring effect on a person's reality. What I used to know is no longer, replaced by a million foreign objects that now need to embed themselves into my psyche. I can't help but wonder how constant upheavals in one's life effect one's ability to ever feel grounded, to feel secure, to trust in one's latest version of reality.

So much is out of my control right now. Things are not going the way I've hoped or planned. The only thing I can do is continue moving forward each moment, each second, with the belief that Mikayla will be found. That the life I've planned will once again become my reality. That I haven't lost everything. That I can trust my instincts.

I stand in the living room window, staring out at the guard dog sitting behind the wheel of the marked squad car. I'm desperate for answers that are not in this house, but I can't leave with him outside. Wide awake and watching.

I feel like a prisoner. My actions are being monitored. One wrong move, and things could get so much worse.

The guard looks my way, and I move away from the window.

What do I do now?

The boxes waiting to be unpacked are really the only thing I can focus on. The stuff inside needs to come out, and directing my attention and energy is the only way to curb the looming anxiety attack I feel weighing heavily in my chest.

I tie my hair back and start on the boxes in the living room.

From the first box, I take out several of Malcolm's trophies and read the inscriptions on the gold plaques. Softball coach of the year, 2016. Track and field, 2014. MVP of his baseball league three years in a row. So athletic. His body is built for sports. He spends a lot of time at the gym or training or with his sports teams . . .

That can take a toll on family life, when one parent is so focused on themselves, their hobbies and indulging in their own leisure time away from the home.

I empty the box, arrange them all on a shelf on the wall, and stare at them. I position them slightly farther apart, then move them closer together.

Then, with one violent swipe of my forearm, I send them all crashing to the floor.

He has the baby girl. I can feel it. He has run off, and he has taken Mikayla with him.

My arm throbs, and a bruise instantly forms. Fuck Malcolm. I'm so angry I could kill him.

I'm not this person. This anger, this fear, this sudden hatred I'm feeling is not who I am. He has done this to me, brought out this side of me. People need to stop doing this!

I clutch my head as my inner voice grows louder.

I need answers. I need to fix this.

I slowly lower my hands and take a deep breath. I bend to pick up the track and field trophy. The tiny gold head of the statue has broken off. I place the bodyless token on the shelf, alone. Then I toss the rest of it, along with the others, back into the box and carry it out to the trash.

Guard Dog Cop is looking at his phone inside his car. He doesn't even notice me. I'm tempted to creep up to his car . . . see how close I could get before he sees me, see how long he'd remain vulnerable.

Back inside, I sit on the floor next to another box and take out several photo albums.

Most people keep their files digitally now, but there's something nostalgic about real photos. Ones you can touch, ones you can feel in your hands and know that the people in them are just as real. On a computer screen, things can be manipulated. Images lie.

These photos show the truth of the moment. Good or bad.

Of course the ones in here are all good. Why would anyone keep and purposely display the bad ones? Ones with closed eyes or an unhappy expression.

We only like to remember the good. Capture the best moments in life.

Like these from the past. Ones I barely feel connected to. Images of a dancer with passion and talent fill this album. Commitment, dedication, and drive coming through the shot of that one moment in time . . . I stare at the picture and wonder where she has gone. I barely recognize her anymore. What was so deficient in her that caused the success to all crumble and decay . . . what made her such a magnet for tragedy and despair, chaos and destruction?

Was it fate? Circumstance? Or her own doing?

The album is devoid of pictures of family or friends. Just a mirror-reflected image of solitary focus on a goal. Dancing was the only thing that mattered, reducing everything else to insignificance back then.

Was that why Malcolm stopped caring? Why he ran away?

I close the album and reach for another one.

A white lace-adorned cover with the names Kelsey and Malcolm and the date August 5, 2016, woven in silk threads on it. I hesitate. Do I want to see the love on Malcolm's face or the happiness radiating from the bride on her special day? Can I reimagine those moments in my mind, drawn in by the images? Or will I just hate Malcolm even more?

I put it back in the box and kick it away from me. Suddenly the past isn't something I want to remember.

September 6—10:56 p.m.

The place is dark when I pull into the driveway of my father's house, but I know he's still up. He's been an insomniac ever since his rotating shifts on the force permanently messed with his sleeping schedule. I suffer the same affliction of unsettled sleep patterns. But for different reasons.

My cell rings as I shut off the car. The station number lights up the call display. "Yeah?"

"It's Carlisle."

"Who?"

"The officer on the scene today . . . at the day care."

Oh right. Rookie Cop.

"Just wanted to let you know that the search of Fran Gallant's place came back clean. No sign of the child ever being there. The woman has no priors."

So much for the lead. This one is going cold fast.

"We did charge the son with possession, though. He's in custody, and we confiscated about two thousand dollars' worth of cocaine from the property."

The duffel bag in the closet. Unfortunately, I'm not sure if her son getting arrested will make life better or worse for poor Mrs. Gallant. "Okay . . . thanks." I disconnect the call and climb out of the car.

I unlock the door and go inside.

"Hey, Pop, where are you?" I set a bag of takeout on the kitchen counter and head to the stairs leading to the basement. "Hey, Dad, I brought food!"

"Be there in a minute," comes his reply.

"I can't stay. I'm on a case. I just didn't want you to starve to death," I call down to him.

"Come down."

Shit. He must have another "lead." I stare down the steps, and my shoulders strain to support the weight of my day so far. If I don't bring the food down to him, he'll let it sit there for days until I end up throwing it away, so I grab the double bacon cheeseburgers and head downstairs.

He's turned my teenage hangout into a home office, despite being retired from the department for ten years. Gone is the old sectional sofa and projection screen where we used to watch movies as a family every Friday night. My gaming consoles are unplugged and stacked next to old board games on a dusty shelf in the corner. Movie and rock band posters have been taken down from the walls.

He's moved several desks down there and his favorite armchair, which has seen better days. The walls are now covered in pegboards with information from a missing-case file that he shouldn't still have access to.

He's in underwear and an old cardigan. His usual.

"Take a look at this," he says.

"I just came to drop off food." I'm not sure he ever leaves this basement. And I know he's not cooking for himself. A housekeeper stops by once a week to clean, but my father only keeps letting her come because she needs the money, not because he really gives a shit about the state of the house.

I can't give him a lecture about any of it. It's his life to live . . . or not. The man is almost sixty-five, but his mind is still sharp and his body is in better shape than mine. A veteran detective, his six-foot-three frame and body built of solid muscle were always a source of admiration and fear for me growing up.

I never messed with my father. I still wouldn't. Though I'm also not here to get dragged down this rabbit hole with him.

"This location north of Bowie—we've never sent anyone out there. All these years . . ."

I open the bag and remove the burgers. Three of them. I'm not sure when I'll get here next. At least if I take them out and leave them in plain sight, he might reach for one when he's frantically following a thread. "That was one of the first areas we searched, Pop." Damn, I hope his mind is not going. I know he has no retirement savings, and his pension and my salary combined wouldn't get him anywhere better than Fran's home . . . I shudder at the thought of him being in a place like that.

"Nope. We searched Columbia and Glen Burnie . . . and all the way up to Middle River, but this area was sectioned off for that new housing development at the time. The one that never went up because the developer decided not to build. The land's still private property and has been sitting there all this time."

I reluctantly look at the point of the map he's suggesting. He's right. We've never searched there.

I'm relieved that his mind is sharper than ever. His forced retirement was solely a policy thing. His obsession with one particular case made him a liability.

It still angers me when I think of the way the station treated him in the end. Like he was crazy. Thirty years on the job, risking his life every day, 349 solved cases to his credit, and they let him go with a lousy severance and a stale grocery store cake.

I check my watch. "I'm on a case, Dad, so I can't stay long."

He finally turns his attention to me. "Does the victim match?"

He's convinced my sister's disappearance and those of all the others fifteen years ago are connected to any recent ones that occur. The truth—that no evidence points to that—would break his spirit, so I let him search. Connecting imaginary dots from one cold case file to another. "No. This missing person is a child."

"Since when do they assign those to you?"

"I was the only one available."

"Parental abduction?"

"Not sure yet." Though each hour that passes without a sign of Malcolm Jennings is certainly pointing in that direction. Unless he's missing too. But why would someone abduct a man and child and not the mother? In my ten years in this job, I've never seen that happen. "I gotta go. Eat."

He picks up a burger and bites into it before turning his attention back to the map. "Yeah . . . ," he says as he chews. "I'm going to head out there this weekend."

"Pop, it's been fifteen years. You know these cold cases . . ."

He's not listening, instead mapping out his route—starting at the perimeter of the property and moving in. Burger sauce drips from his chin. He wipes it against his shoulder. "You'll get me my permits to survey the area."

It's not a question. He knows I'll find a way to get the illegal warrant he's asking for. While the rest of the Ellicott City Police Department has written him off, my respect for him is deep rooted. And a tiny part of me obviously still has a glimmer of hope that he might eventually find my sister's body. We'd finally have some closure at least. "Yes, sir."

I grab a burger, knowing it will all be wasted if I don't, and unwrap it as I climb the stairs. "See ya later, Pop," I call out.

No answer.

In the squad car, I turn on the wipers when it starts to rain and head back to the station.

September 7—9:13 a.m.

I don't know why they bother to knock. It's not like I have a choice about letting them in. I peer through the keyhole in the front door at the woman in a gray pinstripe suit standing next to the guard dog on the front step. Two-inch heels, short hair, no jewelry, very little makeup, and a soft briefcase in her hand. She's definitely a psychiatrist. I've seen enough of them to know.

I release my hair from the ponytail, mess it up, and smudge my eyeliner before opening the door. "Hello?"

"Hi, Mrs. Jennings . . . I'm Candace Thompson from the Ellicott City Police Department. There's been a request for an evaluation to be conducted."

Play dumb. "An evaluation?"

"Of your mental health."

I've reported a missing child. There's suspicion of parental abduction. And they want to evaluate my mental health?

"Who ordered that request?" I shoot a glance at the guard cop, but he quickly shakes his head and looks away.

"Detective Ryan," Ms. Thompson says.

So, he still thinks I'm crazy. "Is this evaluation mandatory?"

"You are not a suspect, Mrs. Jennings; therefore, you can refuse to speak with me. However, we do need to rule out every possibility quickly . . . it's in the child's best interest."

I step back to let her in. I have nothing to hide in this house or in my mind.

And even if I did, I could fool my way to a psychological clearance. The trick is believing what you say is true and never saying how you really feel.

September 7—10:56 a.m.

I scan the psychiatric evaluation report on my desk. Kelsey Jennings is
not crazy.

Which means there are things she isn't telling me.

September 7—12:56 p.m.

It's been over twenty-four hours since I reported Mikayla missing. It feels like twenty-four days. I know that standard protocol is to believe that Malcolm and Mikayla are either in danger or that the child has been abducted by her father. The police department will now initiate a search beyond the local authorities.

It takes every ounce of resolve not to lash out. If they'd believed me right away, Malcolm and Mikayla wouldn't be so far away by now.

Since the evaluation this morning, I can feel my sanity slipping away . . . as though I was forced to use the last of it to pass the psych test. My mind keeps going in circles. I'm questioning every move I've made since the day before.

Maybe I am confused. Maybe Malcolm mentioned they were going somewhere, and I forgot. Maybe Malcolm decided not to accept the job from the school, and I wasn't paying attention . . .

Sometimes fact and fiction intertwine in my brain, and I get the two mixed up.

I clutch my hands together and shut my eyes tight.

No. I won't let them confuse me. I know the truth. I know this life. Malcolm, Mikayla, and I are a family. We just moved here. Malcolm was supposed to be working at the school.

He lied. He took Mikayla. *I'm* the victim.

I stand at the window, shielded from sight by the thin curtain. Media and news reporters line the street outside the house. I'm sure the neighbors are annoyed by the disruption to their quiet, high-end neighborhood. We haven't been here long enough for them to get to know us. Now we may always only be the dysfunctional family that moved here and created a stir within weeks.

I shouldn't care what the neighbors, these strangers, think, but I do. I've been foolishly hoping that for once I'll be accepted as one of them. I'd be seen as a caring wife, loving mother . . . someone who fits in with this life.

I watch as reporters and camera crews set up recording devices and camera equipment along the street, in the driveway, and on the lawn for the statement they said I'd be giving to the press today. It appears every station in Maryland has sent someone out to capture my story . . .

Which is a good thing. The more coverage, the better. Someone, somewhere has to know something about their whereabouts.

I see Detective Ryan's vehicle pull up. He gets out and approaches Guard Dog Cop, who keeps his post, protecting the space directly in front of the stairs leading to the house. He's created a perimeter to keep reporters back.

I slowly, quietly open the window to listen to their conversation.

"How was last night?" Detective Ryan asks him.

"Uneventful," Guard Dog Cop answers. "I don't think she got much sleep. All the lights were on all night."

"I don't suspect parents sleep well when their children are safe in bed, let alone under these circumstances."

Detective Ryan's hint of understanding and empathy catches me off guard. So far, all I've gotten from him have been suspicion and doubt. A clean psychiatric report goes a long way with him, apparently.

"You're right about that," Guard Dog Cop says. "I have four of them at home. Not a wink of sleep has been had for ten years. Any updates?"

I move closer to the window.

"Not yet." Detective Ryan says, scanning the gathered crowds. "We're not releasing any info right now, though."

Guard Dog Cop shakes his head. "I don't get it. Did the husband have any priors?"

"Florida's running a scan. Still trying to track the cell phone."

"He'd likely have ditched it by now."

"Yeah, but we need to start somewhere," Detective Ryan says. He taps the guy's shoulder. "Go home. Get some sleep. You're back here tonight?"

"Nope. Captain's pulling me off. Says there's no reason to keep her under surveillance."

Surveillance. Not protection.

"Okay," Detective Ryan says. "Thanks."

I close the window and move away from it as I see him approach the door.

He knocks, and I wait thirty seconds before opening it. "Detective Ryan, come in. Any news?"

"Nothing yet. Have you heard from your husband?"

"No. The calls go straight to voice mail now, and the mailbox is full. What about Fran? Did you see her?"

"She is still a suspect, but we couldn't hold her," he says. "We didn't find anything when we searched her house—no indication that your daughter was there or could have been there . . ."

Once this media statement is over, I may have to do some investigating on my own.

"But the woman must know something. Did you ask her about Malcolm?"

"She says she's never met him, and she didn't see him yesterday morning. She says she didn't see you or Mikayla either."

I swallow hard and look away. We're back to this again. "I'm not crazy." My voice breaks, and he steps forward. He touches my shoulder.

The first physical contact. A sign of understanding, support . . . getting him on my side may be a little easier than I thought. "Do you think she's lying? Do you believe it could have been a setup? Do you think the woman I met with is working with Malcolm somehow?"

He looks reluctant to make any predictions, but I can read his tells already. That's exactly what he thinks is going on. Anything else would be too complicated. Require too much digging. He's not ready for what he might find if he explores other possible scenarios. "It's a possibility," he says. "Your description of Fran checks out with the woman I met with last night. And she admitted to being at the day care yesterday morning and meeting you last year."

"Last year?"

He frowns. "When you and Mikayla checked out the day care?"

"Oh right . . . of course."

His cell phone rings in his pocket, and he reaches for it. "Detective Ryan . . . hey, Parsons. What have we got?"

I stare at him as he talks. The day before, my mind was a fog, my thoughts were a mess—next steps, how to act; the missing pieces of this puzzle had all stolen my focus—but today my mind is clear, and I know I need to see this through.

With his help.

He'll know more as the investigation progresses. He's trained to uncover clues. Secrets. He'll find out what's going on, and I need him to share that information with me.

Therefore, I need to know him, understand him, get him to trust me or at least feel sorry for me . . . not see me as a threat. He's a good-looking man . . . or could be if he gave a shit about his appearance. No wedding ring isn't a surprise. He doesn't strike me as a romantic type. I've heard the divorce rate among cops is high—married to the job or unable to connect with people because of the shit they see on a daily basis . . . I take in his build—six foot, muscular . . . I could never fight him if it ever got physical. Vulnerable and weak, damaged and destroyed . . . that's the way to play this one.

"Okay, thank you . . . call if you find anything else," he says into the phone.

Anything else?

He disconnects the call.

"What is it?" I ask.

"Your husband's phone is untraceable. I'd like to take a look at any phone records . . ."

I shake my head quickly. "I'm a financial adviser. Or used to be . . . we shred everything right away—credit card statements, bills . . . anything with confidential information on it."

"Paranoid?" he asks.

"Cautious. Identity theft is a lot more common than you'd realize." He's a cop; shouldn't he know that?

"Are there copies available online?"

Not that I have access to. "No."

He doesn't look entirely convinced, but he nods. "Okay. I'll get a warrant for the phone records from the phone company. Do you know if he had any other cell phones? A burner phone, perhaps?"

"No."

"Have you noticed any suspicious activity in any bank accounts? Big withdrawals, or use of a credit card?" he asks.

"Malcolm and I don't share an account. I don't have access to his financial information."

He frowns.

No doubt he finds that odd. Most married couples have joint accounts to pay bills . . . especially when one person is the primary breadwinner in the family.

"Okay . . . well, I'll get a warrant to access that information from the bank as well. Which financial institution is it?"

"Bank of America." I pause as he makes a note of it. Then I ask, "What about the evaluations you ordered?" I resist the urge to punch him in the face for ordering one in the first place.

"All clear. Though the drugs we found in the medicine cabinet, prescribed to you, are a concern."

"I don't sleep well, that's all. I never have. Insomnia. And the anti-depressants were for . . . postpartum." It's natural. A lot of mothers go through it. It doesn't make them less competent as a parent or cause them to love their children less.

He nods. "We may need your doctor in Florida to confirm that."

That won't be happening. This needs to end soon, before things get out of hand.

A knock on the front door; then the department's media-relations adviser, a young woman dressed in a neutral gray pencil skirt and jacket, enters. "The press are ready for you both now," she says.

"Thanks, Jann," Detective Ryan says.

My heart races, and I swallow several times. I'm not ready. How could anyone be ready for something like this? No one ever thinks they could be in this situation. Worst-case scenarios, tragedies, all happen to other people.

Jann still waits by the door. Detective Ryan gestures for me to go ahead, but my feet are frozen in place.

Maybe I shouldn't do this. Maybe I should never have called the police . . . reported Mikayla missing . . . but the day before was stressful and intense. I acted on instinct.

I blink a wave of dizziness away.

Mikayla is missing. I need to stay focused. I did the right thing.

"We'll be right out," Detective Ryan tells Jann. She nods and exits.

He turns to me. "It'll be fine. Over before you know it. We'll just stick to the script," he says. "No more. No less. There are a lot of report-ers outside. They have . . . questions."

"They think I'm guilty of something, don't they? That, or crazy." I'm not sure which I'd prefer. Someone fully believing in me and my story seems far too much to hope for, so I can only pray that putting myself out there like this will help bring Mikayla back.

"We haven't released any details regarding the case yet, so they haven't formulated any opinions yet. They want a story. Just read out the prepared statement."

The statement. The somewhat cold, factual account of the disappearance and the slightly less cold plea for information on the whereabouts of my husband and daughter.

"Ready?" he asks at the door.

I nod.

Outside, cameras flash in my face, and microphones are extended my way. This is my worst nightmare. One I've had before . . . too many times. Calling attention to myself again now is the last thing I want to do, but Detective Ryan says the public is our number one form of assistance at this point. Someone somewhere could have seen Mikayla. Or Malcolm. Or his car. Anything to help further the investigation.

Validate my claims, at least.

He speaks first, but I'm not listening. I blink and jump every time a camera flashes. Heat creeps up my neck, and I'm sweating beneath my plain blouse and dress pants. My gaze shifts left and right, and my hands are in tight fists at my side. I'm not sticking to the cool and calm facade he asked for.

But how the fuck can I?

In minutes, my face will be splashed across every newspaper and media outlet across the state. I'll be judged and criticized for losing my child.

For inventing a child, by some. Maybe murdering a child, by others . . .

I glance at Detective Ryan. I think he might be starting to believe me, and having him on my side is in my best interest. I need to pull it together and get this right.

He turns to me. "Okay, we're ready for you," he says.

I step forward and face the crowd. I clear my throat and try not to stare directly into any of the cameras. I stare over the heads of the hungry, greedy, whoring eyes looking for their next high, their next payday garnered from tragedy.

"My name is Kelsey Jennings. On the morning of September sixth, my husband, Malcolm Jennings, left for work." Or at least that's what I believed. "At around seven fifty-five a.m., I dropped my daughter, Mikayla Jennings, off at Paradise Day Care on Maple Street. I ran some errands, took a yoga class . . ." I don't know why my business that day is necessary . . . to show I'm just an average woman, wife, mother, perhaps? I continue with the script. "When I returned to the day care at a little past eleven, my daughter was no longer there . . ."

"Isn't it true that the staff say your daughter was never there?" a young male reporter calls out from somewhere in the crowd.

I stammer as I search the sea of faces for the speaker. "Um . . ."

Detective Ryan touches my arm. "Don't answer anything. Keep going. Stick to the prepared speech." To the crowd, he says, "Please, no questions at this time."

"Okay, um . . . my husband, Malcolm, drives a blue Toyota Prius . . . license plate, T3ACH3R." I pause for a breath. "I love my husband and daughter. I pray for their safe return. Please, I am asking the public's assistance for any information they may have. If anyone has seen my daughter or my husband, please contact the Ellicott City Police Department."

Detective Ryan hands me a slip of paper. I glance at it and read, "Anonymous tips, no matter how small, will be kept in confidence."

That's it. I'm done. It's over.

I step away from the podium, and Detective Ryan's hand burns into my back, steadying me.

Questions fly.

"Isn't it true that your husband has your daughter?"

"Why would your husband take your child?"

"Did you kill your little girl?"

"Are you making this entire thing up?"

Detective Ryan leads me inside and closes the door. I can still hear the reporters calling out.

I can barely breathe. The fabric of the blouse sticks to my sweaty skin. I'm dying in the itchy, tight fabric of the dress pants. I want to claw them off my legs. My feet are cramped in the low-heeled shoes, and I'm desperate to take everything off. Shower to wash away the feel of judging eyes and lies . . .

Detective Ryan is too close. I need an escape from him too.

"You okay?" he asks.

"Are we done?"

"That part is over." He studies me. "Why don't I make some coffee? You take a moment . . ."

Coffee is the last thing I need, but I definitely need a moment.

September 7—1:12 p.m.

I hear water running in the upstairs bathroom as I make coffee in the kitchen. I should go, but I want her to lock the door behind me. The media have yet to disperse; they're recording their own versions of the statement they've just heard, imposing their biases, with the backdrop of the Jenningses' home behind them. I can't leave and risk someone entering the house.

The tar-like coffee drips slowly into the carafe, and I hope she likes it strong. I scan the kitchen, but everything looks the same as it did the day before. I wonder if she's eaten in the past twenty-four hours . . .

The water shuts off, and I open several cupboards until I find the coffee mugs. Odd that they are all alike. Generic, off-white, standard-size mugs. No special themed ones from places they've visited. None with family pictures on them or with marketing messages on the side. No "Best Teacher" mugs that belong to Malcolm.

This is the only mug cupboard I've ever opened that looks like this.

I'm not sure why it hits me as weird, but I can't shake it off. As though this somehow proves that the family isn't who and what they say they are.

"Sorry, I needed to freshen up." Kelsey's voice behind me makes me turn.

She's changed out of the dressy clothes and back into a yoga set, like the one she was wearing the day before. Only this one is steel blue and matches her eyes perfectly. The pants cling to her curves, and, as all expensive workout clothing is meant to do, they accentuate the tiny waist and her hips and ass. Unlike yesterday's tank top, she's only wearing the matching sports bra, and there is no way my gaze isn't dipping to the large breasts barely contained within it. Her hair is still wet, slicked back away from her face and hanging long and loose down her back, and, for the first time, her face is completely free of makeup.

She knew I was still in her home. She's comfortable walking around like that in front of me?

Alarm bells ring, and I can only hope they aren't ringing too late.

I clear my throat. "Coffee's almost done. I'll get out of your hair. I just wanted to make sure you locked the door behind me on the way out."

She nods. "Thank you." She walks toward me, her gaze locked with mine, and I stare at her. What is she doing? Why am I still standing in her kitchen?

But it's not me she's walking toward; it's the coffee maker. Right. Time to go . . .

I watch her hand shake as she reaches for the pot.

"Here, let me," I say. After all, the woman has had a rough morning. Tough couple of days.

"Thank you," she says again as I pour the coffee into the cup and hand it to her. She immediately sips it, and I watch her. Watch the pale, pretty, bare lips part as she blows softly on the boiling-hot liquid and then wraps them around the edge of the cup.

She looks up at me as she swallows, and the look of vulnerability in her eyes rocks me to the core. She's scared, confused, desperate . . . I've seen it countless times on the faces of family members in these situations, but this time it affects me more than usual. I clear my throat again. "I'll go now."

She nods. She's not asking me to stay.

Does she want me to?

Fuck. What the hell is wrong with me?

I'm making a beeline out of the kitchen, into the hallway, and toward the door when my cell phone rings. I stop and answer it.

Kelsey sets her coffee cup on a hall table and looks at me expectantly.

"Detective Ryan," I say into the phone.

"It's Parsons."

"What have you got?"

"Not much. Neither Kelsey nor Malcolm Jennings have any priors. Their credit scores are great. However, three years ago, police were called to their previous residence in Palm Beach . . . a domestic dispute that turned violent."

I take a few more steps away from Kelsey in case she can hear.

"No charges were filed at the time," Parsons says.

"And that's it?" I ask.

"Sorry, man. I'll keep digging," she says.

I disconnect the call.

"What is it? Have they located Malcolm?" The tone of Kelsey's voice gives nothing away. If she's worried we've uncovered something, it doesn't show. She looks as eager for answers as I am.

"No," I say, turning back to face her. "The Florida office ran a search on both of you for any prior convictions."

Her face clouds.

I wait. Will she admit to something? Will she confess that she's not completely innocent? What have you done, Kelsey Jennings? What are you hiding?

She's silent.

"Nothing was listed," I say, "except for a domestic dispute call a few years ago, but no charges were filed." Those are the worst kind of calls. Officers hate leaving a situation, knowing they will most likely be called to the residence again, and who knows what they'll find the next time.

Her gaze lowers.

I walk toward her. This is the first bit of information we've received that could be the start of unraveling all of this, and I want answers from her. "Kelsey, this could be important to the investigation, so you need to be straight with me. How is your marriage? Is there a history of violence?"

She doesn't answer. She keeps her gaze on the floor.

"Kelsey, I need the truth. Is Malcolm a violent man?"

"His job can be really stressful."

Dude is a teacher.

"Or the search for one, anyway, and I wasn't always supportive."

"What do you mean?"

"Well, I'd be home all day while he went to interviews and filled out job applications, and he'd just expect certain things—dinner to be ready, the house clean—and I've struggled with being a wife and mother at times."

"Has he ever hit you?"

Kelsey is quiet. She seems to be struggling with the truth, with the realization that maybe she's seen this coming. That maybe there were signs that she's ignored. That somehow this is her fault. "Yes," she finally whispers.

Not surprising. The next question is the one that matters most right now. "Has he ever hurt Mikayla?"

Her head shoots up, and her eyes are wide. Frantic. "He'd never hurt Mikayla." Like a dam breaking, tears run down her cheeks. She steps forward and immediately sinks into me. Her firm yet soft body pressed to mine. Her bare arms wrap around my waist, and she buries her head into my chest. Her wet hair and her tears make my shirt damp. My hands reluctantly find her bare back, and then they seem to have a mind of their own, massaging her silky skin gently. Soothing her.

I should not be holding this woman, consoling her. She should not so readily be in my arms, accepting this comfort. But she's alone. She has no one else.

Malcolm's been abusive. Their marriage clearly was in trouble before all this happened. Kelsey is obviously hiding pieces of her past while trying to survive this tragedy. And she's clinging to me as though I'm a life preserver.

I move my hands to her shoulders and gently push her away. I'm a cop. Not a therapist. Not her friend. Not someone who should be getting involved like this. "Kelsey . . ."

She stands on tiptoes, and her lips press against mine. Surprise registers, immediately followed by common sense. What the fuck am I doing? I don't blame this on her for a second. I should have left right away.

I move back, and she falls slightly off balance.

I let her steady herself. Afraid of what could happen if I touch her again.

"Sorry . . . ," she mumbles, embarrassed as she wipes her lips with the back of her hand.

I'm not ready to remove the slightly damp traces of her mouth from mine yet. "I'll see myself out. Lock the door behind me."

I turn to leave, but her hand reaches out for mine.

"Wait. Shouldn't we talk about what just happened?"

"In the grand scheme of all of this, nothing happened." I need her to believe that. These last two and a half minutes and our ill-timed, impulsive actions are nothing compared to a missing child and parental abduction. They were fueled by stress and anxiety, uncertainty and a need to seek comfort in any form. "These things happen in these emotionally charged situations."

She looks slightly disappointed at that.

The breaking of glass sounds in the living room, and I put myself between her and the entryway.

"What the hell?" she says, almost breathless.

"Stay here," I tell her.

I leave the kitchen and see the broken glass and a large brick on the hall floor near the door. The small window in the door panel is broken. Sharp shards of glass still jut out from around the frame.

Kelsey appears in the hallway behind me. "Someone broke the window?" She stares at the glass.

"You're in bare feet. Go back to the kitchen." I usher her inside and go to the back porch, where I find a broom and dustpan. "I'll clean this up. Do you have something we can put in the broken frame?"

She looks slightly stunned as she nods. "I'm sure I can find something."

Ten minutes later, the mess is cleaned up and the window is boarded. I've called in the vandalism and have talked to the remaining reporters outside, but no one will accept responsibility or admit to seeing what happened.

"You might want to consider staying somewhere else tonight," I tell Kelsey.

She's standing at the window. Her arms are folded protectively around her body as she stares outside, as though preparing for another attack.

I drag my eyes away from her sexy concave stomach.

"How long will these people stay out there?"

"They tend to stick around. Lurk nearby . . . they're usually harmless—just trying to get more information for their networks."

"Can't the police do anything about that?"

"Afraid not. Do you have a friend you could stay with?"

"I already told you: I don't really know anyone here."

"Can someone from your previous hometown come and stay?" She has to have a friend somewhere who can be here for her during all of this. I'm shocked no one has shown up already.

She shakes her head now. "I kinda wish I'd made more of an effort to have people in my life . . ."

Isolation is part of abusive relationships. Now that I know about Malcolm's history of abuse, I wonder how much of her loner ways is her choice.

"Okay, well, a hotel . . ."

She holds a hand up to stop me. "I'm not leaving the house. They might come back. I need to be here when they come back." The strength in her voice surprises me.

Good. She'll need to be strong through all of this.

"I understand." I pause as I head for the door. "If you do feel threatened or unsafe, call me." I already regret the offer, especially when a look flashes in her eyes. One similar to the look she'd had in the kitchen before she kissed me.

"Okay." She follows me to the door, and I open it. "Thank you, Detective Ryan. For everything." She cradles a coffee cup between her hands, and her wedding ring hangs loosely on her finger.

Best for me to remember that ring the next time I'm tempted by her.

I step outside and head down the stairs.

"Detective Ryan?"

Fuck. "Yeah?"

"What are the chances I'm going to get my daughter back?"

I don't know the answer to that. "They get a lot better if you cooperate as much as possible." I study her. "Are you sure there's nothing else I should know?"

Tormented indecision reflects in her eyes, and I can tell she's conflicted. Whatever she's hiding is taking a toll on her conscience. I wait. It's only a matter of time before the truth will all come out.

After a long moment, she shakes her head. "No. There's nothing else."

Six months earlier . . .

I've been Kelsey Jennings long enough without anyone from my past finding me that I thought I was safe.

I was wrong.

The Facebook profile picture attached to the unread email in my "message requests" folder is a side shot, but I'd recognize my sister's face anywhere.

I should delete it and block her right away, but I'm terrified of taking any action. As though if I even touch the laptop, she'll suddenly appear. For real.

A chill I can't escape follows me all day as I ignore it. Unwanted memories return, and I have to remind myself that I'm *not* the person she's looking for. I've moved on from the past. But the tingling on my flesh grows stronger, and a morbid curiosity deepens, compelling me to find out what it is she wants.

Hours later, I glance over my shoulder, making sure I'm alone in the bedroom before clicking on the message.

My name is Holly Beinfeld (Sterling). I was born on April 2, 1991. I think you are my sister.

So, she's not entirely sure that I'm the person she's looking for. Good. Testing the waters, maybe? Wondering if I'll respond. Wondering if I've been looking for her as well.

I haven't been, and I can't let her know she's found me. She's not coming back into my life. I've worked too hard to keep my secrets and not let my past ruin my future. Reconnecting with her could destroy everything.

The baby cries down the hall, and I shut down the app and close my computer. I leave the room and go to Mikayla. She's awake, wailing in her crib. I reach for her and pick her up, and immediately she stops crying. I cradle her in my arms and go sit in the rocking chair in the corner of the pale-pink, ballerina-themed nursery.

Her eyes slowly drift shut as the gentle swaying of the chair lures her back to sleep. I stare down at the tiny, peacefully sleeping face, and all I feel is the weight of all my lies threatening to destroy my plans.

◆ ◆ ◆

Three days later, there's another message waiting for me. This time, I read it immediately.

> Dear Kelsey,
> I know you saw my last message and I know my reaching out might come as a surprise, but I've been looking for you for so long. I don't expect anything from you. I would just like the opportunity to know you again.
> Your Sister, Holly

An opportunity to know me again *is* expecting something from me. It's expecting a lot. Too much. I've never told anyone that I have a sister. I've been an only child since my parents—*our* parents—died. How would I suddenly tell everyone about her? Tell them I've been lying all these years? The adoption process that my foster parents went through years ago when they chose to adopt *only* me ensured that my birthright would remain a secret. She would remain a secret. It was to give me a chance at a future without our family stigma. Without her stigma.

Hearing Malcolm in the hallway outside the bedroom, I type quickly before shutting the laptop.

Dear Holly,
I'm sorry, but I think you're contacting the wrong person. I wish you the best with your search.
    K

The next morning's message is a photo. One of the two of us playing in our family yard in California before our parents died. Matching pink dresses and black Mary Jane shoes, white frilly socks. Hair in pigtails. In the photo, I'm smiling and she's crying.

I never cried. She did all the time.

I stare at the picture, my focus narrowing in on the million-dollar home in the background. Hollywood money.

Even from that young an age, I knew we were living on borrowed means. I'd hear our parents argue all the time about having no money. I wasn't sure how that was possible, when we lived in a house big enough that we didn't even need to see one another for days. We had a house-keeper, a cook, and a personal trainer, and my mother shopped all the time. Nothing came into the house that didn't have a designer tag on it.

And I knew the white powder they sniffed constantly had to be expensive, because they always fought over the last of it, and I'd see the cash that they took from an ATM weekly to pay the scary-looking guy who delivered it to our house at all hours of the night.

But I always felt that at any moment, it could all disappear.

Just like everything I have now could all disappear if my sister's decided not to keep our secrets anymore.

I ignore the message, but I can't ignore the mounting tension in my chest and shoulders, making my migraines worse, my anxiety levels rise to an unhealthy level. It was too much to hope that she'd stay a ghost from my past forever.

Days later, just after midnight, another message arrives. My hand trembles as I hover the pointer over it. Nothing is worse than the unknown, so I click on it.

Dear Kelsey,

It's been a few days since my last message. I know you've seen it. I know you've seen the photo. You know it's me. And I know you're the one I'm looking for. I'm sure you're busy and you haven't meant to ignore me, maybe you're even in shock a little, but I'm desperate for your reply. I just want to know you are okay. That your life is good. That you are happy. If you could just respond, it would mean everything to me. Please. Just respond.

Your Sister, Holly

I've finished reading it when a new one pops up, actually startling me with an eerie feeling of being watched. We are both online at the same time. She can see my active messenger profile, and a shiver runs down my spine. I turn around to look behind me in the room, but only Malcolm's sleeping silhouette, illuminated by the moonlight shining through the bedroom window, occupies the space with me. Yet I know she's closer than ever as I read:

Dear Kelsey,

I've asked nicely. Don't make me angry.

H.

September 7—3:23 p.m.

Loud music pounds against my brain, sweat drips from my forehead, and my legs propel my body forward. I'm desperate to outrun the feel of Kelsey Jennings's lips and drown out her words, a pleading echo from my past.

What are the chances I'm going to get my daughter back?

So many ways to ask that question, yet the words were exactly the ones my mother used.

Unlike that officer years before, I wasn't able to lie.

I increase the speed on the treadmill.

My mother knew she'd never see Julia again. Being married to a police detective for too many years, she'd learned that only a small percentage of missing people were ever found. Alive, at least.

By the time the case had been deemed a cold file, my mother's heart was already solid ice. For three months, she'd quickly spiraled into a maddening depression. Committing herself to a hospital where they'd kept her sedated had been her way of coping. For years, she *coped* in a small, whitewashed room, barely cognizant of her own surroundings, until the day she'd checked herself out and was found facedown in a river three blocks from the hospital.

Apparently my father and I weren't enough to fuel a desire for life in her.

But while I couldn't give Kelsey more hope, I also couldn't destroy any she might have had. I can't make promises that I'm going to bring her daughter back, but more than ever, I want to find Malcolm Jennings.

My hands clench, and my jaw tightens.

I shouldn't be surprised that the guy has a mean streak. It explains the immaculate house, the way he moved his family back here when it clearly wasn't what Kelsey wanted.

Was this abduction of their child another way to abuse her? Torture her? Make her suffer? Pieces of this case are slow to fall into place. It feels like weeks I've been working this one, when really it's only been two days.

I told her to call if she needed anything. I hope she doesn't. At least the sensible part of me hopes she doesn't. I'm not sure I can be around her without giving in to the urge that I had to fight in her kitchen hours ago.

I'm not sure Kelsey Jennings would want me to fight it.

September 7—10:45 p.m.

It's dark and quiet, the air still and thick with humidity. Heavy clouds block the moon and stars from view. They're desperate to break at any moment. A thunderstorm threatens. This weather makes it impossible to get comfortable. Too cold to turn off the heat in the house, but too humid for a lot of clothing. Not that the temperature had anything to do with my choice of outfit earlier that day. That was all for Detective Ryan.

I can still feel his eyes on my cleavage and ass. Still feel the way his fingers gently but purposefully touched my bare skin at my back when he hugged me.

He wanted me . . . he might have had enough resolve to push me away when I kissed him, but how long can he resist temptation?

I know he wants me to need him, to call him . . . but I won't. Not tonight.

Tonight, I have other things to do. Important things.

I walk outside and look around. All the reporters have given up and gone. The neighbors' lights are all off. It's dark out. No one is watching.

Finally.

I bend next to the potted plant on the step and reach deep into the dark, damp soil. My fingers touch metal, and I retrieve the set of buried keys. I shake off the dirt into the pot and pat it back into place around the wilting flowers.

I approach my vehicle and go to the back to unlock the trunk. I take out an old duffel bag with a Bowie High School logo and quickly shut the trunk again. A light flicks on across the street in an upstairs window, and I duck low behind the car.

I see the older lady across the street peer outside through her curtain. She glances up and down the quiet cul-de-sac . . . then the light flicks off again.

I wait a second longer to make sure she's not still standing there, watching me in the dark, but all is still in the window. I stand up and hurry back inside the house. I lock the door and check that the piece of wood Detective Ryan placed over the broken window is secure.

Then, I carry the bag upstairs to the master bedroom. Everyone has a "go bag"—whether physical or metaphorical. Or at least they should. No one should ever feel so safe in their reality to think that someday the rug can't get pulled out from under them, that their walls will never crumble . . . everyone should prepare for the worst.

I lay it on the bed and open it and then take out the clothing I've packed. All my best outfits. Special-occasion dresses and high heels. Things I've been looking forward to wearing. I've wanted to look nice.

I hang the clothes in the closet and move several pairs of shoes around on the shoe rack to make room. I've been so looking forward to showing off these shoes. I have great taste in shoes . . . now, who knows if I'll ever get the chance to show them off.

A grieving mother and abandoned wife doesn't get dressed up and go out alone. She doesn't laugh or have fun. She doesn't kiss the detective on the case . . . I need to be careful.

I return to the bed and reach into the bag. At the bottom, wrapped carefully in a T-shirt, is a small handmade box with my initials carved into the lid, next to an image of a little bird. I hide it beneath the bottom drawer of the dresser.

Then, I carefully take my gun out of the bag.

I packed it in case things go sideways. For protection in the worst-case scenario that I need to prepare for. To defend myself if needed . . .

Turns out I didn't even consider this turn of events. That Mikayla could go missing before I had time to execute my own plans. Use my own go bag. Apparently, despite everything I've ever been through, lived through . . . survived, my mind still can't come up with the most horrible things, the devastatingly disastrous events that could happen to me. I still believe that people are basically good. Somewhere deep within everyone, there are good souls and the best of intentions. People just do bad things sometimes. They make bad decisions, make the wrong choices.

When will I learn?

I carry the gun downstairs and put it in a drawer under several notebooks and envelopes. The police have already searched the place. They have no reason to search again.

September 7—10:50 p.m.

I stare at the warrant to search the Bowie development property site on my passenger seat as I drive through the neighborhood toward my father's house. I need to stop enabling him and this insane quest he's on, but the guilt I feel over my sister's disappearance and my desperate need for closure on her case keep me breaking the rules for him.

Last time . . .

It's always the last time. It's never the last time.

I stop at the sign on the corner and glance in the rearview mirror.

My sister's face stares back at me from the back seat. I don't even jump at the apparition. I see her all the time. She appears more often when I'm stressed. In dreams, in visions like this one, in shadows, and in the prickly eerie feeling when your hair stands on end and goose bumps cover your flesh . . . that feeling that you're not alone, that someone else is there.

She doesn't say much. Mostly she just stares with this disappointed, expectant look on her face. Why didn't I stay and walk her home? Why didn't I believe that the night and the darkness were unsafe for her? Why haven't I found her yet?

Sometimes, it feels as though she's leading me . . . but all leads end up in dead ends.

I turn my attention back to the road, and when I glance in the mirror again, she's gone. The clouds break, and rain pelts the windshield as I continue driving.

Faith's car is parked in the driveway when I pull up in front of my father's house.

A quick mental tally confirms that it's Tuesday. Right. Cribbage night. A tradition Faith and my father started when we first started to date six years ago. Their mutual passion for the game made them fast friends, and I'm grateful that, for at least one night every week, Faith's visits get my father out of the basement.

I can't believe she keeps coming. The relationship ended a year ago; still, Faith visits every Tuesday night. Which means it's the one night of the week I definitely stay away.

I should leave. Drive away. I've only seen Faith a few times since the breakup, and those times weren't intentional. Walking into Carla's Restaurant for late-night pasta takeout after a shift and seeing Faith enjoying a meal with some guy I didn't recognize had fucked me up in more ways than I'll ever admit. Avoiding her, pretending she doesn't exist, forgetting about the best five years of my life are the only way to move forward.

I'll never get over Faith. I just need to manage to survive in a world with her in it and one where she's not with me.

Seeing her will only set back any progress I may have made.

I should leave and come back later. But instead, I get out of the car and go inside.

Her laughter hits me like a bullet to the chest.

Soft, floaty, like a helium balloon running out of air. Drifting along at midheight, making it special but attainable. That's what Faith is. She is someone you should never be able to reach, yet she is kind and compassionate. Always available.

Her laughter was the first thing to draw me to her. She was sitting in a coffee shop, alone at a table near the window. She was watching something on her phone, and she laughed out loud, covered her mouth, and glanced around apologetically.

No one needed her apology.

Her laughter enhanced the atmosphere in the coffee shop. It raised my shitty mood. After twenty hours on shift, I'd just gone in for the caffeine fix, but I left with this unusual sense that I'd just been in the presence of someone special. The feeling lingered with me all day.

Then, seeing her again as she crossed the street in front of the court-house solidified my need to know who she was.

I found out sooner than I'd expected.

She was the social worker for an underage minor who'd disappeared from a foster home weeks before. I'd found him and was in court on behalf of the foster home as a witness—not that I believed the poor kid should be returned to the shithole he'd been living in. Hell, I was hoping the kid would turn into a cold case after I met the foster parents and saw the environment he was forced to endure, but luckily, Faith worked her magic.

Instead, the kid was placed in a temporary group home, since he was turning eighteen in three months. The look of gratitude on the boy's face when he hugged Faith outside the courtroom tugged at heartstrings I didn't know I still had.

Faith thanked me for my work in finding the boy, and I asked her out.

To my amazement, she agreed, and for five years I pretended I could be good enough for her, and she gave me every chance to prove it. In the end, I didn't. I could never live up to the person she thought I was, wanted me to be. My existence had been too wrapped up in grief and pain and anger for too long for me to truly feel the love and affection for her that she deserved. She wanted to get married, have kids . . . I knew I would never want those things, so out of mercy I ended our relationship.

"Hello?" My father's voice coming from the living room snaps me out of the trance. Thank God. If Faith turned around and saw me standing there, staring at her side profile, she might get renewed energy to try to work things out, start over, pick up where we left off. What else did she beg for in those first few weeks after the split?

It should have been *me* groveling, begging, and lying by claiming I could change to make things work. Not her.

I cleared my throat. "Hey, Dad . . . I just stopped by with that paperwork you asked me for." He's actually wearing pants with his usual oversize cardigan, and I can't be sure, but he may even have showered. His thinning hair is combed over the balding patch in the middle, and the usual stale smell that follows him around is missing this evening.

I enter the living room, and Faith's smile is genuine, warm. She holds no ill will toward me for breaking things off, and as long as I don't give her any false hope, we can maintain this sense of stalemate, where we both secretly accept that I still love her in my own closed-off way, but a future is not possible. "Sorry to interrupt your game."

"Not at all," she says. "We were just finishing. I won."

"She cheated," my father says.

Faith can't cheat. She is incapable of anything dishonest. But she laughs and hugs my father tight as she stands. The irrational jealousy I feel can take a hike. "I'll let you believe that, old man," she tells my father.

She reaches for a pale-pink cashmere sweater. I recognize it. I gave it to her for her birthday the first year we were dating. Actually, she bought it for herself, wrapped it, and then gave it to me to give to her, knowing I'd forget what day it was. She was always letting me off the hook like that. She turns to me as she puts it on. "Walk me out?"

Shit. "Yeah . . . okay." I place the envelope with the warrant on the coffee table, and my father shoots me a look that I can't . . . or won't decipher. "I'll be back in a minute, Dad."

"Take your time," he calls after us.

I'm grateful for these brief portions of time in which Faith can bring him back to the land of the living, but I know he'd like us to get back together, and I hope she's not encouraging him.

Outside, I walk her to her car and reach for the door handle. The faster I can get her in the car and on her way, the better. But she wants to talk. "It's been a while. How are you?"

"Good." I will never admit to her that my life has been a void without her in it. That would be selfish, and I was selfish long enough. "You?"

"Great . . . work is busy."

Are you seeing anyone? That guy in the restaurant? The one in your recent Facebook pictures? Is it serious? Do you know he has ten unpaid parking tickets and a shit credit rating? I rein in my crazy. I can't background check every man she decides to date. It's none of my business . . . and also illegal. "That's good . . . hey, you know you don't have to keep doing this." I nod toward the house. "Coming here, I mean."

"Are you kidding? I look forward to kicking that man's ass every week."

Ass. She swore, and her cheeks turn bright pink when she catches herself. Profanity's so rare for her that it actually sounds adorable coming out of her mouth. I refuse to get hung up on it. "Well, I appreciate you keeping him company. I know he loves seeing you." So do I, and I have no right to feel that way. Five years of her life were wasted with me. And yet, she stands here, smiling, open . . . the Faith I remember, with no anger or resentment toward me.

No sign of wanting me back, though, either. Which is a first.

"How are you, really?" she asks.

"Fine. Why? What did that old man say?"

"Just that you were on a case. A missing child, and I know how those get to you." She touches my arm. It's meant to soothe, comfort. All it does is make me rock hard. I try to pretend it's leftover attraction from seeing Kelsey Jennings fresh from the shower, but Kelsey spurred a physical response in me, not this deep, aching need that feels like a huge sinkhole the longer it remains unfilled.

I shrug. "It's not a big deal. Treating it like any other case."

"If you ever want to talk to someone."

"To you?"

"About the job, I mean . . . the pressure, the stress . . . I'm always here if you need me, Paul."

"I don't." Too abrupt. Too harsh. Too late.

Her hand falls away. She frowns. "Okay . . ."

There's more she wants to say. I wait.

"He said he found another area . . ."

"Yes he has."

"And I suppose you're helping him?" She doesn't approve of that. She never has. She doesn't believe it's healthy for him to keep holding on to the past. I know she tries to talk to him about it on these Tuesday-night visits; I'm not stupid enough to think it's all about the card game.

"Do I have any other choice?" I ask. "If I don't, he'll just find another way."

She sighs and nods reluctantly. "You're right about that."

For once, I would like her to argue with me. Convince me that helping him is wrong. Give me a reason to stop.

She stares at the car keys in her hand, and I take my cue. The conversation's over. I reach for the handle, and this time I open the door.

"Well, take care of yourself, okay? And it was nice to see you," she says as she climbs in.

"Bye . . . thanks again for visiting with Dad."

She smiles as I shut the door.

I stand in the driveway and watch her drive away.

I shouldn't have gone inside. Now that I've seen that smile, heard that laugh, been the recipient of her thoughtful concern, seen her interact with my father, it will be hell pushing it all to the back of my mind. Stomping down the resurfacing emotions and what-ifs that have no business coming back.

The worst part is that Faith doesn't understand. There wasn't anything really wrong with us. We didn't implode like other couples do. We rarely fought. We were good together. We worked together.

But this job makes relationships impossible. Not the hours or the stress or the demands or putting our lives at risk. Those things make having a relationship impossible for other cops.

For me, it's the secrets I know that reduce relationships to just another aspect of life that I'm not good at. Hidden dark desires of the evil mind that make fully trusting anyone impossible. In one year, I've investigated six missing person files. I've found three. All dead. Fifty percent in this line of work is not good enough, especially when the most likely outcome of locating the missing is that we find them without a pulse.

It's arguable that I'm not good at my job, and fuck if I don't feel that in my core. Disappointment radiates through my bones at my inability to return the lost to their homes and families safely.

It's enough to wonder why I keep doing this. Why I keep working in a career where my failure is guaranteed more than fifty percent of the time.

But it's that failure that keeps me trying. Maybe one day I'll get it right. Maybe one day I'll find the missing and they'll be still alive. Still breathing. I'll get to see a family reunited. Get to see relief and joy on the faces of loved ones. Tears of happiness instead of sobs of despair.

But even if that doesn't happen, I'm not the villain.

Families never hold my failures against me. They know it's not my fault their child or sister or brother or friend is missing. They know there's true evil out there, and I'm not it.

They put their faith in me, and even when I fail, they thank me for trying. They see me as the good versus the evil, and when I fail to do my job, they blame it on evil winning once again. I, too, am a victim alongside them. They never blame their pain and suffering on my inadequacies.

Still, relationships are not an option for me. I see evil everywhere. I know not to let my guard down. I know everyone has a dark side. Everyone is capable of snapping if pushed to their breaking point.

And even if they aren't evil. If their body and soul are pure and right and true, then they will eventually be a victim. Not having an ounce of evil, the truly good can't see evil coming. They can't feel it, can't sense it. They don't know what to look for when it approaches in a dark alley at night or in the presence of someone they trust.

They trust. They love. They forgive. They rest.

They aren't on guard. They aren't ready. Therefore, they leave themselves open to being a victim.

Like Faith.

She is one of those rare truly altruistic spirits—full of love and optimism. She only sees the good in others. Saw the good in me.

But, of course, I'm not like Faith. I let my sister down. I sat back and let my mother spiral into a crazed depression that eventually took her from us as well. And I encourage my father's madness in this never-ending search for peace.

I let Faith down every time she tried to comfort me, love me, take care of me by pushing her away—slowly, silently. I didn't want the stains of my sins to tarnish her, damage her.

I couldn't love someone as good as Faith.

Because loving Faith meant I was the villain in our story.

September 8—8:47 a.m.

I almost don't recognize myself as the woman on television pleading for the safe return of my daughter.

So much for living a normal, quiet existence here in Ellicott City. I crave an opportunity to just blend in. A time when the spotlight isn't being shone on my life and my mistakes.

My parents' death was all over the news. Therefore, so was my face, tear stained and desperate on every television set and newspaper. The reporters in California showed no mercy. Young, scared, the daughter of movie stars . . . no one had much sympathy. The accident was their own fault. They were drunk and high and chasing a well-known paparazzo down the crowded streets of Beverly Hills, seeking revenge for all the illicit, career-damaging photos the man had taken.

Tragedy and the spotlight seem to follow me everywhere I go. The darker the nightmare, the more brightly the media shines, illuminating every crack and tear in my world. Poking, prodding, and determined to shatter it all, break it open so that everyone can see inside.

The poor little rich girl who had no one to care about her has grown up to be a pathetic, stupid housewife with a similar fate.

On the screen, the cameraman has zoomed in on my face. My terrified, nervous, lying face . . .

I turn off the television and throw the remote control across the room. I stand up and pace as I feel my blood pressure rise, my pulse thundering in my veins.

How is this once again my life? How have I let this happen?

This is all my fault. I was naive. I was trusting in a reality that doesn't exist.

I let evil back into my life.

Six months earlier . . .

I know it's a mistake to respond. Better to keep ignoring the emails, to block her and keep denying I am who she thinks I am. If I open any door to her at all, she may not stop at revealing just one secret from the past that I've buried.

But maybe she's telling the truth when she claims to just want to know that I'm okay. She was always concerned about me. She was always the worrier. She was the soft-hearted one. Back then, my sister didn't have one bad bone in her body. Maybe all she wants is to be acknowledged. If I give her something, even the tiniest bit of information, then maybe that will be enough.

Dear H,
I am married. He is a high school teacher. We have one daughter. I am happy.
K

It wasn't enough. Less than an hour later, she replies:

Dear Kelsey,
How wonderful to hear! I am truly happy for you. I have hoped and prayed for these things for you. I wish I could give you the same reassurance that I am doing well too. But unfortunately my life

has gone in a different direction from yours. I've had three serious relationships. One in high school to a boy named Billy West. Ha! He even sounds like a bad-boy doesn't he? You know I've always been attracted to that type. The ones all wrong for me. Billy was everything I knew I should avoid. He was three years older and at fifteen, I thought he was a man of the world. He knew so much more than I did. He wasn't book smart. He was street smart. He smoked and drank. He said he did drugs heavier than pot, but I think he was just trying to be cool. I never saw him sniff things from a mirror or shoot things into his veins like that horrible boyfriend of the lady at the house where we lived. Remember how gross he was? He always smelled so bad. Sometimes I think I can still smell him on my clothes or my hair . . . Anyway, back to Billy. He was gorgeous. Dark hair, dark eyes. He wore a leather jacket all the time. It didn't matter the weather. Hot or cold, he wore the leather jacket.

The jacket was what first attracted me to him. Like I said, I loved a bad boy and there's just something about leather. Unfortunately, that same jacket was what he used to trap my arms next to my body while he did what he did. He tied the sleeves really tight. I didn't think leather could be tied like that.

Anyway, he broke up with me afterwards.

The next guy was when I was eighteen. I know big gap between boyfriends, right? The truth was I was afraid of boys after Billy, so I dated a few girls, but I couldn't make myself like it. So then there was Fred. Boring name. Boring guy. Safe. I thought that was what I wanted, but he was constantly trying to change me. He didn't like my hair or the way I wore my makeup. He kept trying to make me dress like his sister. He bought me the same perfume and insisted I wear it. It creeped me out, but I wanted a boyfriend so I went along with it. Things were going great until I saw him kissing his sister. Not like a brotherly kiss, but full on, with tongue.

I didn't end it though, I just asked to be a part of whatever they had going on. I know, completely pathetic, right? He said no and dumped me.

So, a few weeks later, I met Erik. I still think I fell for him partially because of his name. It sounded nice, normal. Not boring like Fred or dangerous like Billy. Erik. It's nice, right?

He was my boss at Chick-fil-A. He was the manager there and he was really driven. He worked really hard and he said one day he might promote me. That's not why I dated him though. It was more a convenience thing. He lived in the small apartment at the back of the restaurant and he let me stay there with him. That one lasted the longest. A full year. Until I got pregnant. I told Erik when I was five months along, after it was too late to have an abortion. I was starting to show by then and couldn't keep pretending I was just gaining weight from eating Chick-fil-A for every meal. He freaked out. He said he was working on his career and didn't want a family right now. He was worried about what his parents would think. He dumped me, fired me and kicked me out and then I lost the baby a few months later.

So, that's my relationship history. Men, huh?

Oh but not for you! Your husband sounds perfect! I'm so so happy for you.

And I'm an aunt! Aunt Holly! I can't believe it. I mean, I totally can believe it. What happened to me never happened to you so you can totally have kids. And I'm Aunt Holly.

I bet she has our hair coloring and blue eyes, right? I bet she looks just like us. I can't wait to see her. Maybe you could friend me so I can see photos. I noticed you changed your profile picture to an image of a flower. It's really pretty, but I'd love for you to change it back to the picture of yourself. I love seeing your face.

Anyway, think about it. The friend thing, I mean. I'd send you a request, but your profile doesn't allow it. So, no pressure.

Anyway, I've rattled on forever and you have a husband and a daughter to spend time with, so talk to you soon.

Please write again. I miss you and I love you!

Your Sister, Holly

I've made a mistake. I know it immediately. I feel my past reaching through the computer screen and strangling any peace I've found. Responding has only led to her wanting more. She was always so pathetically desperate for my time and affection.

And now that she thinks my life is perfect, she'll only be more motivated to become a part of it.

I don't respond, and I certainly don't send her a friend request. This has gone too far already.

The next day, a new message is waiting for me. I stare at my computer as though it could explode any minute, with the pressure of a bomb, blowing me to pieces. It's the only way she can contact me, and now it's become a thing I fear most. My heart races. I know that I have to open the message: the only way to make sure she hasn't actually found me yet is to keep checking the emails to see if she's still wanting more info . . . digging . . . looking for clues. The minute she stops messaging is when I'll really have to worry.

Dear Kelsey,

I'm so sorry that I didn't ask you any new questions in my previous email. Please know I am always interested in learning more about your life. I want to know everything. Where are you living now? Did you ever make it back to a coast? Everything else has worked out for you so I bet you did—which one? Do you still swim? (Remember how I could never swim? How I would freak out when you'd do that floating facedown thing. I'm so glad you never actually drowned.) Did you ever become a dancer? You always wanted to be one. You were always so talented and driven and dancing was really the only thing you cared about, so I bet you did become a famous ballerina. I bet you perform under the stage name you always loved—Ariel Barbarac. I've searched that name so many times, but I've never found you. But, I'm sure I'm searching wrong . . . or maybe you decided on a different stage name. Something just as elegant and beautiful as you are. If you'd friend me, I could see pictures.

Just a thought. No pressure.

Write back, okay? I promise to always ask more questions so you'll know to keep responding.

Your Sister, Holly

I shut down the message, and my screen saver makes my heart hurt. The picture taken three years before at my last ballet performance—meant to be inspiration, a visual goal of a life I'm desperately trying to get back to—only taunts me with thoughts of what may never be again.

All I ever wanted was to dance. I had God-given talent and the means from wealthy, famous porn-star parents to make it happen. Despite my embarrassment over their low-class reputations in Hollywood, I was set up for success with no chance to fail. I was the prima donna at the dance academy. The other little girls hated me, envied me, wanted to be me. Even I was sometimes jealous of me. I was chosen as lead dancer in every production the academy performed, and from the age of three I knew I was something special. My arms and legs moved gracefully as if on their own. I never felt like I was in control of my movements when I danced; they controlled me. And for a child with zero discipline or guidance at home, I craved the power of the dance when it took over. It gave me focus, led me in the way I needed, made me stronger, determined.

That's not to say that dancing came easy.

Countless missing toenails and blood-soaked ballerina shoes proved otherwise. I was going through new shoes quicker than anyone else. Even the older girls at the academy didn't work as hard or practice as long as I did. I didn't feel the pain while I was training, but it was agony after I'd stop. I never wanted to stop.

In addition to the torn flesh on my feet were the muscle cramps and aching bones, which felt like my limbs were being torn and stretched. They were, in a way. I was building a dancer's body. And that meant pain and persistence and not showing any sign of weakness.

By age five, I was on every dance company's radar as the child to watch. I was working around the clock on multiple productions, performing two or three shows a night for forty-eight weeks of the year. When our parents took us out of the regular school system, three months into kindergarten, and my sister started learning with a home tutor, my parents insisted that I didn't need to worry about the lessons right away. While my sister was stuck inside learning to read and write and do math, I was dancing. It was the only thing I cared about. It wasn't a passion; it was an obsession. It was really the only good parenting my parents ever did—recognizing that I had potential and not forcing me to focus on useless things. For another four years, everything was perfect.

But then, true to their nature, my parents had to fuck it all up.

The night of their accident, I wished I had died in the car along with them. Not because I was devastated by their deaths. All I ever needed—all I'd ever received from them—was their financial support and their somewhat questionable connections to continue my own dream. The luxury, the lifestyle, the joy of dancing. And their fatal car crash brought all that to an end.

My sister wouldn't stop crying at our parents' funeral. I cried, too, but it was only for show. Tears ran down my face, as strategic and as perfectly placed as they had when I performed on the stage.

Unfortunately, they didn't work.

No one came to my rescue. I would even have settled for one of my parents' rich friends—seedy Hollywood royalty—to step up and take me in. But no one did. Despite the talent I possessed, the promise . . . no one wanted me.

I begged Madam to find other dance parents to adopt me. After all, I was a better dancer than their children were. They could raise a star. But their jealousy ran too deep. They resented me for stealing their children's spotlight for so long. They didn't want me either.

Worse: they knew what was about to happen. I was about to disappear. I was about to leave a big, gaping hole on the stage for their children. The spotlight I'd stolen all for myself would now get redistributed among the less talented, the less deserving.

They snickered and sneered now when they saw me at the dance studio those first few days after the funeral, when my sister and I were still in limbo, stuck in the care of our parents' executor—their talent agent, a man who was desperately struggling to find any money in the will at all. They whispered when they saw me pack up my things from my locker at the academy for the last time. Even Madam Ellouette was happy to see me go. She'd never reached the potential I had, and she knew it. Now, she could focus on the talents she could contain. Make them great, but never like me. Never phenomenal.

Creatives are sick like that. The professional jealousy runs deep.

The other little girls laughed and reveled over my expulsion from the academy. They all knew I was suddenly poor and would never be able to afford to come back. They teased me as I gathered my things. Still dressed in their tutus and ballet shoes, hair pulled tightly back in buns, makeup on their faces as they got ready for dress rehearsal of the first show of that season—the one I was set to star in. The one my replacement would now get the spotlight in.

They called me names and shoved me as I passed by them on my way out of the studio.

So, what choice did I have but to wait the two hours, hidden behind the studio door until they emerged after practice, and then push them one by one down the flight of stairs?

The broken bones piled at the bottom where six screaming girls lay meant that mine wasn't the only dance career that ended that day.

◆ ◆ ◆

Psycho. Soulless. Crazy.

All words that were used to describe me after the incident. And no one wanted to adopt a child described that way. Our parents' reputation continued to haunt us, and now, with my unfair assessment, the local foster homes didn't want to take in either my sister or me.

Suddenly my sister developed a voice and a backbone. She yelled at me that it was my fault no one wanted us. She threw insults my way. As if she was anyone in the world. I knew she was nothing. This was just a minor setback for me. I would rise to the top again.

So, I calmly, quietly waited until she shut up; then I punched her hard in the face, several times.

She never took that tone with me again.

After we'd spent a few weeks in an overcrowded home for runaways, our social worker located a family member in Maryland. Our mother's great-aunt. We lasted about six days with her. She told social services that she felt threatened while she slept, just because she'd woken every night to find me watching her.

Once again, I was to blame for my behavior. The reason the Maryland social workers couldn't find a new place to put us. No one understood that, in a matter of months, I'd lost my parents' borrowed money, been forced to leave California to move to one of the most boring places on earth, and had had my dreams ripped away.

Finally, at age eleven, we were placed. In a home with two lawyers who couldn't have children of their own.

Jackpot. Finally, more money. I'd show them my talents, and they would love me. Not that I wanted their affection. I just needed them to pay for dance again. I couldn't go back to an academy because of those stupid clumsy girls in California, but I would ask them to hire a private dance teacher. They could afford one, and they would want me to have only the best. Personal attention. No distractions.

Besides, in Hollywood, memories are short. Six months after my parents' death, people had long forgotten about them. In another few years, my misunderstanding at the academy would be a thing of the past. Just a tragic incident by a young girl devastated by recent life events. When they made a movie about my life and my rise to fame, they'd spin it in my favor. That's what Hollywood does. If anything, I was learning to see my parents' death, my incident, all of it, as just fodder for an amazing biopic someday.

The foster couple lived in a huge house. They had a pool. They had a housekeeper and a cook. They had nice clothing and expensive things. They were perfect.

My sister was still missing our parents, but even she was relieved that we finally had a nice home again. I told her to be good, to listen, to try not to be so stupid; then they might even adopt us.

The home had so many bedrooms. As we walked down the long hallway, I could see into each one. I was already envisioning how I would decorate my room. I prayed I'd get my own and wouldn't have to share with my sister. I made her promise not to tell the foster parents that she was afraid of the dark and of being alone. She had to grow up. It wasn't my job to take care of her.

The woman stopped at the end of the hall and opened a door, and my heart raced. This was it. The beginning of my climb back to stardom. My dancing career had been on hold, but I could feel life was about to get better again. And with these two, I wouldn't have to feel embarrassed. Lawyers weren't as fabulous as doctors or philanthropists, I thought, but they were better than having drug-addicted, washed-up movie stars for parents. Maybe when they adopted me, I could take their last name, and my tarnished past would be erased.

The foster mom told us to go inside, and I pushed my sister aside to go first.

But the room was full of junk. Unlike the rest of the house, this space was filled with collectibles . . . movie posters covered every inch of the walls, rows of shelves held miniature figures of action movie stars. I stepped farther into the room, and my chest tightened at the sight of a movie collection a preteen should have known nothing about.

Our parents' porn movies. I had seen them all . . . they'd been filmed at our home.

That day, we became the newest addition to their Hollywood collectibles.

With the threat of death if we told anyone or tried to escape, the foster parents would take us to dinner parties. Rich professionals who shared their passion for all things Hollywood. They'd loan us out for the evening, and we were expected to do whatever was asked of us. Sometimes, the people would just ask us questions about our parents and our lives in LA. I couldn't remember everything about those days, so I'd make things up. Make everything sound glamorous and exciting—the way they expected. Other times, they'd want to touch us . . . brush our hair . . . stroke our skin.

We were props. I knew it, but I played right along. I did whatever they wanted me to do. I'd seen the things my parents had done—how they'd used sex to get what they wanted—so I learned to do that too. Only a few of the really odd ones asked for sexual stuff, though. Most were content to just be around us. Living Hollywood royalty dolls. I believed that if one of the other couples could see my brilliance, they'd stop seeing me only as a toy to pass around and would adopt me. Take me away from these people. Give me everything I longed for and deserved.

They wouldn't take my sister, of course, and I wouldn't ask or expect them to. It was her own fault. She was too shy and scared and cried the whole time. She didn't try at all. But at least she didn't fuck it up, for once in her life.

I even danced for the "borrowers" at every dinner party. Unfortunately, I was rusty and clumsy. My limbs didn't seem to work right, and my timing was off. No one was going to want a failed ballerina. A mediocre child with only minimal talent.

Without my formal training, I could feel every ounce of skill swooshing away. Without regular practice, without the right teacher, and without the opportunity to be on stage, where the spotlight added fuel to my passion, I was losing the only thing I'd ever cared about. If I didn't get back to it soon, it would all disappear. Years of hard work, dedication, and determination would have meant nothing. If I wasn't a dancer, I was no one. I couldn't let that happen.

I couldn't count on my sister to help. She just grew more withdrawn and moody and helpless as time went on. She'd lost hope of having a real family. People who would truly care about us. Well, I didn't give a shit if she stayed a living doll for these people forever. I had to get out.

The next time I was brought as entertainment to one of their dinner parties would be the last time.

I'd noticed a trend.

The man and the woman seemed to enjoy time together in the bathroom at these events. They had a routine. One would slip off unnoticed. The other would wait three or four minutes, then sneak away to take a call. They'd fuck in the bathroom, then return at different times. It was their thing, I guess. I didn't care. At least I didn't have to watch them.

Quite honestly, life with the man and the woman really could have been much worse. If they'd just given me my own room and allowed me to continue my dance lessons, I may have reconsidered my next moves.

That day, almost a year after they'd taken us in, we were at the man's boss's house. He was an old guy. Kind eyes. I almost chickened out because I felt bad that he'd have to clean up blood in his bathroom, but he had a housekeeper, and I assumed it would be her job. And she didn't have kind eyes. She had judging eyes. So, I carried out my plan.

As predicted, sometime after dessert was served, my sister and I were handed to our borrowers. I pretended I was sick but sneaked into the kitchen instead. I grabbed two knives; then I weighed my options. Kill them all, or just the foster parents?

I was still holding out hope that the older man with kind eyes might take me in once this was over, so I headed upstairs to the master bedroom, where I knew the foster parents would end up.

Hearing footsteps on the stairs, I hurried into the en suite bathroom and hid behind the door. My less-than-seventy-pound frame served a purpose. My body was completely unnoticeable, pressed against the wall.

I held my breath and clutched the knives tightly in both hands. The minute the man entered and closed the door, I had to attack. If I hesitated or delayed, it was game over. I'd be killed or locked up forever in a glass case in their collectibles room. I had to be fast.

Footsteps drew closer, and I could feel my heart bursting through my skin. I knew it was him. I could smell the cologne. I could discern the slight limp he walked with.

He entered the bathroom, and as he closed the door, I lunged. Catlike. Two knives pierced the skin at his back at the same time. In the mirror, I saw his wide-eyed reflection. Surprise, fear, terror.

I yanked the knives out quickly and kept stabbing. Blood seeped from the wounds, covering the fabric at his back. He fell forward, then tried to turn to face me, to fight me off, but I kept stabbing. I got him in the waist, then the stomach as he turned. He fell to the floor. Bleeding out. I think he called me a bitch or something, but I was too hyped on the adrenaline of my actions to really focus on what idle threats he was making.

I was the one holding the weapons.

Finally, his body convulsed on the bathroom floor and then went limp. Pools of blood covered the floor beneath him. Served the house-keeper right for her judging eyes.

Then came the hard part. Rushing to pick up his feet, I dragged his two-hundred-pound body as best I could away from the door, enough so that I could close it again.

Then I climbed up onto the counter, bloody, dripping knives in both hands, and waited. I kept an ear to the door and an eye on his body in case he moved.

Four minutes later, more footsteps.

The door opened, and I lunged. One knife landed in the side of the woman's cheek. The other missed her shoulder. She gasped in fright, and I quickly stabbed her stomach. The first knife was lodged in her cheek, trapped between her cheek- and jawbones, so I just used one to finish her off.

Seconds later, the man and the woman were no longer an issue.

Except for the housekeeper.

The next few weeks were a blur. Once again, my sister and I made headlines—for all the wrong reasons. I was a hero. I'd saved my sister's life and my own. However, I was the only one who saw it that way. Everyone else thought I was a psychopath. This new double murder, combined with the incident from the dance academy, didn't put me in a very good light. Apparently everyone thought I was crazy. Especially the therapist at the hospital whom social services brought me to after the trauma.

I tried to explain that I didn't need therapy. That I wasn't traumatized at all. Murdering the man and the woman had been my only choice, the right thing to do. I didn't feel bad or guilty about it. No, the sight of their blood all over the bathroom and on my face and clothing hadn't frightened me at all. I was safe now. Free.

Unfortunately, that only made the therapist even more concerned about me. "Lack of conscience," she said.

All I know is that I stabbed those people to get out of the situation I'd been forced to live in. If that made me crazy, then so be it.

The thing that made the situation worse was that my sister had gone silent. She was the traumatized one. So much so that she stopped speaking. Conveniently enough, just when I needed her to back me up the most. Ungrateful bitch. I saved her life, and she let everyone think I'd made up how bad living with the man and the woman really was. Which meant they kept me in the hospital. A danger to myself and others.

Still, cops came and fingerprinted me—juvenile offenses. They started a file on me, expecting to see more of me in the future.

It was bullshit. I'd never hurt myself. Or anyone who didn't deserve it.

September 8—11:02 p.m.

On my computer screen, countless images and articles load about Kelsey Jennings. A former prima ballerina . . . or hopeful at least. She claimed to be a financial adviser . . . but she never mentioned this obvious passion of hers. I can definitely see it. Her body is shaped like a dancer's—tall, lean, tight—graceful in her movements.

Reviews of her ballet performances in Florida all reveal she was on her way to becoming a star.

What happened? Why didn't she continue to pursue her passion? What made her give it all up? Malcolm? Did she leave it all behind for a life as a teacher's wife? A mother? Is this why she needs psychotics to make it through her day?

The last performance listing is for a production of *Swan Lake* four years before. Mikayla Jennings is two, so that makes sense. It is rare to see a pregnant ballerina on stage. Not that I know much about theater.

Next, I search Kelsey Jennings's Facebook profiles. Maybe I'll find some answers there. People treat their social media like private journals, easily forgetting that nothing online is secure. I've never seen the appeal of sharing my personal life and details with strangers, and, thankfully, my career has helped to curb any desire I might have for online dating, should I ever feel that desperate.

Eighteen listings appear under the name. I scan the profile pictures but don't see her. I'm able to eliminate fifteen of them . . . but I have to look at the locations listed for the other three before narrowing it down to one listed as living in Florida. She hasn't updated her information since the move.

She's smart. The profile is locked. No way to friend request her or message her. I click on the personal info, but only the old hometown is listed. No profession. No relationship status. No interests or likes. Her friends list is not visible to the public.

The profile picture is a generic image of a flower. Not a customary family picture or mother-daughter pic. Not a wedding photo from the best day of her life . . .

Why so secretive? What are you hiding, Kelsey?

I click on "Photos of Kelsey," and it's a completely different story. Dozens load in. She obviously hasn't locked her profile as much as she thinks. I lean closer to study the images with her tagged in them.

Kelsey Jennings might be a loner now, but it wasn't always that way.

In one picture, she's on a beach. In a bikini. Not the picture I expected at all. Her expression screams sex, so completely different from any I've seen in the last forty-eight hours. A memory of her in the yoga outfit has me instantly hard.

I keep scrolling through the images. Before Kelsey Jennings was a suburban housewife, she was a party girl. No pictures of boyfriends, which irrationally makes me feel better, but there are several of her kissing other women.

Curious or bisexual?

Which one is it, Kelsey?

Odd that she'd leave these pictures tagged. What does Malcolm think of his wife's former life? He has to have seen these photos. Is that why he is so controlling over his wife? Has she given him reason to feel insecure?

Everyone has a past, but I'm not so sure I'd trust this version of Kelsey Jennings either.

I stop scrolling at an image of her that draws me in with a magnetism so strong that I'm barely breathing.

Those eyes—teasing, taunting . . . even through the camera, Kelsey's gaze is intoxicating. Mesmerizing. Those dark-blue, penetrating eyes.

My cell phone rings, and I close the laptop quickly when I see her number light up the call display. "Damn it."

◆ ◆ ◆

Twenty minutes later, I'm standing on her front porch, responding to noises she's heard outside her home. The pep talk I gave myself about keeping my head in the game doesn't work worth a shit once she opens the front door.

"Hi, Detective Ryan. Thank you for getting here so quickly," she says.

She's in a pair of shorts and a baggy sweatshirt, and her long, tanned legs are a distraction this case can't afford. Her hair hangs loose around her shoulders, and, despite the late hour, her face is made up . . . except for her lips.

"Are you coming in?" she asks when I'm silent. "Or are you planning to do a perimeter search first?"

Muggy, humid yet cool fall air provides no relief for the rush of heat running through me, and the air-conditioned interior is tempting, but I should do the search around the house and get the hell out of here. "I'll take a look around. The noise came from the back of the house?"

"I think so."

"Okay. Lock the door and I'll be back."

She nods as she closes the door. I wait to hear the click of the lock, then make my way around the side of the house. By now an intruder would be gone, but I look for footsteps in the mud. The landscaping around the sides of the house and in the yard hasn't been done yet, so tracks would be easy to spot.

I don't see any.

I reach over the top of the gate and unlock the door, my hand on my gun as I push it open. I move into the backyard, scanning the space.

A slow creaking sound comes from the swaying swing of the play set in the center of the yard. Other than that, there's no noise. No movement.

I leave the yard and go to the other side of the house. In the kitchen window, I can see Kelsey standing there, watching. Her worried expression and the fact that every light is illuminated in the house bring out an insanely stupid urge in me to protect her.

For all I know, she is crazy, but until all signs lead to that as the only conclusion, I'm not dismissing this investigation. Or her. She's scared, and she may have every right to be. I told her to call me if she needed anything, and I refuse to let my attraction to her prevent me from keeping her safe.

A clanging sound startles me, and I swing to my right. The metal garbage can lid rattles against the ground, and noise comes from inside. It would take a small person to fit in there. Still, I'm approaching with caution when the front door opens and Kelsey appears on the step. "What was that?"

"Stay back," I tell her as I approach the garbage can.

A raccoon springs from it, and I bounce back toward the house as it scurries toward the step.

Kelsey screams as it runs toward her and dives out of its way as it goes inside through the open front door.

Shit. Fucking wild animal.

I put my gun back in the holster and head straight toward the car.

"Hey! Where are you going?" she asks.

I don't look back. "You're safe," I call over my shoulder.

"Like fuck I am—I have a wild animal in my house!"

"What you need is animal control." My hand is still shaking from the sight of the vicious-looking thing—sharp claws and savage teeth.

"You can't be serious," she says.

I stop and turn. "Dead serious."

"You're a cop. What happened to 'serve and protect'?"

"Against bullets, not raccoons. Good luck and good night."

"Detective Ryan, I can't go back in there with that thing."

Jesus. The pleading in her voice is something I desperately wish I could ignore. I did not sign on for this. Animals are not my problem. Still, I hesitate at the vehicle. Can't I just leave and let her deal with this rodent problem on her own? It's not trying to kill her . . . just eat her food.

The sound of crashing coming from the kitchen makes us both jump.

"It's destroying the house. Please help," she says.

What the hell does she think I can do about it? I pull out my cell and search for a local exterminator, one that's open twenty-four hours, and place the call.

She listens while I give the guy the info and address. "Now what?" she asks as I disconnect the call.

"You wait. They'll be here in less than an hour."

She nods as she sits on the step. "Okay. Thank you. Sorry to drag you out. I feel stupid." She wraps her arms around her long, bare legs and gently rocks back and forth.

I should go. I've done my job—searched the perimeter, confirmed that she's safe, called a guy—and I'm done.

Instead, I climb the stairs and sit on the top one next to her. It's almost midnight—I can't leave her out here in the dark, alone. In this rich, safe neighborhood. "It wasn't stupid. I told you to call if there was anything."

She raises one eyebrow as she glances my way. "You obviously didn't mean raccoons in my garbage can."

"I said anything."

"So . . . afraid of animals?" she asks, drawing her knees closer to her body as she shivers.

I remove my jacket and place it over her lower body. "Not cute ones, but wild ones that look ready to eat my face—yes."

She laughs. Just a small one, but it's probably the first one in days, and I'm happy I can give her that at least. "They aren't that bad," she says.

"Really? Why don't you go back inside then?"

"I like them better stuffed."

My look of disgust garners another laugh, but this one is slightly nervous. "I just meant my grandfather was a taxidermist. Hunted everything that moved. Stuffed them and displayed them."

Gross. I've never understood the appeal of taxidermy. All those dead animals with cold, blank, unseeing eyes.

We sit in silence for what feels like a long time. I check my watch. It's been three minutes.

"Have you heard anything?" It's almost a whisper.

I shake my head. "Nothing new."

She stares across the front yard. "You know what tortures me most?"

"No."

"That I shouldn't have left her there."

"No one thinks their children are in danger when they leave them with people they trust."

She blinks as though she's confused about who I'm talking about; then her expression changes to one of concern. "Have you found anything more regarding this Fran woman—any connection to Malcolm?"

"No. Her son, George, was staying with her at the Compassionate Care Seniors' Complex, and he's now being charged for possession and dealing, but so far we haven't found any reason to question Fran further or connect him to this case." The hope is that the media's broadcasting will lead us to Malcolm Jennings, and if he lists the old woman as an accomplice, then we can arrest her . . . until then, it's all a waiting game. "Wish I had better news for you."

She sighs and rests her head on my shoulder.

I stiffen as her long blonde hair falls forward against my chest. The soft floral scent of her shampoo tantalizes my nostrils. I want to move away from her, but I can't. I sit here, enduring the torture . . . praying the exterminator arrives quickly. Before I do something stupid.

"Do you believe in karma?" she asks.

"Like a 'getting what we deserve from the universe' kinda thing?"

"Yes."

"No."

"Why not?"

"Because of all the bad shit I see happen to good people on a daily basis." My career makes it almost impossible for me to believe in an outside force dealing out justice. There are just bad people and good people. And not everyone gets the life they deserve.

She lifts her head and looks at me. "What if these good people weren't always good?"

I'm remembering the Facebook images and her wild-child side, but she can't honestly think her past might be the reason this is happening to her. "You can't blame yourself for what happened . . . and you also can't change the past."

Her eyes search mine. She looks like she wants to take comfort in my words, but something is haunting her. She turns away quickly before I might catch a glimpse of what that something could be.

Seeing the van pull into the cul-de-sac seconds later, I clear my throat and stand. "Well, your hero is here. I should go." Watching them take down the animal isn't my thing. "Hope there's not too much damage inside."

She stands next to me and hands me back my jacket. She straightens her sweatshirt and tucks a long strand of blonde hair behind one ear. If she's embarrassed by her display of vulnerability, her neediness, her leaning on me, she doesn't show it. "Me, too, but it's the least of my troubles right now."

"I'll . . . uh . . . check in on you tomorrow."

She nods. "You don't have to . . . I mean, unless there's news."

I know I don't have to. Normally I wouldn't. She knows it. I know it. "I'll check in." I wave as I climb into the squad car and tear out of the neighborhood, the smell of her still on my clothes.

September 8—11:59 p.m.

"So you have a rodent in there?" The thin, short guy standing on the step outside the front door wearing a Tom's Critter Capture logoed shirt isn't exactly what I was expecting, but he looks eager and ready to get to work.

Detective Ryan's ego would certainly have been dealt a blow had he stuck around.

I take in the tranquilizer gun on the man's hip, the roll of plastic in a holder at his side, and the baseball bat–looking club he carries at his waist. The creature is a living thing. It was just hungry and is now trapped inside the house.

Wrong place at the wrong time.

From inside, I close the door slightly. "Um . . . you know, I think it's gone. I haven't heard it in the kitchen in a while."

He frowns. "I should check it out just in case. They can cause real damage to your home, and you don't want to be sleeping and have that thing sneak up on you and attack."

I nod. "I appreciate that . . . and I'm sorry to have wasted your time coming out, but I think it's fine. I'll pay you for your time," I say, and I reach behind the door for my purse.

He looks annoyed, as though he was looking forward to catching his prey. I've ruined his night.

I close the door a little more as I extend a credit card.

He refuses the card. "It's fine, ma'am," he says. "You sure?"

"Yes. Thank you." I close the door and lock it, then head into the kitchen, following the sound of scratching coming from the pantry.

The door is slightly ajar, and I can see the dark, matted fur of the creature inside. Cereal litters the floor, and a glass honey jar has fallen off the shelf and broken—the thick, golden liquid seeps out slowly.

I open the kitchen drawer and take out my gun. Slowly inching closer, I throw the pantry door open and aim. Nothing is creeping up on me while I sleep.

The animal turns to look at me. Cornered. Helpless. Desperate to survive. My hand trembles, my grip tightening on the weapon. I lower it. I can't do it.

I open the kitchen door leading into the backyard and grab some leftover meat from the fridge. I dangle it in front of him and throw it outside. He rushes past me and out of the house.

I close the door and lock it and then put the gun away. Just in case Detective Ryan is wrong and karma does exist, I'll save my dark deeds for something more important.

September 9—11:56 a.m.

I shouldn't be here, but so far Detective Ryan hasn't been doing his job well enough, so I have no other choice. I was hoping to get answers from him, but the investigation isn't moving along fast enough. I need to find Mikayla. It's been three days, and time is running out.

As I enter the Compassionate Care Seniors' Complex the next day, I wonder if Detective Ryan realizes he told me where I could find Fran. Was the slipup a sign that his guard was lowered? What other information might he reveal, given the right circumstances?

I almost gag as the front door closes behind me. Old people have a smell. It's almost like death starts to wrap itself around them as they get older. Sickening, stale flesh already starting to die and decay: the yellowed skin and the deep crevices of wrinkles absorbing the odor, making it impossible to wash it from their pores.

Everyone in this place looks minutes away from death, and I scan the faces for Fran as I enter, but I don't see her. I glance down at my phone, at the Paradise Day Care website that obviously hasn't been updated in a while. Next to a friendly-looking picture of Fran is her full name: *Fran Gallant, Senior Childcare Provider.*

I pretend to scan the brochures along the entrance wall—pamphlets about Compassionate Care Seniors' Complex boasting top-notch facilities and exceptional, qualified staff—as I keep an eye on the check-in desk. It's almost noon. Someone will no doubt be going for lunch soon, leaving someone else covering the desk for an hour.

As if on cue, the minute the clock hits twelve, a middle-aged woman gets up from the desk, and a young girl in a striped uniform takes her seat. A volunteer. Perfect.

She looks a little nervous as I approach. "Hi . . . um, can I help you?" she asks.

Confidence is convincing. "Yes, I'm here to see Fran Gallant."

"Oh . . . okay . . . um. Well, the usual attendant just went for a smoke break. I'm new. I'm just volunteering, actually—for extra college credit . . ."

Of course. Why else would anyone willingly work here for free?

"That's okay. I'm sure you can figure out how to check me in as a visitor."

"Are you family?" she asks.

"Yes. I'm her niece. I've been away quite a bit. I feel so bad for not visiting in so long."

The young girl still hesitates, so I ask, "Did you want to go check with someone?"

She glances toward a staff room down the hall. The sound of a popular daytime soap opera on the television comes from inside the room. "No . . . it's okay . . . can you sign in?" She hands me a check-in sheet, and I see that the last person to visit this place was Detective Ryan, two days ago.

Sad.

Keeping my gloves on, I scribble a fake name. "I believe she was moved. Can you remind me where she is now?"

The volunteer checks the computer system. "No . . . it looks like she's still in the housing units at the far end of the property."

"Are you sure?"

The girl checks the computer again. "Yep. She's still in unit 4B."

"Oh, okay . . . if you say so. Thank you."

I head back outside and walk along the overgrown paths toward the unit 4 complexes. Even in daylight, these trails are dark and eerie. Shadows of swaying trees give the impression I'm being followed. The trails aren't well maintained, and I almost trip over a large tree stub. I reach out and grab a branch to steady myself, and my hand is covered in sticky sap when I pull it away.

Houses appear at the end of the trail, and I'm reminded of the kinds of places I've lived . . . after my parents died. Dingy, dirty, broken-down foster homes. Peeling paint, loose shingles, bedsheets in place of curtains hanging in the windows.

If Mikayla is trapped in this hellhole with a woman who stinks, I won't be responsible for my actions.

There's no one around. No sign of life in any of these homes. No one watching through the windows . . . guess they've all given up on receiving visitors. No one ever comes here.

I'm careful on the crumbling concrete steps, and my hand shakes as I approach the door for unit 4B. I knock and wait. I listen, but no sound comes from inside.

The door is locked, but the wood around the doorframe is old and decaying. It doesn't take much to get it open.

Inside, the house smells damp and musty. Like the air has been turned off. It's dusty, and cobwebs hang in the corners. It's hard to believe someone actually lives here. Dirty dishes are still in the sink, and several flies buzz around an overfilled garbage can in the corner of the kitchen.

If I didn't hate you right now, Fran, I'd feel sorry for you. Who allows you to live like this? Don't you have any real family who can take better care of you?

The house is still. Quiet. Empty. She must not be home. Otherwise, she'd have seen or at least heard me enter by now.

A shiver runs down my spine as I move throughout the small, cramped space. The floorboards creak under my feet in the hallway, and I pause. That sound would wake the dead.

I move closer to the open bedroom door and peer around the doorframe. The bed is unmade, with blankets and a handmade quilt hanging off one side. There's no pillowcase on the yellow, stained pillow, and the headboard has come away from the wall on one side.

A closet door is open, but there's very little inside—just an old housecoat and several cardigan sweaters.

A breeze blows through the room. The bedroom window is open. Open or broken?

I move farther into the room and see pieces of glass on the floor. Sharp slivers still border the window frame.

Then I see her. Dressed in old, soiled pajama pants; a faded T-shirt; and pink knitted slippers, and she's slumped against the bed on the floor. Her head has fallen forward, and her arms hang limp at her sides.

If Fran knows something about where Mikayla is, I won't get the truth from her.

Fran's dead.

September 9—7:34 p.m.

My hand instinctively on the gun and badge at my side, I walk the path toward Fran's house. It's getting dark. Unlike the last time I was here, when I walked the trail with the old woman, this time I feel like I shouldn't be here, like I'm trespassing.

The place has a deserted feel, and I almost expect to learn that there is no one here named Fran. That there hasn't been in years. That the woman I spoke to a few days ago was just a ghost.

When you live in Ellicott City long enough, you start to believe in a lot of crazy things.

But I know she's real, and I know she's had a visitor. A niece . . . supposedly. I was actually surprised to receive the call from the home's nurse an hour ago. Not entirely surprised that Fran had a visitor, seeing as how her son had a lot of "friends," but surprised that Compassionate Care Seniors' Complex actually did what I asked and informed me that someone had stopped by to see her.

Maybe they were on top of things around here, after all.

I need to know who came to see Fran, because the description of the woman—tall, thin, blonde hair, blue eyes—fits the bill for Kelsey Jennings.

Would she really come to see Fran? Try to get answers on her own? Or for some other reason? Perhaps Malcolm Jennings isn't the one working with the older woman . . .

I walk up to the front door and stop when I notice it's open. There's damage around the handle and lock, as though it's been pried open with something. It wouldn't take much. I look around the step and see a dozen old tree branches that could have been used as the tool.

I scan my surroundings but see no one. I listen carefully, but there's just silence within the house. I push the door slowly, my hand on my gun. The house is chilled. The door must have been open this way for a while. I scan the small kitchen and see the microwave flashing.

Your meal is ready . . . Your meal is ready . . .

How long have the words been scrolling past? I open it, and the stench of old chicken stew makes me gag.

"Mrs. Gallant?" I call out. "It's just me, Detective Ryan . . ." I check the living room. It's empty.

It's in the hallway that I smell it. Death. It has a unique odor in the early hours, when the body hasn't been abandoned by the soul long enough to start its decay, but the last breath stinks as it lingers on the air, and any bodily functions that have given way are foul.

I know I'm going to find the old woman dead before I see her body lying on the floor of her bedroom. Her landline phone on the floor next to her. The incessant dial tone now ringing so loudly in my ears I'm amazed I didn't hear it from outside.

I put on my gloves and bend next to her body, rolling her over. The landline cord is wrapped tightly around her neck, the plastic cutting into her flesh and her pale, bruising skin ballooning over it. Her wide-open eyes, sunken deep into the surrounding swollen flesh, hold their final look of terror and panic.

"Shit." I reach for my radio and call it in.

Then, because I can't just leave her there alone, I sit on the floor next to the lifeless body and wait.

September 9—9:34 p.m.

I find more boxes in the garage. There have to be answers somewhere. Some clue, some indication of where Malcolm could have gone and why. With Fran dead, I can't get the answers I need to find Mikayla . . . and it's too risky to go to the other source that holds the key to all this. What if I'm being followed? Watched? I'm feeling more than a little paranoid and tense after seeing the dead woman on her bedroom floor.

I wanted to get help or call Detective Ryan, but how would I have explained my presence in the woman's house? I'd broken in. I didn't hurt her, but would anyone have believed that?

I tear open the first set of unlabeled boxes and find winter clothes and extra blankets . . . stuff I won't need for another few weeks at least, when the weather turns colder and the snow starts to fall. I close them up and stack them near a wall.

Another set of older, worn-looking boxes contain Halloween and Christmas decorations. Multicolored lights and an artificial Christmas tree, faded plastic outdoor display pieces that look like they're from the seventies . . . nothing of any importance if Mikayla isn't found. I can't even think about celebrating anything until my family—the only people I care about, the only people I have in this world—are returned to me.

I open one labeled with my name and jump back.

Baby dolls. Their faces cut off and switched. Unblinking, judging eyes staring out through the jagged, unevenly cut holes in the plastic.

A pair of blood-covered scissors lies on top.

It's your fault she's missing! You did this!

I cover my ears and back away from the box.

My mother's collection. They once belonged to her mother. A woman who died before I was born. Compared to everything else in our home at the time, they weren't anything special, but they were the only material possessions my mother truly cared about. Each with differently colored hair—curled at the ends, vibrant-looking bows. Pretty dresses and matching Mary Jane shoes. Little paper tags sat next to each one with their names scrawled in pink ink. Jasmine, Aredelle, Constance . . .

I wasn't allowed to touch them. Not after losing one of the shoes of my own doll.

Take care of your things! You're so stupid! Why aren't you more careful?!

It was the only time I disobeyed my mother's rules. I loved those baby dolls. Cherished them. I thought it was sad that they sat in there, unplayed with, unloved, day after day.

When I opened the glass display case, whenever my parents weren't home, I was always careful with them. I put them all back where they'd been after I was done. I never hurt them. I never rumpled their clothing or messed up their hair. I never lost their shoes or bows. I was careful.

Now they sit here, destroyed. A warning.

How the hell did they get here? They couldn't have come from the house in Florida.

My blood runs cold, and I shiver as I look around the garage.

Has she somehow come back? Is she in this house? Watching. Waiting.

No, that's impossible.

An image of Fran lying dead on her bedroom floor has my heart pounding so loud in my ears that it sounds like knocking on the walls all around me.

No. She couldn't have killed Fran. I'm panicking. I'm imagining things.

Yet these mutilated dolls are very much real.

The sound of the doorbell echoing throughout the garage makes me jump. I freeze, unsure what to do.

Loud knocking on the door, followed by another ring of the doorbell.

I have to answer it. There's no way I can leave without being seen.

I close the box, stack several others on top of it, and then go back into the house and to the window.

Detective Ryan's car is parked in the driveway. I can see his back as he waits on the step.

He knows about Fran.

Shit. How much does he know?

I can't ignore him. There's no escape. All the house lights are on. He knows I'm home.

I take a deep breath, try to steady my racing pulse. I didn't kill Fran. I have nothing to hide.

A moment later, I open the front door. "Hi, Detective Ryan . . . what are you doing here?"

His eyes scan my face, registering my anxious state, and his hardened expression softens just a little.

Enough to put me at ease. He's not here to arrest me.

"Can I come in?"

"Of course." I stand back to let him enter. "Would you like coffee?"

"No . . . thank you."

"What's wrong? Have you heard anything? Any tips?"

"No." He pauses. "Mrs. Jennings, Fran Gallant was murdered."

The look of shock on my face must be convincing, because his shoulders relax a little as he continues. "Autopsy reveals she was killed two days ago."

While he was here with me. He doesn't think I've killed her. He doesn't know I was there. That I found her body first. I take a deep breath. "Oh my God . . . that's terrible. Do you think it's related to Mikayla being missing?"

"We're not ruling it out . . . however, as I mentioned, her son had been living with her. Turns out he owed some people some money."

"So, maybe Malcolm paid Fran and her son to help him abduct Mikayla . . ."

Detective Ryan nods slowly. "Maybe. We have the son in custody, so we will be questioning him again. But this may not have anything to do with your case at all."

"Okay . . ." It may have more to do with my case than he could ever know.

He turns to leave. "I just wanted to let you know."

He could have called. He could have waited until he had more concrete evidence that Fran played a part in all this . . . or not. He wanted to come here. He wanted to deliver the news in person. Partially to see my reaction, perhaps . . . but he also wanted to see me.

I can feel his hesitation now as he lingers near the front door.

What do you want from me, Detective? How do you want me to play this? What will work better for you?

"Um . . . do you think you could stay?"

He looks surprised.

"I mean, just for a few minutes. This news has me a little freaked out." It's not a complete lie. The baby dolls in the garage have me on edge. If she is somehow lurking . . . watching me . . . taunting me, she won't come around with the detective here. "I mean, do you think whoever killed Fran . . . if it is for money . . . do you think they might come after me? Do you think they will want more cash?"

He shakes his head. "I think you're safe. The two situations might be related, but I don't think you'll have to worry about your safety."

He's never been more wrong. "Still . . . could you stay for a while?"

I can see him struggle with the decision between the right thing to do and what he wants to do. Reluctantly, he nods. "I'll stay for a quick coffee . . . until the shock of this news subsides."

"Thank you."

Ten minutes later, I hand him a coffee cup and sit next to him on the sofa. He shuffles farther away, but the arm at the other end prevents him from getting too far. His legs bounce. He's jittery. Is he like this around all women?

"So, how did she die?" I ask, turning to face him.

"Strangled with a phone cord."

"Shit. How terrible. That poor woman."

He looks at me, a question on his face.

"What? You think I'd be happy that a woman was murdered just because she might be involved with Mikayla disappearing?" That would just be heartless and cruel.

"I don't know," he says, studying me. "I don't know much about you."

That's true. Despite his questioning and probing for the case, he really knows nothing about me at all. I stare into the deep, dark liquid in my cup. "What do you want to know?"

"Anything that can help solve this case, find your daughter faster . . ."

His words fall weak. Right now, he's not interested in this case. He's not seeing me as an investigation. I've seen the way his gaze lingers on my body, the way he looks at me when he thinks I'm not paying attention. His words and reassurances the night before were outside his job description . . . just like his being here now. He is interested in me as a woman.

And I'll use any angle I can to make sure this all works out in my favor.

"Well, I'm not happy that someone was killed—even if she could've been responsible for Mikayla going missing. I blame Malcolm for that."

I add a note of anger in my voice as I remind him that Malcolm and I are not a loving, caring couple. That I am a victim of his abuse and that he has taken Mikayla away.

No matter how this all ends, I won't be sharing my life with Malcolm moving forward. Ever.

I remind Detective Ryan that the ring on my left hand is simply a symbol of an empty, broken promise now. He doesn't need to feel guilty about the way he is attracted to me, the way he wants me. There's no shame in it. I need him to act on it. I've used sex to get what I want, used it to survive, since I was a child . . . it's instinct by now. My default.

"Why do you think he did this?" he asks.

It's Paul asking the question this time, not Detective Ryan. He wants to know who I really am, how I am someone whose husband could take her child away.

"Because he could. It's about control and power with abusive men, isn't it?" My entire life I've been controlled . . . I've seen the way a man can torment and torture, use any means to get what he wants. It's my turn now.

"Usually . . ." He faces me, his expression questioning. "But is there any chance he was protecting Mikayla from something?"

"From me, you mean?"

He doesn't answer. Just continues to stare at me. Waiting.

I put my coffee cup on the end table. I take his from him and set it next to mine.

He watches. Continues to wait.

I move closer until our shoulders touch. I position my body toward him. "Do you think I'm dangerous, Paul?"

He doesn't answer, but something changes in his expression at the sound of his first name.

Good. I want this to be personal. I want to connect with him. Make it impossible for him not to be connected to me. Attraction is a powerful tool.

I touch his leg. He tenses under his faded denim, tight across his muscular thigh. Will he stop me? Leave? Just how far will he allow me to go?

On some level he had to know that staying for coffee might lead to something. Is that why he stopped by? Has he been thinking about my previous advances and untimely kiss in the kitchen?

My hand inches higher—tempting, teasing, daring—like teenagers and their first game of "nervous." Only I'm not nervous. Unlike an inexperienced teenager, I know exactly what I'm doing. Fingers creep higher still, dipping around the edge of his thigh . . .

He reaches for me. His rough hands grip my waist, his fingers digging into my flesh.

"What are you doing?" he growls, the desire in his voice daring me to continue my upward trek.

I could ask him the same thing, but I don't want to spook him. I'm in control here, and as long as it remains that way, Detective Ryan can allow himself to give in, to break these rules, cross this line. "Whatever you want me to do." I move closer and talk into his ear, pressing my breasts against his chest. "I've seen the way you look at my body. I've seen you watching me. I know you want me, Detective."

Excitement flashes in his eyes, and I know I've succeeded in getting him where I want him. "What's your game? Your husband and child are missing. You know something about it. There are things you're hiding . . . secrets that you refuse to tell me."

He's not wrong. "And that intrigues you, doesn't it?" I unbutton his pants and unzip the zipper. He is hard already, and his cock stands out straight in his boxer briefs. He's open and exposed in front of me, and I'm closed off and mysterious. It's an intoxicating combination for him. His gaze locks with mine, daring me to keep going, to finish what I've started.

He has no idea just how far I plan to go. What I'm willing to do to finish what I've started.

I find the opening in his underwear and slide my fingers inside slowly. Allowing my hand to wrap around him.

His eyes close, and a low moan escapes him before he asks, "Why don't you tell me the truth?"

Cute how he thinks he's the one playing me. That I'll somehow give in and tell him everything I know, confide in him, just because his dick is in my hand. He underestimates me, and for now, I'll let him. "Because the truth isn't what you think it is, Detective."

I slide off the couch onto my knees and start to lower my head toward his lap.

He stops me. He picks me up off the floor by gripping my wrists. He moves me aside and stands. He buttons his pants and heads for the front door. "I will find out the truth, Mrs. Jennings—be sure you're on the right side of it."

A second later, the front door slams.

My heart races, and my body is on fire. His rejection has only fueled me even more. He can't resist me forever. His interest in me is too strong, and men can only resist their natural urges for so long.

I sit on the sofa and watch through the open living room curtains as he walks to his car and gets inside. His gaze meets mine from behind the wheel before he drives away quickly seconds later.

I know the detective will be back.

Five months earlier . . .

Dear Holly,

*I lived on the coast for a while. I tried and failed
to be a dancer.*

K.

I sit and stare at the last message between us I sent weeks ago. I only sent it to make sure she'd stop looking into my dancing career. If I ever do find my way back to the spotlight, seeing her in the audience at one of my shows would send me toppling off stage.

But I haven't heard back from her, and now I'm in a panic. I feel her eyes on me everywhere I go. I jump whenever my cell phone rings, and at night, I'm too afraid to sleep. I think I see her in the faces of strangers on the street; I hear her call out to me in a crowd, but when I turn, she's not there.

My anxiety medication isn't working. I can't focus. I can't concentrate.

Malcolm's voice drives me to the brink of insanity. Always criticizing. Never supportive. Mikayla's demands are becoming too much—I have no time alone. No time for myself.

My life is complicated right now, and the pressure keeps escalating. Soon it'll reach a breaking point.

Even my own reflection terrifies me. I see my sister everywhere.

So, my body sags in relief when a new message from her appears a few weeks after the last one arrived.

Dear Kelsey,

Sorry it's taken me so long to respond, but I wasn't sure what to say. I bet the ocean was everything you'd hoped it would be. Remember when we were kids, before our parents died, we'd lie awake in our bunk beds in our shared room and talk about where we would go on vacation if we ever had a chance. If mom and dad ever agreed to take us somewhere. Of course we knew we'd never go on one as a family. Mom and dad barely had enough money left over after buying their drugs and alcohol and paying your ballet school tuition fees, to feed us both. But it didn't matter, we still had fun planning, didn't we? You always wanted to go to a beach, even though we were already surrounded by beaches in California. I wanted to go to a rainforest. I've always been fascinated by the woods and I so love animals. (I'm not allergic like you, remember those cats at the foster home?).

Anyway, I still haven't gotten to the rainforest, but I live in a regular forest. Not outside of course lol. Can you imagine? No, I'm not living like a wild animal. I have a cabin. It's okay. I live in it all by myself now. The man who adopted me (I'll tell you all about him another time), left it to me when he died. He left me a lot of things . . . lots of money, but accessing it would be tricky (long story, I'll explain later), but the cabin is mine and no one bothers me out here in the woods. I have everything I need and sometimes when it rains, I pretend I'm in a rainforest. It's nice. I know what you must be thinking—cabin in the woods all alone sounds creepy, like something out of a horror movie, but it's not like that anymore.

Anyway, I still haven't gone on my perfect vacation . . . But you! You did it! You went to a different beach! An east coast beach. I'm not sure how different those beaches are compared to the ones in California, but you were certainly eager to find out. And now you have! How was the sand between your toes? Did the salt water cover your skin? I bet the waves were terrifying, but not for you. You always wanted to dance in them. Our pool in our backyard wasn't quite the same . . . but I used to love watching you swim. Except for when you did that floating thing. I'm so glad you were never actually dead.

I have to tell you Kelsey, that my heart is so conflicted. I want to rejoice that you made it to the east coast, but I'm filled with sadness that your dream of becoming a dancer did not happen. You deserved that! You worked hard—I know you must have, you never did anything half-assed (sorry, for swearing). And to not succeed must have broken your heart . . . but I pray not your spirit. They say it's never too late and that we must never give up on a dream. I hope you will keep trying. I know you have the talent to succeed. If that is still a dream for you.

Sometimes dreams change. Mine have. When we were kids, you wanted to be a ballerina. You wanted to twist and turn your body into beautiful shapes, telling a story through the flow of music and limbs. Do you remember what my dream was? I wanted to be an archaeologist. Ever since that kindergarten school field trip . . . the one and only field trip we went on before mom and dad decided to pull us out of public school and homeschool us. I bet you must remember that field trip to the dinosaur exhibit at the museum. I've been fascinated with bones ever since that day. Not necessarily dinosaur bones, but just bones.

I think it actually started before the field trip. I think it started that day when we found that dead animal in the woods near our family house. Do you remember? It was the day you went to play with your friends, Kim and Amy. They lived down the street. Mom said we should all play nice together. She wanted me out of the house, remember? But you and Kim and Amy didn't want to play with me. You told me to "get lost!" I remember. Don't worry, I totally forgive you! We were just silly kids back then and kids are sometimes cruel without meaning to be.

I followed you three anyway and you started running away from me. I chased you three through the woods. I even fell once and hurt my knee, but you didn't care so I kept chasing you guys. It was harder to run with a bleeding knee, but I caught up to you.

The three of you had stopped running and were standing in the woods screaming. It was silly really. It was just a dead bird. Decayed. Bones lying on the ground. Not a big deal, but the three of you ran back toward the house screaming.

I stayed with the bones. Touched them. Tried to reconnect them to make the bird.

It was fascinating. Anyway, it didn't last long because you told dad and he came to the woods with a garbage bag and took the bones away. You didn't want them lying there in the woods where you'd have to see them when you played with Kim and Amy.

I didn't become an archaeologist after all, but I think I would have made a great one. The same way you would have made a great dancer.

But like I said, it hasn't been my dream in a long time.

Dreams change over time. Since reconnecting with you, I've actually developed new dreams . . . or maybe just goals. Hearing all about your wonderful husband and beautiful little girl, I think I'd like a family. A husband for sure and I could adopt a little girl. My family will be just like yours. Once again, we will be exactly alike, have everything the same.

You've inspired me, Kels. Just like I know your dancing would have inspired the world, had they gotten a chance to see it.

Write back soon! Oops, I forgot to ask a question. What are your husband and daughter's names? You never did mention that.
Your Sister, Holly

I've had enough of these exchanges and the torment they're causing me. They just prove that she's the same person she always was. Someone I didn't have time for. Someone I've never liked. Someone I shouldn't be so afraid of.

She can't find me. If she could, she'd be here by now.

I block her.

Unfortunately, it's too late. She's gotten to me with these messages. Irritation seeps deep into my pores as I replay her stream-of-consciousness rambling over in my mind.

She thinks my family life is perfect. Why? Because I have a husband and a child? She's so stupid to think that I may have changed over the years. That I actually care about family. That a husband and child were things that I suddenly wanted.

She's right about one thing. I did work my ass off to become a dancer, and it's through no fault of my own that I failed.

It's Malcolm's fault. And Mikayla's.

The family I'm so *lucky* to have, according to my sister, has cost me everything I've ever wanted.

She would have cherished the foster parents that eventually raised me. She would have been so eternally grateful that they'd felt enough sympathy for us that they'd put aside their fears of adopting a preteen with a history like ours and rescued her from the shit that had been our lives up to that point. She would have loved them. But they'd only wanted one of us.

I only saw them as a means to an end.

Two days after they brought me "home," I begged them for ballet lessons. They felt so bad for me, for all that I'd been through, and so happy to finally have a daughter in their lives, that they would have said yes to anything.

Starting over in ballet school was challenging—a blow to my prima donna ego—but after a few weeks, the teacher thought I was a natural. She told my adoptive parents that I was more advanced and placed me with the older girls. I felt clumsy and uncoordinated. Sure, I was better than the rest of them, but I wasn't my best. But it didn't take long before I was back where I belonged. Center stage and performing again.

My life was slightly disappointing, in that the couple weren't rich. Our house wasn't big. We didn't have a housekeeper or cook. I had to go to school, and I was so far behind the others that I was put back a few grades. I felt awkward and dumb at school. The dance studio wasn't full of Hollywood talent, and the performances were amateurish. But I put in the time and effort and danced when I wasn't in school.

My adoptive parents were nice enough. Kind of bland and boring, but they felt sorry for me because of my troubled past, so they patiently tried to help me and bailed me out of all the trouble I constantly found myself in.

Drugs, alcohol, sex with strangers. What the hell did anyone expect? I was the walking poster child for the effects of abuse, neglect, and abandonment. Only shitty parents would have turned their back on me, given the circumstances.

The new therapist was amazing. She helped convince them that I'd been through hell and that my actions were a result of trauma. My "symptoms" were similar to those of soldiers with PTSD. All I had to do to solidify her diagnosis was cry once in a while in her office while recounting tales of my torture and abuse as a child and then claim to have nightmares and social anxiety.

In truth, I slept like a baby, and I just hated people.

My new parents scrimped and saved enough to send me to college in Florida, where there was an amazing dance studio, the one I demanded to go to. My grades sucked, but they were enough to keep me enrolled, and as long as I continued my courses and sent copies of my grades to them quarterly, they continued to pay for my schooling, my housing, and my dance membership. I couldn't wait until I wouldn't need to do things their way anymore.

I graduated with a business degree in finance, because it was the easiest and because it pleased my adoptive father, who was an accountant. Both of my adoptive parents died that same year, but any hopes of inheriting a windfall of cash quickly disappeared—they had barely been able to keep up with their financial obligations. So I got a job at a firm in Florida and was saving to move to New York when I met Malcolm.

He was good looking, in a traditional, boring, teacher kind of way. He was nice and kind and pleasant enough to talk to. But none of that was what attracted me to him. It was his parents who appealed. He'd come in to talk about his financials, which weren't impressive at all, but he let drop info about a trust fund account in his name. Once he'd left the office, I'd googled him and learned about his rich parents, his privileged upbringing in Ellicott City. I called him to schedule another appointment for the next day.

I was desperate to meet his parents, see their big mansion of a home in Ellicott City—enough that it didn't bother me that we'd have to return to the site of all my crimes and troubled past in Maryland, if it meant finally being part of the wealthy again. But Malcolm's parents were the kind of rare rich people who suffered from a conscience. They had retired early and were traveling to third-world countries as missionaries. They'd just left for a six-month trip.

Still, I knew I'd hit the jackpot if I could land Malcolm. I googled him further, found out who his previous girlfriends were, and discovered his type and became it. Six months later, I met his parents, and within weeks, we were married.

His only pitfall was that he wasn't at all interested in my dancing career. He attended one performance, then claimed the theater wasn't for him. Therefore, I had to downplay my love of performing whenever

I was with him. Curb my enthusiasm. Pretend my financial adviser career was the dream, the goal I had for myself. Every day, sitting in that cubical sucked the very life from my soul. I hated walking into the office filled with middle-aged, balding men who had coffee stains on their shirts and yellow teeth and who eyed me as though I'd ever consider letting them put their dick inside my body.

None of them were that rich.

I watched the clock. My efforts were lackluster at best. Most of my day was spent envisioning my latest routine in my mind. Dancing from the water cooler to the coffee maker and back to my desk again. Stretching during my breaks and watching ballet performances on YouTube whenever I got a break between clients. I knew I'd eventually get fired, but I didn't care. I hated the job anyway.

I thought it wouldn't matter for much longer anyhow. We'd been married a few months, and I'd done all the right things. I was supportive of Malcolm's search for a teaching job, encouraging him to look at opportunities in New York City. I paid all our bills in the meantime while he struggled to find work. I massaged his shoulders at night when he was stressed and did whatever he wanted in bed, which was easy, because he never wanted much—missionary and a blow job every now and then. I learned to cook his favorite meals . . . I had no problem taking over some of the household domestic chores when I became a full-time dancer . . . at least until I was successful in convincing him to hire a maid.

For months, I was doing everything right, and Malcolm was falling more and more in love.

It was time to talk about investing in a house together. I was a financial adviser and had just enough money saved to make it look like (a) I knew what I was doing, and I convinced Malcolm that buying a home we couldn't really afford was the right idea, and (b) that I was willing and able to help with the mortgage down payment. I didn't actually think we'd need to borrow money from the bank. His parents were multimillionaires. Didn't that mean they were expected to help out their children?

We found a house in Florida well above our means. I convinced Malcolm it was the right thing—our very eager Realtor was a great help in that endeavor. Then we told his parents.

I waited. Waited for their excitement and a check.

Neither was forthcoming.

They advised us against it. They didn't offer to help with the money part. They were completely useless.

Apparently Malcolm's parents preferred to donate their money and time to charity and to let their only son figure out his own life. What the fuck had I done? How could I have been so wrong about this? Something so important?

Now, I was an inch away from being fired. I was married to an unemployed teacher. And we'd just bought a house we couldn't afford. I was tied to Malcolm. A poor, boring man who didn't support my passion. When I told him I wanted to pursue dancing full time, he laughed.

I'd killed two people at twelve years old, but never in my life had I wanted to stab again until that moment.

Dancing is not a real career, Malcolm said. Time to think about a family, he said. Time to look for a new job with medical benefits and find a more suitable home, he said. Time to consider moving back to Maryland.

When he spoke, all I heard was the sound of everything I'd thought I was getting with a life with him fading away. All my hopes and dreams once again vanishing into thin air.

He was supposed to be rich. He was supposed to tell me to quit my job and dance. He was supposed to feel lucky to have a young, beautiful, talented wife who owned the stage and could have had anyone she wanted but was slumming it with him.

At that point, I'd have settled for just the second one.

I was on the pill, so I wasn't worried about kids. But the big house in Florida quickly disappeared, and I got a new mind-numbing, soul-crushing job at another finance firm.

I still danced, but knowing I'd screwed everything up started to take its toll on my mental health. My confidence waned, and I spent more time figuring out how to keep paying my dance-academy tuition than on perfecting my routines. I was no longer soaring . . . and other dancers started to catch up.

I was feeling desperate and on edge.

And it trickled into our homelife. We fought about everything—mostly finances. We argued about Malcolm's inability to care for us . . . he'd yet to find a full-time teaching position, and he ignored all the employment opportunity links I sent him for New York or Boston or anywhere near where I wanted to be for my dancing career. Needed to be.

Things got violent—on my end. Verbal abuse turned to physical abuse. I'd hit him over and over, hoping to knock some sense into him. Couldn't he see that he was no better than the foster parents who'd rented me out to their friends, who got what they wanted but never gave me what I desired in return? He was stifling me, torturing me . . . slowly killing my desire and spirit.

He threatened divorce, and I immediately wanted to jump at the opportunity to get out of this pointless, loveless marriage, but his trust fund still dangled like a carrot in front of me. I pretended to be a better wife. We stopped arguing. I started massaging his shoulders and cooking dinner and held back my screams of rage when he failed job interview after job interview.

Sex resumed. The biggest of all my mistakes.

My birth control failed. I was pregnant and wanted an abortion, but he found the positive pregnancy test in the trash.

Suspicious fucker! Going through my private things. I was enraged. We fought again, and once again, I was violent. Who could blame me?

My husband deserved the black eye for snooping, for invading my privacy, for insisting that an abortion was not an option, and for trying to tell me what I could and couldn't do with my own body.

Somewhere deep down, though, I still held out hope for the money. Other dancers had had babies, and their bodies had bounced back. I'd rack up credit card debt on diet pills and a personal trainer after this leech was out of my body, if I had to. The important thing was that if Malcolm's parents had a grandchild, they'd pony up finally, right?

We sought counseling, under my tearful, apologetic pleas. Malcolm would have preferred a divorce, but he was worried that he wouldn't have the access to his daughter that he'd want. He longed to be a father, and shared custody wasn't appealing to him. He knew that the courts would favor the mother, especially when he was still unemployed. He'd have to take any job at all just to afford the child support payments . . .

Mikayla was born. Cute enough baby. I didn't care. I just hoped that after sixteen hours of childbirth (I'd refused the C-section because I'd heard it could further destroy abdominal muscles), I now held the golden ticket in my arms, sucking on my breast (I'd heard breastfeeding was a way to get skinny quickly again—something about the uterus bouncing back). Grandparents spoiled their grandchildren, right? And any trust funds they set up for Mikayla, I'd have access to . . .

Still, Malcolm's parents were a disappointment. No big windfall. No trust fund. No expensive push present that I could pawn for cash.

Then I found the papers. Stacked one on top of the other in his office desk. Not locked. As though he could trust me not to snoop.

He'd gone ahead with his plan of filing for divorce. I read all the terrible accusations he was filing against me. I saw the receipt from the law firm where he had his retainer and the insane amount he'd had to pay. He didn't have that kind of money. His parents were helping him leave our marriage.

Sole custody. He wanted to take Mikayla with him.

That child was the only hope I had of getting money. And these papers were a sure bet that he'd get everything he was asking for. The house, the baby, seeing as how he'd been her primary caregiver—a stay-at-home dad—while I'd quickly returned to work. He was even asking for child support, and alimony, seeing as how I'd been supporting him all this time.

Unfortunately, he'd called the police after several domestic disputes, and the neighbors had been witnesses to my behavior, so there was proof of his claims. I was screwed.

And the amount I was being screwed out of on the next set of papers—his trust fund account that he now was being given access to, on the condition that he divorce me—was astronomical.

Mommy and Daddy were finally ponying up.

Anger coils through me now as I hear Malcolm playing with Mikayla in the nursery down the hall. I can hear her giggle and the sound of his parents' voices coming through a Skype connection. They are all so close. So loving. They want to save their son and granddaughter from this hell of a life with me. They think I don't know that I'm going to be served with divorce and custody papers. That their money can help Malcolm escape and take Mikayla with him. That I'll be once again left with nothing.

They have no idea who they are dealing with. Malcolm could leave me, all right . . . but he'll be doing it in a coffin.

September 10—11:23 a.m.

If the Jenningses want to help their son and granddaughter disappear, they certainly know how to do it. And they have the money for it.

No word or sign of them in four days. I'm starting to wonder if their overseas mission trip is a cover this time. Kelsey Jennings claims to be trying to reach them, and if they aren't in on this, what grandparents wouldn't at least return a phone call if their son was suspected of parental abduction and their granddaughter was missing?

Getting a warrant to search their premises didn't work out. Apparently there wasn't enough evidence of their involvement for the judge—whose campaign for mayor is being significantly funded and endorsed by the Jenningses—to sign off on a search of their home while they're overseas, saving the world.

How many rich do-gooders hide dark deeds among their charitable actions?

Still, I'm here at their home. There might be something here—a clue that I could use to convince the judge that this search is warranted. I tug at the big iron gates leading to their house, but they're locked. I can see the multimillion-dollar home in the distance, but it looks quiet. An empty house has an aura about it—cold, slightly haunting. This house has that feel.

But my gut tells me there's something here . . .

I walk along the side of the privacy wall, along a well-maintained path toward the back of the house. The backyard faces a ravine, and with no back-facing neighbors, the privacy wall gives way to a glass wall to provide a spectacular view of nature.

Inside the yard, a covered pool and hot tub are off to one side; an outside grill and bar area for entertaining are on the other. Why have such an extravagant home with all these luxuries if the Jenningses aren't around much to enjoy them?

Then again, all the homes in this area are never fully enjoyed. The owners are workaholics who are either busting their asses to pay for their luxurious lifestyles or else are away on vacations.

I keep walking until I see a detached garage at the back of the property outside the wall. The only thing not well maintained. Overgrown shrubs and vines creep up the exterior, and I have to push them back to get to the door. It's dead bolted. So are the garage windows, but, using the flashlight on my key ring, I shine it in through the dusty, dirty glass.

There it is.

A car matching the description of Malcolm Jennings's vehicle. A blue Toyota Prius. The front end is damaged. Was Malcolm Jennings in an accident?

Without overthinking the consequences, I crowbar the garage door open.

I gag as the musty, damp air of the unventilated space fills my lungs. It's been a while since anyone was in here. A thin layer of dust covers the vehicle.

I move to the back, but the license plate has been removed. I peer inside through the back window.

A child's car seat.

I take the VIN number from the front before leaving the garage and securing the door the best I can with the broken lock.

My coffee from the café a block away is barely cooled down enough to drink when I get my answer.

"Yep. That car was last registered to Malcolm Jennings," Parsons says over the phone, "but the insurance and registration weren't renewed when it expired months ago. No record of the plates being registered on any other vehicle either."

"Okay, thanks." I disconnect the call and get my coffee to go.

I know where to get the truth . . . but this time I'll have to get creative in how I ask the questions.

Ten minutes later, I'm parked outside the Jenningses' house. I can see Kelsey in the living room, but she hasn't noticed me yet, so I watch her. She hangs a photo on a wall, standing on tiptoes, long body outstretched to reach the nails in the wall. She stacks books in what looks like a new bookshelf near the fireplace, pausing to read the back covers . . .

She leaves the living room, then returns with a glass of red wine.

It's barely noon, Kelsey . . . a little early to be drinking.

Not too early for other sins.

She turns suddenly toward the window as though she can feel the weight of my thoughts. Sense my intentions.

She drops the wineglass. It shatters on the floor at her bare feet, but her gaze is locked with mine.

I'm inside her house in seconds. The door closing behind me is the only sound.

Her body presses to mine, and her mouth makes contact with my lips as my hands dip inside the waistband of her tight yoga pants, cupping her bare ass beneath.

No underwear.

She wraps her long, slender arms around my neck and holds my face to hers. She hungrily kisses me, her tongue exploring my mouth.

I'm rock hard.

I lift her and back her against the door. My hands squeeze her breasts. Hard. Harder. I wait for her to tell me to stop. Tell me I'm hurting her. She doesn't. It completely drives me wild.

I don't think there's anything I could do to this woman that she wouldn't let me do, wouldn't enjoy, wouldn't beg for more of. That lack of inhibition is the sexiest part of her, and the most terrifying. I don't want to stop. I want to keep going.

Find out how far she will let me go. Find out what secrets I'll uncover in the process.

September 10—4:03 p.m.

For someone who spends his life around the scum of the earth, the detective is unusually trusting with his things.

He's showering, and he's left his badge, gun, cell phone, and wallet on my bedside table.

I've already been locked out of the cell phone for multiple wrong attempts at his pass code, and I can't risk trying again. I never really expected to be able to guess it right, but I had to do something while I waited for him.

I pick up his wallet and don't feel even the littlest bit guilty as I open it and riffle through. He's combed through every inch of this house. He had no problem with the idea of invading my privacy, and I know he's here today because he's looking for something. He wanted me, but he wants to get to the truth of this case even more.

I wonder if he's figured anything out . . .

There's forty-six dollars inside the wallet, tangled among dozens of receipts. All from the same place—the coffee hut near the police station, where they serve the shittiest coffee I've ever tasted. Too weak. Too bland.

Way to perpetuate the stereotype, Detective Ryan.

There's a bank card, but no credit cards. That's different. Based on his salary, I would assume Detective Ryan would have debt coming out of his ears. People who serve those in need really should get paid more.

I flip through the side compartment and find several condoms. The packaging looks new. They haven't been in there for long.

Did you buy these for me, Detective?

I can tell I'm the only woman he's currently sleeping with. His eagerness borders on starvation, and his orgasms came much too quickly.

I won't tell him that, though. Men don't like hearing honesty about their performance in bed.

There's an old Ellicott City Library card, his driver's license, a health card, and several photos.

Funny, I didn't peg him as the sentimental type who would carry family photos around. I look at the first one, a fairly recent one that looks to have been taken with one of those new Polaroid cameras that are primarily bought for nostalgic purposes by people who miss the good old days when you took a photo and could have it in your hands immediately, but without the benefit of a redo or the filters of a digital camera.

The woman in the photo is pretty. Not gorgeous, but girl-next-door looking, with shoulder-length brown hair, green eyes, a plain face partially covered by glasses. Not the big stylish frames that women are wearing these days but normal, boring black-rimmed glasses. She's smiling and looks genuinely happy . . . but far too innocent for the detective's liking. Obviously she means something to him, though, if she's featured in his wallet.

I flick to the second one—looks like the detective's parents . . . the black-and-white image is old, fraying at the edges. The man and woman stand in front of a hospital. The woman holds a baby. A little boy stands next to the man.

A family photo. From a million years ago.

Don't have anything more recent, Detective? Or was this the only one?

The next picture is of a vibrant, smiling young girl in a cheerleading outfit with the same dark hair and dark eyes as the detective. So pretty. Something magnetic about her, even through the picture. It's like being sucked in.

The fashion sense and hairstyle suggest the nineties.

The detective's sister?

Something in the photo catches my eye, and I lean closer. I peer through the plastic covering. I can't be sure, but the necklace dangling on her chest looks familiar.

Very familiar.

My blood runs cold, and I shiver, feeling as though I've seen a ghost. I shut the wallet quickly and put it back beneath his badge on the table, exactly the way he left it.

Is that why Detective Ryan is on this case? Does he know something?

I shake my head. No. He's here because of Mikayla. And Malcolm. Not because of his sister.

His missing sister.

His dead sister.

September 10—4:36 p.m.

She spends a long time in the shower. She's been in there for over twenty minutes. The water must be running cold by now.

My blood is.

Thinking about what I just did makes me slightly nauseated, but not enough to know it won't happen again. She has an intoxicating effect on me in her mysterious, misleading way of only revealing what she wants to reveal, and I'm desperate to get closer, to learn the truth.

I walk around the bedroom, looking for something—anything—we might have missed. A clue. Not about the case. About her. The boxes have all been unpacked, so maybe there's something . . .

I open the drawers in the dresser. Men and women's underwear mixed in together.

Malcolm is a tighty-whities kind of guy.

I pick up a pair of boring, white full-bottom underwear. All of Kelsey's are the same—boring and white.

So not representative of the woman I just fucked.

Was it the woman she was trying to be? The woman Malcolm wants her to be? An image of the Facebook photos of a more adventurous, daring Kelsey flash in my mind. Which one is she really?

I put the underwear back and reach farther into the drawer. I yank my hand back and see a thin line of blood surface on it.

A paper cut.

I reach in again and find a business card buried among the undergarments.

Sheffield and Burke Law—divorce lawyers in Florida.

Any guilt I may have felt vanishes. Malcolm is filing for divorce? He is going to throw her away . . . I know it has to be him. If Kelsey had been the one calling an end to her marriage, she'd have told me. She would have wanted me to understand any motivation Malcolm might have to take off with their daughter.

Does she even know her husband has been wanting out?

I tuck the card into my pocket as Kelsey comes out of the bathroom.

"Are you hungry? Do you want something to eat?" she asks.

"No . . . I have to get to the station." I stare at her, but all traces of the naughty woman I've just had sex with are gone.

Standing there in a towel that covers her entire body, water droplets visible on her arms and legs, her wet hair combed back away from her makeup-free face, she looks pure and innocent.

Which one are you, Kelsey Jennings?

"Okay," she says simply. She turns away from me and goes back into the bathroom. She shuts the door, and I stand there staring at it like an idiot.

What was I expecting? I found something new to investigate. That's the reason I came here in the first place. Time to leave.

Three minutes later, I lean against the hood of my car and dial the Florida number on the business card.

"Sheffield and Burke, how may I direct your call?"

"I'm calling for Mr. Sheffield. Is he available?" It's after four thirty; if he hasn't packed it in by now, he's the only lawyer I've ever heard of to work a full day.

"He's not. He had to leave early today."

Sure he did. He probably came in late and took a long lunch as well.

"Can I take a message?" she asks.

"Maybe you can help me . . ."

"Probably not; I just answer the phones."

And clearly, she'd been hoping to leave early too.

"If you'll hold the line, I'll put you through to Sandy, Mr. Sheffield's assistant. Who may I say is calling?"

"Malcolm Jennings."

"One moment, please."

I slide my sunglasses down over my eyes as the late-afternoon light glares off the roof of the car. I've committed more sins in the last eight hours than I'm proud of, but this case is getting to me. I know everything is not as it seems, and I'm desperate to figure out the truth. In three days, it feels as though I've spiraled into a mess that will eventually lead nowhere.

"Hello, Mr. Jennings," another female voice says. "If you're calling about your retainer with us, it's been over six months, and as I mentioned, we donate all unused retainer funds to pro bono organizations after that time if the account remains inactive."

"Sandy?"

"Yes."

"I'm not calling about the retainer . . . I was just calling about the status of the divorce?"

"Status? What status? We filed the paperwork, and you never came to get the documents to serve Mrs. Jennings. We closed your file months ago. We assumed there was a reconciliation." She says the word as though it's bullshit. I'm sure their firm sees a lot of couples deciding to reconcile once they see the bill attached to their desired freedom.

Months ago . . . he didn't show. Offered a position at the school and just didn't show up. The car parked in his parents' shed . . . my blood chills. Is Malcolm Jennings still breathing? I glance toward the house and see Kelsey's silhouette in the upstairs window. "Sorry . . . I know. Things got . . . better for a while." She must have heard this story over and over as well, and she sighs heavily into the phone. I add, "Um, could you send me a copy of everything?"

"You want us to reopen your file?" Now she's interested.

"Not yet. I'd just like to review everything again."

She sighs. "I can email you a copy of the paperwork. Again."

"Actually, could you fax it?"

"Are you sure you wouldn't rather use a pigeon courier?"

"A fax is fine, thank you."

"What's the number?"

I give it to her as I climb into the car.

"I'll send it over right away," she says.

"Wait about twenty minutes . . . if that's not too much trouble."

"It's too much trouble. It's Friday afternoon, Mr. Jennings; you're lucky I'm not telling you to wait for Monday. Also, we will be sending out an invoice," she says, and then the line goes dead.

Twenty minutes later, I hear the fax machine as I unlock the front door of my father's house. "Pop! You home?"

"Downstairs."

Where else? I take the stairs two at a time and reach the fax machine just as he does. "That's mine."

He scans it, his dark eyes reading quickly.

"Hand it over, please."

"This for your case?"

"Yes."

"I assume you didn't bother getting a warrant?" His eyes are glued to the printout, and he frowns as he continues to read.

"Don't start, Dad. We both know time's wasting . . . if we have any chance of locating . . ." My excuses are all there on the tip of my tongue, but he holds up a hand to stop my bullshit.

"This woman sounds like a piece of work."

"What? Give me those."

He hands the papers over, and I read quickly. There are ten pages of an affidavit sworn by Malcolm Jennings accusing his wife of a lot of terrible things. Adultery? Attempted abduction? Abuse.

"You sure she hasn't done away with this husband and child?" my father asks as he reads over my shoulder.

I don't answer the question. Truth is, I'm no longer sure of that at all.

September 10—6:07 p.m.

It's rare to see a man filing for divorce on the count of abuse; yet, parked a block away from Kelsey Jennings's house, I'm staring at a sworn affidavit from Malcolm Jennings that claims just that.

May 5, 2017—Kelsey in a drunken rage throws all of his clothing out the bedroom window out onto the lawn. Locks him out of the house.

May 27, 2017—Kelsey shows up at a school where he is substitute teaching for the day, demanding to see him. Screams at him in front of his students in the middle of his class.

July 8, 2017—Kelsey punches him in the face several times.

There's a photo attached of Malcolm's black eye. I stare at the picture of the man, trying to understand how this happened. Was he abusive first? Was Kelsey's extreme behavior a reaction to his manipulation and control? Or am I simply making excuses for her?

January 10, 2018—Kelsey locks herself in the bathroom with a gun, threatening suicide.

September 4, 2018—Kelsey doesn't come home with Mikayla.

I flip through the supporting documents attached to the affidavit. One police report for a domestic disturbance call, and then just informal statements from their neighbors in Florida. All claiming they witnessed the same behaviors. Kelsey enraged. Kelsey violent.

Kelsey a threat to Malcolm and Mikayla.

Yet no charges were ever pressed against her. Why, Malcolm? If your wife was so horrible, why didn't you have her arrested? Put a stop to it?

Was the man really that terrified of his wife and what she might do that he resorted to abducting their child? Or was he building a case to make it look like his wife was the unstable one? The unfit one.

And where the hell is he? Is he dead, or has he been "missing" longer than Kelsey Jennings claims? Without being able to reach his parents, I'm at a standstill in my search for answers. There's no evidence to suggest that Kelsey Jennings murdered her husband, yet there's also no trace of him anywhere but in her life.

I run a hand through my hair and toss the papers into the passenger seat. I hit the steering wheel with my fist. What the fuck is going on?

I throw the car in drive, and a minute later, I park in front of her house.

The front door opens before I have time to knock.

A surprised look registers quickly before she smiles. "Back so soon?"

"Going out?" I ask, noticing a small duffel bag on the floor and a Tupperware container of food in her hands. She's dressed in a pair of jeans and a loose-fitting sweater, stained white canvas running shoes on her feet.

"No . . . just about to heat this up, and I saw your car pull onto the street through the kitchen window," she says.

I point to the duffel. "The bag?"

She raises an eyebrow. "Am I under investigation again?"

She's never not been. I wait for her to answer.

She sighs. "It's my clothes for yoga. I haven't been sleeping, and I thought it might help."

At this point, I don't believe anything she tells me, but I need her to start opening up, so I force a laugh. "Sorry . . . suspicious minds never take a vacation. Can I come in?"

"Of course," she says, moving away to let me in. "Coffee? I just made a pot."

"Sure." I carry the divorce papers into the kitchen behind her. I watch her as she pours two cups and carries them to the counter.

I place the divorce papers on the island, and her gaze falls to them. No recognition registers on her face. Is it possible that she doesn't know?

"What are those?" she asks.

"Malcolm was filing for divorce last year."

Genuine shock registers on her face now, and it would take an Emmy winning actress to pull it off if it wasn't real. "You didn't know." Somehow that makes me feel better. At least she hasn't lied or withheld information about this. And if she's never been served with these papers, she hasn't had time to defend herself against the accusations.

Damn, I have to stop giving her the benefit of the doubt, when she's done nothing to deserve it.

"No, I had no idea," she says. "Last year . . . so he changed his mind?"

"You tell me."

"I don't know. I told you: I never knew he'd wanted one in the first place." Her hand shakes as she reaches for the papers.

I sit on a stool and sip my coffee, letting her read her husband's words. I watch her face. A pained look that slowly gives way to anger. Eventually she sets the papers back down and takes a deep breath.

"Everything in here is one sided."

I notice she doesn't dispute all the claims that have been filed against her. "Then tell me your version of the truth." She has no other choice now. I know all her dark secrets, her anger issues, her abusive tendencies, and her control issues over her husband . . . or at least, I know Malcolm's version. The trouble is that I can't equate the woman described in these pages to the one standing in front of me.

She hesitates and then climbs onto a stool across from me. Her hands cradle her coffee mug, and she stares into the depths of the dark liquid. "When we met, I had goals for myself. For my future. I had a degree and a promising future as a dancer. Malcolm was supportive of all of that. He encouraged me to pursue my passion . . . until we got married."

I wait. So far it sounds like a familiar story. Hook, line, and sinker. Classic abuser strategy. But who was manipulating who is still unclear.

"Then things changed. He wanted me to give up dancing. He said I should focus on my finance career. I was hurt. I thought he'd believed in my talent. When we were dating, he'd been nothing but encouraging."

Not unusual. Often the way things go in relationships.

"I did both," she says. "I continued to work and started dancing with a group in south Florida. Nothing big. Not Broadway performances or the Royal Ballet or anything, but small shows that received glowing reviews."

I know all this already. I've read the reviews. Seen the photos online. But I don't tell her that.

"I thought if I could prove to him that I was good enough, he'd be on board with me pursuing it as a full-time career."

"But he wasn't?"

"He started talking about starting a family. He wanted a baby."

"You didn't."

"After so many years of . . . setbacks . . . my dancing career was finally going somewhere. It wasn't the right time for me to get pregnant. I wanted to wait."

"So why did you change your mind?"

"I didn't. I wasn't on the pill . . . it made me crazy, hormonal . . ." She gestures toward the divorce papers as though the pill were to blame for her mental instability.

I'm not a woman, and I have no idea what they go through, so I don't comment.

"One night after a performance, Malcolm took me out to celebrate. He bought one bottle of champagne after another. I don't know how much I consumed . . . I was drunk. Passed out."

"He raped you?"

"No . . . I mean, I don't remember . . . maybe. Anyway, weeks later, I found out I was pregnant."

"Why didn't you have an abortion?"

She shakes her head. "I don't believe in that."

"So, you were stuck."

"Career over, and carrying a baby I wasn't ready for. I was angry at Malcolm. So, yes, I admit to some of his claims about abuse. I did yell at him. Lost my temper."

"Punch him?"

She nods. "He isolated me from my family and friends. He took away my internet access. He wouldn't allow me to go anywhere without him."

"Why the sudden change?"

"He thought I'd do something to harm the baby . . ."

Would she have? Has she? I stare at the woman, who just keeps getting more and more complicated as the hours tick by, with no sign of her husband and child. I'm nowhere close to getting answers . . . just more puzzle pieces that don't seem to fit.

"After Mikayla was born, everything was different. Once I held a baby in my arms, I didn't care about anything else. My dancing career no longer mattered. I settled into life as a wife and mother, and things got better."

"That's why he didn't go through with the divorce?"

"I guess so."

"What about the move here? Was that something you wanted?" The principal at the high school didn't think so. Neither did Fran. Will she be honest?

"I don't know," she says finally. "But it doesn't matter now." She breaks, and I stare at the tears running down her cheeks. "I'm here. And I'm alone."

Crocodile tears or real?

She could have lied, denied Malcolm's claims, but she didn't. I want to believe that, despite her questionable actions from the past, they were just the actions of a manipulated, abused woman. But I know I can't trust her.

"Divorce," she whispers. "He was always planning on leaving me." The desperation in her eyes, the pleading—along with the suspicious duffel bag in the hallway and the already-hot food in the Tupperware container—makes one thing clear.

She was headed somewhere this evening, to see someone, and for multiple reasons—some stupid, some strategic. I'm not leaving her tonight.

September 10—6:53 p.m.

Too many lies are a liar's downfall. Tell one and it's easy. Tell more and suddenly they start to overlap, intersect, contradict. Fortunately, no one's ever cared about me enough to call me out on anything. My connections to those around me have been entirely too surface for my truths to be discovered.

But I can tell by the look on Paul's face that he could be the exception. He was listening to every word I said. Scrutinizing. Evaluating. He wants to believe me now.

They say everything changes for a woman after sex. After the physical connection, her hormones start to make her believe that she's in love. She's imprinted part of herself on her mate. That's why rejection after a sexual relationship is harder on women.

Detective Ryan looks like he might be suffering from the same affliction. His objectivity has been compromised. His practical clearheadedness clouded by our intimacy.

His sympathetic gaze makes me ill. I want him to sympathize with the fact that I've lost Mikayla. I don't want him to sympathize with lies. Ones I'm forced to make up because he keeps prodding, keeps searching. I needed to defend against the accusations in those documents with the best possible version of reality I could come up with quickly, based on the bits and pieces I can fabricate, weave together.

I need to change Detective Ryan's expression to something else, and I need to solidify his belief in what I've just told him.

I slowly reach for the hem of my sweater before lifting it up and over my head.

He watches every move, and I see the conflict in his dark eyes. He wants me. Just like before. Am I more desirable to him now, or less? Does he crave twisted and broken, or simply abused and abandoned?

I stand up and remove the boring, plain white bra. He swallows hard. I watch his Adam's apple bob several times.

"Kelsey . . ."

"I know what you're going to say. That we shouldn't be doing this. It's wrong." I move closer and rotate the stool so that he's facing me. Wrapping my arms around his neck, I straddle his lap, bringing my bare breasts just inches from his face in the process.

I can feel him harden between my legs as he looks back and forth from my eyes to my exposed body.

I take his hands and put them on my bare breasts.

"I think that's what you like about it. The fact that it's wrong. You're the kind of man who seeks justice, who's trained to do the right thing all the time. Giving in to temptation, when you know you shouldn't, turns you on," I say, running my hands through the back of his hair and pressing my hips forward.

His hands massage my breasts now. His fight is over.

I wrap my legs around his waist and kiss him hungrily as he stands and carries me out of the kitchen . . . up the stairs . . . into the master bedroom. He lays me on the bed, and his body falls on top of me.

When his gaze meets mine again, I've succeeded—the look of sympathy is gone. Replaced only by lust.

September 10—8:09 p.m.

"Are you married, Detective?"

I stare at her, at first confused. If I were married, would I be here in bed with her? But then the reality sinks in, and I answer her question. "No. I was in a long-term relationship once, but it didn't work out."

"Why not?"

I should have simply stopped at no. "The same reasons most marriages fail for people in my line of work. I'm a workaholic, obsessed with my cases, emotionally unavailable . . ." What other reasons did the ex-wives of my coworkers throw around?

She nods, her long blonde hair falling into her face. "I could never be married to a cop."

Her words don't bother me. I have no misconception about why she's lying here next to me naked. We're both playing a game. I'm not sure who is winning.

"Do you have other family, Detective?"

"Just me and my father."

"Has it always been that way?"

Now we've moved into uncomfortable territory.

"I mean, obviously you had a mother at some point at least."

"She died in a psychiatric hospital." I spare her the details. How we thought she was getting better. How she'd convinced the nurses, the doctors, my father, and me that she was actually okay. That she was ready to rejoin the living, move on in the best way she could, the way my father and I were. Then we discovered it was all just a lie. She'd successfully fooled us all into letting her have her freedom, just so she could end her life in a nearby river.

"What happened?" Kelsey asks.

No sympathy or empathy in her voice, just curiosity.

She doesn't want to hear this, which is maybe why I decide to say it. She's poked a wound with her nosiness, so I'll poke back with the unsettling truth. "She went crazy when my younger sister went missing fifteen years ago."

I've hit my mark. I should apologize for the bluntness, which has hit far too close to home for her. Explain further. But I don't. She's opened a wound that has never fully closed.

Kelsey tenses in my arms. "Went missing?"

"Years ago . . . there was a string of abductions from different neighborhoods. All teenage girls."

She shudders. "I remember. I was terrified."

"Everyone was." I wasn't terrified enough to keep Julia safe.

"Did the police ever find any of them? Their bodies?"

"No." I know I'm not instilling much confidence in the department, but what can I say?

"What was she like—your sister?" she asks after a long pause.

I don't want to talk about her. I haven't in so long. The only conversations I've had have been with my father, and those were only to discuss the case. Julia doesn't feel real when we talk about her as a cold case file; only when she haunts me do I let myself remember that she was real. Some part of me obviously craves the opportunity to tell someone, as I don't shut down the conversation immediately. The way I used to when Faith would ask about her. "She was funny and smart. Athletic. She was a cheerleader."

"Younger?"

"Yes. We were two years apart."

"Did you look alike?" she asks.

We did. As kids, people thought we might be twins. "Yes. We both took after my mother's side of the family. Dark hair. Dark eyes."

"Do you have any pictures?" she asks, moving her body away from mine.

I hesitate, then reach for my wallet. I open it and bypass pictures of my family and one of Faith and take out the old school picture of Julia in her cheerleading outfit. The last photo taken of her, from the week before she disappeared.

Pom-poms out, big smile, jumping high into the air.

Kelsey studies the picture. "She's gorgeous."

"Yeah . . . my grandmother used to say she prayed for ugly grandchildren because no one took ugly children. Ironic how eerily accurate she was about that." All the teenage girls who went missing that fall were beautiful.

"You both grew up around here? Went to school here?" she asks.

"Yes."

She stares at the photo. "So sad that she was never found . . . none of them were ever found . . ."

A chill runs down my spine at the words . . . or maybe it's the odd way she says it. Either way, it has me putting the picture back in the wallet and sitting up. I reach for my pants on the floor.

"Do you want something to eat?" she asks.

If she's noticed my abrupt change, she doesn't say anything. I grab my badge and gun. "No. I should go."

She swings her legs over the side of the bed and stands. "I'll see you out." Once again, like before, she's not upset. She actually looks relieved that I'm not planning on spending the night or staying any longer.

Clearly, we've both gotten what we wanted.

But at the door, moments later, she hesitates. "I had a sister once too," she says.

Admittedly, not what I was expecting. She's said she has no family.

"We were in foster care after our parents died, got moved around a lot," she continues. "She was adopted first, and we lost contact."

I don't say anything. The only information I care about is anything that can help solve this case. The sooner I find her daughter, the sooner all this ends, and I know in my gut that the sooner this ends, the better—for both of us. I nod and reach for the door.

She stops me. "What did you do?"

"What do you mean?"

"Well, your mom went crazy. I assume your dad did as well, in his own way. What did *you* do? How did you deal with your sister's disappearance? With not having her in your life anymore?"

"I had no other choice but to continue living."

She seems to breathe easier. Her body relaxes. It's as though she'd been waiting for me to give her that permission.

September 11—9:04 a.m.

Once again I'm learning how to live after tragedy strikes. Until my secrets, my mistakes, catch up with me, there's nothing else I can do. Detective Ryan is moving in closer; he's digging into things. I know he's monitoring my every move. So my movements need to look natural. Not raise any flags or suspicion.

I should be good at this by now, but I'm not sure what to do with myself. What would other mothers with a missing child do to try to survive the hours of worry and uncertainty? Go to yoga? Read a book? Go shopping for groceries? Act like everything is normal, when their world hasn't just been irreparably altered?

Nothing will ever be the same after this. Everything has changed. And not knowing the outcome or how long all this will last has me feeling lost and unsettled.

What do I say when I run into strangers or people in town who might recognize me from TV?

Hello? Nice day?

It's not a nice day, and I want everyone to know it. I want to scream for the world to stop turning around me, for people to stop what they are doing, stop living so casually, unaffected by the most devastating thing that's ever happened to me. Or at least happened to me recently.

How cruel that no one else cares. The media hounds who keep showing up outside the house only want a story. They don't care that

Mikayla is real. That I'm real. And even they've lost interest, which is even worse.

Being in the house is safer with other people around.

A few days ago, our case was the hot topic. We at least mattered to the world in a twisted, warped, train wreck sort of way. No one cared, but at least they took notice.

Today, they've moved on to another hot topic. Something they can fill the airwaves with. More white noise that everyone eventually no longer hears.

Tragedies happen every day. Children go missing. People die.

No one cares.

So, I'm left to wander around in this fit of uncontrollable angry energy with no outlet. No comfort. No reassurance that things will be okay. Just uncertainty and waiting.

I have to leave the house eventually, so I lock the door and get in the car. The grocery store is as good a spot as anywhere else to join the life of the living . . . integrate into my new community.

Unfortunately, the nearest one in town is in the Enchanted Forest Shopping Center, and I sit in my car staring at the fat old king pointing the way toward the long-closed and abandoned Enchanted Forest Theme Park, with its Mother Goose–themed attractions.

I fucking hate this place.

As a teenager, I didn't have any friends. Friendships had already been formed by the time I attended school nearby, and no one was willing to open up their close-knit circles to allow in a newcomer. The popular kids acted like I didn't exist, and the outcasts all seemed to shun me as well. The damaged foster kid vibe seemed to linger on my clothes and hair despite all my attempts to wash it away. Other children thought I was weird, and parents thought I was trouble.

The day Shelly Bishop gave out her sixteenth birthday party invitations, I'd held my breath. One by one, she handed them out to the kids in the class as she made her way down the aisles between the seats, and I could see the Enchanted Forest logo on the invites as the kids all around me removed them from their envelopes.

We were at the age where you chose who you invited. You weren't expected to invite the entire class, like when we were younger. So, getting an invite to the most popular girl in school's birthday party meant something.

I waited. My hopes started to rise when it seemed everyone was getting an envelope, even the booger-picking boy everyone teased. I saw the stack getting smaller. Until they were all gone.

Surely, Shelly had made a mistake. We weren't great friends, but she wouldn't invite everyone else in the class and not me. I walked up to her and asked for my invite, but it turned out she hadn't made a mistake. She was the mean-spirited bitch I'd always known her to be.

The snickers around me made me angry, but I held my temper, the way I was supposed to.

The day of the party, I sneaked away from home and rode my bike to the Enchanted Forest. I followed several other kids with their parents to the front gate, and when the attendant asked for my ticket, I said I was there for Shelly Bishop's birthday party.

He let me in . . .

I climb out of the car now, and instead of going into the grocery store, I head toward the grave site of an amusement park. Entry gates are permanently open now for visitors to walk through—to reminisce about fun times or appreciate the eerie nostalgia that surrounds the place. Most of the attractions are still there, but some displays have been moved to an old farm outside town.

I enter the park, and overgrown brush tickles my bare arms as I walk along the trail. Run-down, broken, graffiti-covered displays and rides all around me.

In my mind, I see them as they once were. Lit up and magical.

The day of the birthday party, I rode all the rides by myself, making sure to avoid the other party kids—the ones who'd been invited. No one doubted my story that I belonged there, just like all the other teens. That day, I was able to forget that I wasn't like everyone else, that I didn't have what they had, that I wasn't loved and accepted the way they were. That day, I was just another sixteen-year-old laughing as I spun as fast as a spin top or screaming as the roller coaster car plunged to thrilling depths.

I was about to leave when Shelly Bishop's mother saw me.

She recognized me from the class, and the look in her eyes told me she knew my name was absent from the guest list . . . yet here I was.

"Hi . . . ," she said.

"Hi, Mrs. Bishop."

"Um . . . we're going to have cake now, if you want to join us over at the picnic tables."

Part of me wanted to say no. I know I should have. I'd come to the party uninvited and had spent hours having fun on my own. The day had been perfect.

But another part of me wanted to let that bitch Shelly know that I'd won.

So, I followed her mother to the picnic grounds, where the other kids had gathered around tables draped with birthday-themed tablecloths and festooned with balloons. Hot dogs grilled on a portable BBQ, and a big pink-frosted birthday cake sat in the center of the table, with "Happy Sweet Sixteen" scrawled across the top in bright-pink gel frosting.

Shelly was mad when she saw me there.

I smiled as wide as I could . . .

It was the last time I'd ever smile that wide.

I stare at the secluded part of the forest where Shelly and three other girls beat me with tree branches that day. Where I threw up the birthday cake and hot dogs and lay bleeding until a park attendant found me at closing time.

Bile rises in my throat now, and I turn and run out of the forest.

In my car, I force several deep breaths before getting out and going into the grocery store.

I push the cart down the aisles, my hands reaching for all the items we are getting low on at the house . . . or that the raccoon ate or destroyed.

Lucky Charms. Mikayla's favorite cereal. Caramel-flavored rice cakes. The only treat I allow myself. Frank's RedHot for Malcolm.

The bottle shatters on the floor. Orange-red paste-like liquid splatters against the tiles, on the shelf below, and all over my white canvas running shoes. Shards of glass have another customer—a young mother—struggling to maneuver a cartful of groceries around the mess. She pauses to shoot me an annoyed look.

Her day is interrupted by my little accident.

Her judgmental stare is in my peripheral vision as I stare at her blonde-haired little girl sitting in the front of the cart. She's looking at the mess on the floor while absently twirling the tangled dark hair of a half-naked Barbie doll around her finger.

Tiny little hands. Tiny, innocent face.

Precious darlings like her should never experience pain or fear, like Mikayla must be feeling.

My heart nearly stops. Is Mikayla afraid? Or is she relieved to be away from me? Happy to be with Malcolm . . .

The little girl's blue eyes are curious as she looks up at me. Shy, slightly sympathetic, as though she understands my situation.

I've dropped things and broken them too, they seem to say.

A hand on my shoulder makes me jump.

A grocery store clerk stands next to me with a mop. "Excuse me, ma'am . . . I'll clean this up."

I nod and move out of his way. "Sorry . . . it slipped from my hands."

"Happens all the time." He gets to work. "Did you need another bottle?"

Do I? Will Malcolm ever be in the house again to use it? Will I ever need any of the things in the cart? "Uh . . . no, that's okay." I move my cart around him, forcing the other woman to back up a little to let me pass.

The little blonde baby girl reaches a hand toward me, and I instinctively touch it. But then, I don't let go. Can't let go. I bring it to my nose and breathe in the sweet, baby powder–fresh scent of her skin. I trail the back of it against my cheek and lips. So soft. My gut clenches and my vision blurs as the aisle circles around me.

"Hey!" The mother slaps my hand away from her child. "What the hell are you doing?"

I blink and step back, away from the child, away from the crazed-looking mother. "Sorry . . ."

The woman glares at me as I pass by them quickly. She's still staring at me when I turn back to look at the little girl. I barely see the mother, though. All I see is the tiny face, bright-blue eyes, and little outstretched hand as the baby girl waves at me.

Almost as though she's taunting me. I abandon the shopping cart in the middle of the aisle and hurry out of the grocery store, across the parking lot, and back to the car.

This nightmare has gone on long enough. I need to get Mikayla back. Now.

September 12—3:00 a.m.

You're standing at the edge of my bed. Through the open window blind, moonlight illuminates the shape of you. I can't see your face—it's hidden in shadow—but I can hear you. Asking me to get up. Asking me to follow you. I know it's no use. These dreams lead nowhere I haven't searched before.

But you're persistent. You won't be ignored.

Another night of restless tossing and turning, searching woods and back roads and all the places you used to go . . . never finding you.

I wish you'd leave me alone. I wish you'd go visit Dad in his dreams. Take him on these voyages. He'd find peace in it. Hope. And maybe eventually he'd realize what I have—that we are never going to find you alive.

You beckon me to follow you out of the bedroom, and I know this trail by heart. Down the stairs, out the front door . . . through the trees, and past the river that flows through town, carrying away secrets. Your secret?

Is that what this is about, Julia? Do you want me to know your secret?

I follow you through the last minutes of darkness, and light crests the hill in the distance. We are near the old tree house we built in the woods so many summers ago. You climb the ladder and motion for me to follow. I have no choice. Dreams don't give the dreamer a choice.

But I know what's inside, and my legs feel heavy as I climb the decaying wood to the top.

Your expression changes to a look of fear as I enter. Piles of unidentified bones are stacked high. Bones of victims long missing—like you—waiting to be found. Bones waiting to be identified. Bones that are all that remain of the missing people I have failed.

206 of them are yours.

◆ ◆ ◆

I get up and go to the kitchen. I don't need to look at the clock to know what time my sister's apparition woke me up. It's always the same. Three a.m. The hour of spirits, the undead, the unsettled, lost souls wandering between this world and the next.

I pour a glass of water from the tap and drink the lukewarm, unfiltered liquid. Then I sit at the table and reach for her file.

Case file of Julia Ryan.

I've read this thing so many times. Nothing changes. Nothing new. But other than her hauntings, it's the only thing I have that reminds me of her. I don't want to forget.

AA (Amber Alert) CA (Child Abduction)

Age: 16

Reported Missing Date: December 21, 2008

Last seen: St. Bishop's High School

Medical Information: Eating disorder

Those fucking cheerleaders did that to her. Constantly told her she was fat, that she needed to lose weight. She believed them. She was desperate to fit in, to be one of them.

She was perfect the way she was. I should have told her that.

Personal Description: Five foot six inches. 115 pounds. Shoulder-length, dark brown hair. Dark brown eyes. Athletic build. Bitten, chipped fingernails, pierced ears, no tattoos.

Personal Belongings Description: Backpack, wallet or purse, earrings, and locket, engraved with "Happy Sweet Sixteen."

The locket—a birthday gift from my parents to her, two weeks before she went missing. The last thing any of us ever gave her. She'd worn it every day for those two weeks.

Was she wearing it now? In death?

Hours later, I climb out of my father's truck and follow him toward the old housing development property in Bowie, long abandoned due to insufficient cash flow. The company had barely broken ground on it before the project had dried up.

Research into the company revealed that the contractor, Doug Beinfeld, had a history of buying land and then never actually developing it. Rumor was that a gambling problem haunted the old man. He died years ago. No employees could be located to meet us out here, and the number for the old man's next of kin, Holly Beinfeld, is out of service.

My father uses bolt cutters to break the lock on the wire fence, allowing us to enter the only area of these woods that has never been searched for the missing girls.

"Which way do you want to start?" I'm tackling this search with as much confidence and enthusiasm as if I were on the hunt to prove the tooth fairy's existence, but my father is jacked. In his old hunting reflective vest, his shotgun at his side for any wildlife we may encounter, he's more alive in this moment than I can remember seeing him in forever.

This futile expedition into the woods is worth it just for the renewed sense of purpose it gives him. Combing these areas could take us weeks with the overgrowth and uneven terrain, and it gets him out of the basement, at least. I just hope the crash after he doesn't find what he's looking for isn't the one that finally destroys him.

"We'll start south and head north," he says, cutting at the overgrowth with a machete as we start to walk.

Eyes down. Move slow.

Any sign of clothing or jewelry—anything we can find to validate we might be onto something. Finally searching the right area.

"How's that woman holding up?"

I don't want to talk about her or the case, but my father's interests are few and far between. Bridge and missing people are basically the extent of his vocabulary these days, and I didn't bring a deck of cards out here with me. "Kelsey Jennings? As well as can be expected, I guess."

"Any new leads?"

"No. We suspect the older woman's death was the result of her son being involved with dealing drugs, but we have nothing to connect her to the missing child, except for Jennings's claims that she left her daughter with the woman."

"What about the son?"

"Drugs were his thing, not kidnapping. And he had an alibi for that morning when the child disappeared. He was at the unemployment office submitting urine samples."

"So, it's the husband?" my father asks.

Was it? He certainly had motive, if everything in the divorce documents, his claims against his wife, were true, but why not just go through with the divorce and leave her? Why put himself at risk of doing jail time and of never seeing his daughter again?

Kelsey's history of violence toward him, and the medication found at her home suggesting that her moods and mental health weren't exactly stable, have me pondering options I'd rather not consider.

Parsons ran a search for obituaries for a Malcolm Jennings that morning, but she came up with nothing that matched a profile for the missing man. So much of this isn't adding up.

Luckily, my father's forgotten all about his questioning. He's approaching a large tree on the side of the trail. He stops to examine the bark.

"What is it?" I ask, moving closer to see deep, long scratch marks in the wood. "Bear?"

He shakes his head. "Not unless it was a cub with especially small fingers."

I move closer and inspect the markings. Definitely deep fingernail scratches, with brown, dried-up blood in the thick grooves.

My father pulls out an acrylic fingernail. So old it flakes apart in his hand.

He bags the pieces and gives me a look that I refuse to encourage, despite the fact that my heart has started to pound in my chest. At least one woman was in this area of the woods, and she didn't seem happy to be here.

We keep moving in silence. Examining every inch of the trail and surroundings as we go.

No sign of struggles or attack . . . no sign of anyone having been on these trails, except for the scratches.

"More scratches here," my father says.

"Odd. If the woman was being chased, attacked, or dragged through these woods, why stop to carve up the trees?"

"Leaving evidence behind the best way she could is my guess," my father says.

Leaving evidence behind. Of her existence. Of her being here. She obviously knew she was going to die . . .

Did my sister know? How long did she live after being abducted, having to endure the torture of a psychopath . . . knowing she was going to die?

It starts to rain, and the ground becomes slick on the trails beneath our feet. Thick, heavy, fall clouds make it dark as night in the woods. I don't know how long he planned to be out here before, but now that there might be some evidence that we're looking in the right area, I doubt I'll drag his old ass out of here until we find something more concrete.

A body?

We walk for hours. Our flashlights the only source of light as we trudge through the thick bush. Morning gives way to afternoon, and there's nothing else to be found. Just scratches on trees. It's dark, and thunder rumbles in the distance. I'm calling it. "Dad, thunder means lightning's next. We need to call it a day."

"A few more minutes. Just don't get too close to the trees," he says.

"Dad, other than the scratches, we haven't found anything else . . . we'll submit the samples to the lab . . ." I'm disappointed. The first possible sign of the missing teen girls sparked more hope in me than I'll admit. How could there be nothing else? Unfortunately, time and weather over the last fifteen years have made this search fifteen years too late. "Dad, are you hearing me?"

"Over here," he says.

Stubborn old man. "Dad, listen to me. We're done for today." I have no idea how I'm going to stop him from coming back here every day. Now that he's gotten a little something to sink his teeth into, he'll be even more obsessed than before. "There's nothing else here."

"You're going to change your mind when you see this." He's standing at the edge of a slope at the side of the trail, staring down at something.

I move closer, and my blood turns to ice in my veins as I stop in front of a graveyard of human bones at the base of a deep tunnel.

"I estimate eight bodies," my father says.

"At least." I count ten skulls among the misshapen heap of decayed bodies that look as though they were trampling and climbing on one another to get out of this deep hole.

"I think we just solved some old case files," he says, and I know he's praying for one in particular.

So am I.

September 12—9:08 p.m.

Three Bowie police cruisers and several forensic vans are parked along the street. Lights are off. No one's around. They are all in the woods.

I sit in the car, staring at the wire fence bordering the perimeter of the property. The locks have been cut.

Someone finally thought it was time to search this area of the woods. Fuck, it took them long enough.

Though by the time the teenage girls made it here, it was too late for them. The hunt had started, and no one ever escaped.

Scientists now believe that the brain continues for minutes after death. Therefore, a person knows when they are dead. They know that they've taken their last breath. They know how they've died. They probably still feel the pain of whatever killed them.

That knowledge saved my life.

I might have ended things a long time ago if I didn't believe that the scientists were right.

I can live with dying. I just don't think I could continue to be aware of the fact that I was dead. The thought alone of being trapped in my own mind, perhaps feeling remorse for what I'd just done, perhaps feeling pain for the bullet lodged in my skull or the blood that's seeping out of my wrists . . . drives me to the brink of insanity. What if I change my mind about dying? What if I've forgotten to do something? What if I can hear the voices of those who are still alive all around me? What if I stay that way—caught in a terrifying limbo for eternity?

I see a beam of light from the trees and several shadows heading toward the parked cars. I start the ignition and drive away.

I won't be able to come back here for a while. Hopefully, the police won't discover my secret in the meantime.

September 13—9:03 a.m.

I comb the woods. Searching. I hear your scream. I hear your footsteps. I start to run, following the sound. I can even smell your shampoo on the wind. I see your hair first, flying behind you in the wind. Then the rest of your body comes into view. Naked. Bloody. Bruised.

You turn and your eyes are wild with fear. You can't see me.

I move closer. I call your name. But you don't hear me. I'm close enough to touch you, but you're unaware.

Frantic, desperate, you start clawing at the trees until your fingernails fall off and your fingers start to bleed. You're smart, Julia; you're leaving a trace for us, in case at the end there's nothing left of you for us to find. To know you were here.

To know you are one of the bones.

The feel of a hand on my chest has me instinctively reaching out and gripping it tight. My eyes snap open, and I'm breathing heavy. Sweat covers my body and the bedsheets beneath me. As though I have actually been running through the woods.

"Hey . . . it's okay. I think you were dreaming."

It's Kelsey next to me. Her naked body beside me in her bed. I release her wrist and take several deep breaths. Continuing to be with her is a mistake, but I didn't want to be alone and I didn't want to be around my father. I know part of him wants closure, but if some of those bones belong to my sister, I don't know what he will do next.

Searching for her has been his mission for so long—what happens when he doesn't have that anymore?

"Was it about your sister?" Kelsey asks, sitting up and covering her body with a bedsheet as she turns to look at me.

I shouldn't have told her about the search or what we found. Has it made her feel even more scared not to know where her own daughter is? Or has it restored some of her faith in me? That eventually mysteries can be solved.

Either way, I needed to talk to someone, and she was there . . . open door, open arms. Unfortunately, now I'm regretting it, and I no longer want to talk. "It's always about my sister," I say.

She reaches past me and picks up my cell phone from the bedside table. "This was ringing. That's what woke me."

I take the phone and sit up. Two missed calls from the forensic lab. I get out of bed and grab my clothes off the floor. "I have to make a call."

"I hope you find the closure you're looking for, Paul," she says. It's barely above a whisper, and a deep chill runs through me.

I go into the bathroom and lean against the sink. For years, we've waited for closure, some sort of finality to my sister's disappearance, but now that I may be getting it, I'm sick.

I throw up. Then I splash water on my face and dial the lab.

"Hey, man . . ." Parsons's voice gives nothing away.

"Is there a match to my sister?"

"No. I'm sorry, Paul. She's not here. We ran DNA testing on all the femoral bones for her first . . . but unfortunately . . ."

I disconnect the call and throw the cell phone across the bathroom. It smashes against the ceramic tub, and the screen breaks.

I'm shaking, and air struggles to get into my lungs. I knew not to get my hopes up. Part of me is relieved that my sister wasn't one of the bodies running scared from the predator in those woods all alone. One of the victims tossed into that deep, dark hole in the ground and left to die a slow, painful death. I'm happy that the blood-soaked bark is not my sister's doing, and I'm glad that she hasn't been that close all along.

But now I'm left with the same empty hollowness as before, wondering if her disappearance was worse . . . if her death was even more painful and cruel . . . or if she's still out there enduring her kidnapper's punishments.

I grip the edge of the sink and close my eyes, but images of her frantic, terrified face reappear behind my closed lids. I used to think the uncertainty of it all would drive me crazy . . . like my mother and father . . . if I let it.

I realize now that it has.

The bathroom door opens, and Kelsey's arms are around me before I can attempt to push her away.

"It's okay," she says softly. Her hands gently caress my lower back, and her soft lips kiss my cheek, my earlobe, my neck as she whispers it over and over again.

I don't respond because the only thing I could possibly say is that one day she may know how this feels, and then she won't think it's anything close to okay.

September 13—10:23 a.m.

I could have given Paul his answer about his sister. I was tempted to. When he'd shown up at the door looking exhausted and anxious, but also slightly encouraged . . . I'd wanted to put his fears to rest and squash any hope before it got too big. Before it consumed him and made the fall even harder when the news came in from the forensics lab.

But I couldn't do it.

How could I without jeopardizing everything? I'd have to tell him the truth. About my past. About me.

Maybe he'd understand. Maybe he wouldn't hold me responsible.

Shower water runs in the bathroom, and I keep an eye on the door as I sit on the edge of the bed. The necklace in my hand. The one his sister was wearing in the picture he carries around.

How would Paul react to seeing it again?

I stand and pace the room, my head aching and my palms sweating.

Can I put everything at risk by giving him the information he so desperately craves? I like him. I haven't liked anyone like this in a long time. I have no pretenses about what's happening—he doesn't trust me, but he likes fucking me. This thing we have going isn't real. It's not going to last.

But he's the first person I've felt connected to in a long time.

Telling him is the right thing to do.

Since when do you do the right thing? Do you even know the difference between right and wrong anymore?

I shut my eyes tight and press my fingers to my temples to try to stop the voice that plagues me. The chain dangles from my fingers and catches the light of the early-morning sun shining through the window.

It could all be over . . . for both of us.

I hide the necklace away in the small hand-carved wooden box; then I stash the box back under the socks in the dresser drawer as the water shuts off.

I can't do it. His sister is long gone. Dead somewhere in another pile of bones left to be discovered.

I'm not, and this is my one shot at a future.

September 13—11:18 a.m.

Telling my father is the hardest part.

I knock once on the basement door before heading down the stairs. "Pop, you down here?" The basement is almost unrecognizable. All the pegboards have been taken down. His years of diagrams, news articles, and missing person files that were scattered about three desks are all free of paper.

"Where is everything?" I ask. I'm stalling, but I'm not sure how to hit him with the news.

"Didn't need it all anymore."

Every part of me wants to let him believe that. What good would it do to tell him the truth anyway? He's found peace. He actually looks lighter, his spine looks straighter, as though the heavy weight he's been carrying for so long has been lifted. He's given up this never-ending search. It's over for him.

It could stay that way.

But I'll know the truth. And if he ever found out, it would kill him. I refuse to disrespect my father that way.

"Dad, the lab couldn't confirm a match to Julia."

He shakes his head. "We counted twelve victims. All female. Any one of them could have been her."

"They matched all twelve bodies to other cold case files." Twelve missing teen girls from that fall finally found. DNA testing identifying their murderer as the already deceased Doug Beinfeld. Not exactly the justice these families craved, but at least the man couldn't hurt anyone else. "Dental records, the DNA from the tree samples, some clothing . . . they were able to identify all of the girls."

He's silent.

"We still haven't found her, Dad."

He reaches for his shotgun, and I know there's no point in trying to stop him. So I move aside as my father passes by me and heads upstairs. A moment later, the front door slams.

He's going back out into the woods.

"Damn it," I mutter as I scan the now cleaned-out basement. My cell phone rings, and I'm in no mood for more bad news or dead ends. "What?" I say into the phone on the second ring.

"Hey, man . . . where are you?"

The station. "On my way in . . . what is it?"

"Washington/Baltimore International just called in. They have the little girl—Mikayla Jennings."

What? My mind being preoccupied, I've almost forgotten about the current case I'm working. "Trying to leave the country?" That was ballsy. Malcolm Jennings had to know that the local authorities were searching for them.

"Coming back into the USA," Parsons says.

"Is she with the father, Malcolm Jennings?"

"Nope. Apparently, she's traveling back from Haiti with her grand-parents—a Meredith and Walter Jennings."

The overseas do-gooders have the child? "Any sign of the father?"

"He's not with them."

"Where are they now?"

"Holding room four at the airport."

I take the steps two at a time as I hurry upstairs. "I'm on my way."

"The guards say they can only keep them about an hour for questioning, as the grandparents have documents saying they are the child's legal guardians and they have travel consent."

I trip over the top step. "What? How is that possible?" The child hasn't been abducted all this time? She's been with her grandparents. Her legal guardians. What the hell is going on?

I leave through the front door.

"I don't know, man," Parsons says. "And it gets even weirder. We just received Malcolm Jennings's phone records. The only calls made to the number in the last two months are from Kelsey Jennings and some spam calls. But the calls weren't answered, and there haven't been any outgoing calls from the number. No texts out either. Kelsey Jennings's calls have only been this week . . . since the kid went missing."

"Were there any other numbers attached to his cell phone account? Maybe this was an old number."

"No others listed. Just the family plan. His number and Kelsey's number."

"Okay, thanks," I say, climbing into my car. I have less than an hour to get to the airport, so I put my light on the roof and tear out of the driveway.

"Hey, at least the kid's safe—that's good news, right?" Parsons says.

"Yeah." Unfortunately, I'm not sure what Mikayla Jennings is safe from.

September 13—12:34 p.m.

"They're in there," the tall, intense-looking border guard says, pointing to the small holding room near US customs at the Washington/Baltimore International Airport. "You just made it. We were ready to release them."

"Thank you." I knock once and open the door.

A man in his sixties, dressed in a pair of wrinkled khakis and an army-green button-down shirt, paces. He spins toward me as I enter. "What is this about?" He glances at an expensive-looking watch. "We've been traveling for almost twenty-four hours. We'd like to know what the hell is going on here."

So would I. "Walter Jennings?"

"Yes. Who are you?" He eyes my badge and gun.

"Detective Ryan from the Ellicott City Police Department. This is your wife?" I glance at the woman. She's in her late fifties, holding a sleeping little girl in her arms. Mikayla. The missing child is safe. According to these people, she's always been safe.

"Yes, that's Meredith. And my granddaughter."

I look at the paperwork from the guards. A court order granting the grandparents the right to travel with the child without further parental consent. "And you both have custody of . . . Mikayla?" Keeping my hand and voice steady is a challenge. The child has been found, but now there are so many unanswered questions. Why did Kelsey Jennings call the police and report her child missing when she knew where she was the entire time? This crazy act of hers the last few days, the extent she went through to convince us the child had been abducted, makes no sense.

"That's right," Walter says. "Now, please explain to me why we are being held." His tired expression is full of justified annoyance, but I still need my answers.

"And where is your son? Malcolm Jennings?" He's still missing from this equation. I'm reluctant to take all this at face value. Hesitant to believe a woman would just make all this up for no reason. Kelsey Jennings was adamant that her husband and daughter were missing, and I'm tangled up with her and her mess, distracted by my own tragic mystery over the last forty-eight hours, so I'm not seeing what's in front of me.

Meredith's expression changes to one of grief when she stares up at me, and Walter looks confused. "Malcolm died two months ago."

My gut suspicion is confirmed: none of Kelsey's story adds up. That's definitely information a wife would know. Is it possible that Kelsey Jennings is suffering from some kind of grief-induced memory failure? Denial? "I'm sorry for your loss. Can I ask what happened?"

"There was a car accident. He was on his way back to Florida. They'd been here looking at new houses after Malcolm had been offered a job at the local high school." There's an edge to his voice, as though he's not happy about having to recount the details of their personal life.

"What about his wife . . . Kelsey?" Her name sticks on my tongue. Hours ago, my hands were all over her body . . . the body of a woman I don't know anything about. Except that she's a liar.

"She was in the accident too. But she escaped with minor injuries," Meredith says in almost a whisper as she glances at the sleeping child. "Thank God, Mikayla was with us at the time."

I stare at the child—pink cheeked, her hair slightly sweaty on her forehead. "Is there a record of the death?"

Walter frowns. "Yes. Why? What's going on?"

"The department ran a search for an obituary—"

"Are you trying to imply that we're lying to you about our son's death?" Walter's voice rises as he advances toward me.

His wife shoots him a look. "Walter, relax." She turns to me. "You wouldn't find one under Malcolm Jennings," Meredith says. "Our son's real first name is Frank . . . Frank Malcolm Jennings. Named after his grandfather. We call him by his middle name." Emotions evident in her voice, she pauses. "Called him by . . ." The rest of her sentence trails off.

"What is going on?" Walter asks again, obviously fighting for patience.

I ignore the question. My thoughts are spiraling as I try to make sense of what I've been told and the reality in front of me. I should never have let myself get involved in this case the way I have. "How is it that you both have custody of Mikayla?" My blood runs cold through my veins as I ask the question. Just how crazy or dangerous is Kelsey Jennings? All the accusations in the divorce file—were they all true, as Malcolm claimed?

"We were granted sole custody of Mikayla because our daughter-in-law has . . . limitations that prevent her from being a suitable parent," Meredith says.

Like she's batshit crazy, perhaps? "Limitations?" Why are they sugarcoating things? Abuse and attempted adultery seem like perfect reasons to lose custody of a child. Are they trying to protect her from something? Or are they just that good of people?

"Kelsey has never really been the maternal type. She didn't want a child," Meredith says, cradling Mikayla into her chest, as though feeling the need to protect the child even now.

"She has anger issues, and Mikayla isn't safe with her," Walter says. He releases a slow, deep breath. He's annoyed and rightly so . . . but my world has been tilted in the last few days, rattled around until I've felt like I've been in a constant confusing nightmarish state. Missing child. Dead old lady. Bones . . . no answers. Nothing adding up.

Lies and truth undecipherable.

"According to Mrs. Jennings, your son was the abusive one," I say. Desperate to find something in Kelsey Jennings's story that isn't a lie. I'm not sure why I need it. Maybe to feel like I haven't been completely fooled. Manipulated by this woman.

Meredith shakes her head. Her dark curls fall across her makeup-free, tired-looking face. "That's not true."

"Did you know your son was planning on filing for divorce?" I ask them.

They exchange looks.

"We were helping him leave the marriage," Walter says reluctantly.

"We didn't want it to come to that. We think a child needs both parents," Meredith says quickly, defending their actions, "but Kelsey has a temper. She can be manipulative . . ."

You're telling me.

"And we believe she could be a danger to Mikayla," Walter says.

Hence the sole-custody judgment in their favor after Malcolm Jennings's death.

"The truth is, Kelsey didn't really fight our application for custody," Meredith says. "She's fine with seeing Mikayla a few times a week . . . when we're not overseas."

That's not the mother I've spent time with, questioned . . . the one who needed to be sedated at the day care, who allowed us to open the investigation to get her daughter back, the one who made a heartfelt plea to the public . . . was she having a change of heart or a nervous breakdown?

"Can you please explain to us what's going on now?" Walter asks firmly.

I have no idea. "Turns out it was a misunderstanding." I'm unwilling to provide them with details until I speak to Kelsey and get to the bottom of all this. The important thing is that the child is safe. "You're all free to go."

They stand, and Meredith hands the little girl to her husband. He takes the sleeping child and places her over his shoulder. "We'd like answers about what all of this is about . . . but this little girl isn't feeling well, and we'd like to get her checked at a hospital."

I frown. "She's sick?" She does look pale, except for the flushed cheeks and the blotchy-looking skin on her hands.

"A low-grade fever for the last several days, with upset stomach and dehydration . . . that's why we came back early from the mission trip. We were there just a day before she started to show signs of illness."

At least they were putting the child first. They obviously cherished their granddaughter above all else. Maybe the child was safer with them. What mother simply gave up custody without a fight? "I hope she feels better," I say.

Meredith reaches for the handles of the suitcases and heads toward the door.

"Sorry for the inconvenience," I tell them.

"Don't worry. Your captain will be hearing from us," Walter says as they leave the room.

Shit. What a fucking mess.

September 13—5:06 p.m.

I see Detective Ryan pace outside near his vehicle, parked on the street. He's on the phone. He looks annoyed, confused . . . irritated.

Something's going on. The phone has been ringing all afternoon, but I've been too freaked out to answer it.

Meredith Jennings. Walter Jennings. Detective Ryan. Two calls from unknown numbers. What do they want? Have the police finally reached them? Have they found Malcolm? I know I should answer. Tell them what's going on . . . but I'm terrified.

Would they accept me if they knew the truth? Would they blame me somehow for Mikayla going missing?

I need more time. With the police still scouring the woodsy area . . . I'm at a standstill. I can't go in search of answers yet. Have they already found them?

Detective Ryan heads up the walk, and I move away from the window and meet him at the door.

"I've been calling you," he says.

"Sorry . . . I was napping, and the phone was on silent." I study his expression for any sign of what he knows . . . the depth of what he may have discovered. Have I let him get too close? Let my guard down too much? Does he know everything?

"Can I come in?" he asks.

"Of course. There's news, isn't there." It's not really a question. He's definitely here to deliver news . . . good or bad, I'm not sure. I clutch the handle of the coffee cup. Have they found Malcolm? Mikayla? If so, where are they?

He enters and closes the door behind him. "We need to talk."

The cup shakes violently in my hand, and the hot, dark liquid splashes over the side. "What's wrong? You found Mikayla? Is she okay?"

He runs a hand over his face. His eyes look like he's aged since he left here hours before, and my heart threatens to burst from my chest. "Let's go sit in the living room," he says.

"Tell me." My gut says this is all going to be over soon . . . with an ending I haven't expected or planned for. One that may not go well for me.

"We found her."

I drop the coffee cup, the contents splashing across the floor as the ceramic breaks into a million pieces near my bare feet. I'm surrounded by shards, frozen to the spot. "Safe?" I think I've said the word out loud, but it doesn't reach my ears.

He nods, and my knees almost give way. I cover my mouth as a sob escapes.

"Let's clean this up and talk."

Is he fucking serious right now? This mess can wait. Where is Mikayla? Why hasn't he brought her home with him? "Where is she? Why didn't you bring her here?" I step forward, not feeling the tiny shards pierce the bottom of my feet.

He takes me by the shoulders to prevent me from stepping on more shards and releases a deep breath. "Kelsey . . . she was with her grandparents."

Okay . . . so they were all in on this. They turned themselves in? "Where's Malcolm?"

His grip tightens on my upper arms.

"Where's my daughter?" On the floor, a small pool of blood collects by my foot.

"You've cut your feet. Let's clean this up, clean you up, and then we need to talk."

What the hell is going on? Why hasn't he brought me my daughter, and where is his sense of urgency? I lunge at him, nearly slipping on the coffee. "Where is she, Paul?"

"She's safe. She's with her grandparents." He grips my wrists, but I yank free, taking a step back. "Where she's supposed to be," he says, a sharp irritation in his tone.

I nearly buckle at the waist. "What? No . . . she's supposed to be here with me . . ." I reach for my sweater and car keys.

He blocks the door. "Where are you going?"

"To get Mikayla."

"I can't let you leave. We need to talk. Meredith and Walter Jennings have custody of Mikayla. She's been with them all along. You knew that," he says. "I need to know why you did this. Why did you call the police? Fabricate this entire thing?"

The room spins, and I feel everything crashing down around me. I've been deceived, fooled, made to look crazy. "What are you talking about? These people must be lying. Where's Malcolm?"

He runs a frustrated hand through his hair. "Cut the act, Kelsey! I know Malcolm died two months ago. Stop this."

The room seems to have tilted on an angle, and I'm thrown off balance. My shoulder connects with the doorframe, and I blink. No. That's not right. Malcolm's not dead. "Where's Mikayla?" I grip the wall for support.

I feel Paul's hands on my shoulders as he guides me away. He wraps his arms around me, but there's no comfort in them. Just control. "Kelsey, I need to take you in to the station."

What is he saying?

"Mikayla . . . I need to see Mikayla."

"Mikayla's fine. And I can help you. I want to help you."

By bringing me in? "You've always thought I was crazy. You never believed me." I move out of his arms and take several steps backward. Now, it seems that he's right.

"Kelsey, I want to help. I've gotten too close this time, and I care about you." He runs a hand through his hair and places his hands on his hips. Defeated. "I can help. I want to help. But you're going to have to come in. You reported false information about a missing person . . . that's a crime. I can't just ignore this."

I nod, though nothing he says makes sense. Malcolm can't be dead. Mikayla doesn't belong with her grandparents. This is my life. Malcolm, Mikayla, and me. This is the life I deserve. The one I should have had all along.

He's not taking it away.

"I'll need you to provide a statement. Explain why you did this. Maybe write up a formal apology . . . Kelsey . . ."

He stares at the floor. He, too, had been hoping for a different ending. But I can sense his relief that it's finally over. This thing between us has been wrong, dirty . . . he feels ashamed, guilty. He's happy this whole thing is over.

For him. For me, it's just beginning.

"Okay . . . ," I say, reluctantly. My shoulders sag, and my body language and tone match his. Defeated, giving in . . .

He looks relieved as he nods.

"Just let me change my clothes." I turn and leave bloody footsteps across the hardwood floor as I head into the kitchen instead of going down the hall to my bedroom.

Detective Ryan follows. "I'll clean up," he says.

"Thank you," I whisper. Inside I'm screaming. I'm a fire that can barely remain under control, a blaze ready to engulf everything and everyone around me. This isn't the way things were supposed to go. What the hell do I do now?

Mikayla is safe. With her grandparents. They have custody. Malcolm is dead.

What the actual fuck?

I can't go into the station. Everything has started to unravel, and all Detective Ryan has to do is pull the right loose thread and all the answers, all the truth, will tighten around me, suffocating all the hope I've had for a normal, peaceful existence.

If I tell him the truth now, will he understand? Will he take my side? Believe me, help me?

He goes to the counter and unrolls some paper towels from the holder.

I watch him. Torn. Conflicted. I know our connection wasn't real for either of us. I can't trust him. At the end of the day, he's still a cop, and he will do what he believes is right. He won't listen to my story. He won't understand. He will never take my side.

I open the kitchen drawer and take out my gun.

I feel the slightest hesitation as I raise the gun toward his back. He's a nice guy. He doesn't deserve to die . . . but Come On, Paul . . . how long would it have taken you to figure out I'm not *Mrs. Jennings?*

I see his body sag and fall forward before I hear the shot. His body crumples on my kitchen floor, and his blood seeps out from his waist, making another mess. He moves around for a few seconds, wild eyed, confused. He reaches an arm out toward me—his desperate gaze full of questions when it reaches mine.

I step over him as I leave the kitchen. I don't have time to clean this up right now.

I need to go get answers. I need to go get the life I was promised.

PART TWO

Twelve days earlier . . .

There she is. My twin sister.

From my vehicle parked across the street in the nice neighborhood, I watch her climb the front stairs and unlock the door. Other than her slightly shorter hair, we're still identical. And a haircut is no big deal. If it means we'll be exactly the same again.

Being exactly the same is the only way to pull off a successful switch . . . like we've done before.

I can't believe I'm actually this close to her again. It's been fifteen years since I've seen her, been almost close enough to touch her. And it's been months since our last contact. I'd thought that was the end . . . when she blocked me from sending her new messages.

The FOR SALE sign on the lawn has a big **SOLD** sticker across it. There are currently thirty-six homes for sale in Ellicott City. I spent time outside twenty-one of them in the last week, but I can understand why she chose this one for her family. It's bigger and nicer than most, and in a prettier, safer part of town.

She wouldn't want to raise her daughter in a house like any of the places we lived after our parents died.

My niece deserves so much better than the life we had. Or at least, I had. *Kelsey* at least eventually got to grow up in a house like this again.

When a couple walked into the office at social services after Kelsey had murdered the Hollywood "collectors" and they reviewed our profiles, they only wanted one of us. Me. Obviously. The good girl. The one who didn't murder people or push seven-year-old ballerinas down flights of stairs. The one who didn't need psychiatric help. The one without a criminal record.

But that's when being a twin stole my one shot at the future I deserved. We were identical, down to the tiny mole on the right side of our chins. Markings like that are usually unique to one twin and not the other. A tell. A way to distinguish us. A way to be our own person. My sister and I don't have that. We are identical in every way. No one can ever tell us apart.

So, she told me we were switching places. She left with the nice couple, and I was left to assume her doomed-for-life persona.

But about six months after she left, someone wanted me too. He wasn't the perfect-looking, barren couple who had come for her, but at least this man didn't shudder at "my" record of problematic behavior, as the agency was forced to reveal to him. He didn't even wait to see how things with a teenage girl would work out. He started the official adoption application immediately.

I was nervous. He was older, single . . . never married, no kids. What did he want me for? But he was a wealthy property developer, and I was desperate to get out from under the boys at the foster home every night, so I said yes when they asked if I'd like to go live with Doug Beinfeld in Bowie.

I packed my few belongings into a garbage bag and left the group home. Mr. Beinfeld insisted I call him Grandpa so that people wouldn't wonder about us too much.

Home wasn't what I'd expected. The tiny, loft-style cabin in the woods was so far from everything and everyone. Far enough that no one could hear screams from Grandpa's victims that fall.

I'm not sure how many there were before I arrived, but that year it seemed like he was "hunting" a new girl every couple of days. He'd take them from neighboring towns, so as not to raise too much suspicion in

Bowie, and then he'd listen to the news on the radio about the disappearances . . . about how the police had no clues, no suspects . . .

I was afraid at first. I thought maybe he'd hurt me too. But he never did.

He wasn't all bad. He taught me survival skills I'd never have learned otherwise. He taught me to hunt, to stalk the prey silently through the woods without being seen, without being heard. I learned to observe and later imitate the hunted.

It made the animals feel comfortable when I acted like one of them. Like I belonged there. They didn't fear me. They let their guard down.

Grandpa would hunt the animals, and then I'd help him skin them and hang them below the cabin deck to dry out. I'd sit for hours watching each last drop of blood drain from the animal.

I never ate the meat. It felt wrong somehow to eat something I'd gotten so familiar with.

I'd often wear their skins, though. They helped me hide. Sometimes for hours, I could sit in the woods with the shell of a deer draped over me, waiting . . . but I could never kill one myself.

That disappointed Grandpa. He'd hoped I'd have a thirst for blood the way he did. After all, he'd thought he was adopting my sister.

We spent a lot of time in the woods together, but the year I started high school, Grandpa gave me news that made my heart soar.

I was going to a real school. No more homeschooling under his intense schedule, crazy demands for perfection, and relentless belittling when I got something wrong.

He insisted I wear a uniform to school, even though we didn't need to anymore. He believed in the old ways and refused to let me wear "bumming around" clothes to school.

My uniform was the boy version—pants and shirt and vest. After my ordeal at the foster home, Grandpa wasn't taking any chances with the boys at the school. He cut my hair himself in the cabin. Gone were the inches of silky locks. I was left with barely three inches of hair on all sides. Combined with no makeup, I could have passed as a boy, if it hadn't been for my very well-endowed chest.

I went through the motions of living, but I didn't have dreams. I didn't have passions. I'd learned from an early age that I just wanted to survive.

Though I'm not sure why.

The only thing keeping me moving forward was thoughts of her— my sister. Knowing someday I'd see her again.

I dreaded being in the cabin alone with Grandpa all the time. Especially when he'd come home without a victim, covered in blood . . . with a new story to tell. But then he got sick, and he stopped hunting. I guess he knew his time was coming, and while it was too late for redemption, too late to make peace with God or whoever he may have believed was going to end up with his awful soul, he tried to make peace with me.

I was relieved that there wouldn't be any more guests in the cabin. No more screams. No more girls begging for me to release them, set them free, go to the police. I was thankful that he had given up and was no longer taking his meds. My life could only start to change with him gone. I believed that, along with his body, the guilt he'd bestowed on me would shrivel up and eventually turn to dust. With him gone, I could leave all these horrific deeds in the past and move on with a new life, a peaceful life.

I'd do good to make up for all his wrongs.

But a few days before Christmas, he somehow found a renewed strength, a renewed energy and desire to go out again.

I begged him not to, but he did anyway.

I didn't see this one. He never brought this one home. But when he returned, he had a gift for me. A silver pendant hanging on a silver chain.

It was a sweet-sixteen pendant. I knew wearing the jewelry of a dead girl around town when police across Maryland and her family were looking for her was a bad idea. A mistake. So I was careful. I only wore it on special occasions. The rest of the time I stored it in the only other thing Grandpa ever gave me—a hand-carved jewelry box with my initials next to a bird.

It's one of the few things I've packed to bring into this new exciting chapter of my life where I reconnect with my sister. I guess I want to reassure her that my life hasn't been so horrible. That someone cared about me a little—enough to give me that gift. That she shouldn't feel guilty for making me switch places with her. That I'm happy for her. She deserved a good childhood in a nice home. And now, she has this wonderful home.

It's picture perfect, with its white picket fence and blue shutters on either side of big bay windows in the front. Windows through which I can see her now, moving around the house.

I sit there staring at the house, admiring the big maple tree in the front yard, the wind rustling the branches, causing a spiral of autumn-colored leaves to fall prematurely to the ground. It's so beautiful. I can picture Mikayla playing in those leaves, gathering them all together into a big pile and then running and diving into them. Kelsey and I used to play in the leaves in the backyard at the home we had with our parents. Or at least, she'd play in the leaves with her friends, and I'd hide in my own pile, watching the fun.

Maybe once she lets me be in their lives, we can all play in the leaves together.

I watch the house, trying to see if anyone else is home. Is Malcolm there? Will I get a glimpse of my brother-in-law? Is he as handsome in real life as he is in his Facebook profile picture? Very few people are. Facebook profile pictures are probably the best anyone has ever looked in their lives.

I'm just happy I was able to find him on Facebook. He was much more open and trusting than my sister, with his unlocked profile. After she'd blocked a dozen new profiles from sending her any more Facebook messages, I'd had to learn about her through Malcolm's Facebook posts. It hadn't taken much effort to connect them—a few Google searches . . . amazing what one can discover online if one is motivated enough.

I've seen photos of their early relationship, photos of Malcolm's graduation with his teaching degree, their wedding photos . . . those hurt a little. I wasn't invited to one of the most important days in my sister's life. And then the new baby photos of Mikayla tore me apart with sadness that I hadn't been there for that.

But I'm here now. I peer through the windshield toward the house. Will I see them together? See them laugh, see them touch, see them kiss?

I wonder where Mikayla is. Napping? She's probably exhausted from the move. I wonder if she's happy in her new house, new room . . .

My gaze lands on the upstairs windows. There are no curtains on those yet, either, and I can see that one room's been painted beige, the other a pale pink. Mikayla's room.

I sigh, overwhelmed with happiness for Kelsey. This new house with its bay windows and white picket fence must be everything she's ever wanted. It's everything I've ever wanted.

I won't approach her just yet. I'll give the family time to settle in.

When the timing is right, I'll just need to show her that I can be a part of all of this, too, without ruining things for her. The perfect house. The perfect husband. The perfect little girl. And the perfect twin sister.

What more could my sister possibly want?

From the produce section, I watch as Kelsey walks down the aisles of the grocery store. Every time she rounds a corner, she disappears from sight for just an instant; then my gaze is locked on her again. She doesn't notice me, and I resist the urge to go up to her, to hug her, to feel her to see if she's really real. For fifteen years I've imagined the moment when we'd first see one another again.

But she didn't want me to come, doesn't want me back in her life, so I need to be careful not to upset her by jumping in too quickly.

I watch now as she puts items into her cart. Milk. Coffee. Cereal. Bread. Hot sauce.

I make a note of the kind of bread they eat, the brand of coffee . . . I try not to judge the sugar-filled cereal she selects for Mikayla. We never got the good, sugary kind as kids in the foster homes. Just stale, no-name-brand puff wheat that tasted like cardboard. Maybe she's just overcompensating for the things we didn't get.

Better be careful, though, not to spoil Mikayla. I'll talk to her about it.

I smile thinking of all the amazing, meaningful conversations we'll have. Like real sisters. She'll ask my advice on things, and I'll help her. I'll be here for her. Moving to a new city must be tough, and having me here to help will make her feel better.

She just doesn't realize it yet.

And I've already forgiven her for blocking my attempts at contact. I know she was just scared and worried. She may have gotten away with her actions in the past, but will her husband and daughter still love her if they learn they're living with a liar? My hands clench tight at my sides.

Of course I'll never tell.

I turn away quickly as she approaches. I can't let her see me just yet. I need to try to learn more about her first so that we can truly connect.

Her cell phone rings. She stares at the caller ID and silences the call. Who was it?

From the corner of my eye, I see her go to the cash register. I study her face, but her expression is unreadable. Blank almost.

It's a shock. My sister doesn't look happy. She looks slightly lost and confused.

The cashier says something to her, but she barely responds.

Come on, Kelsey, don't be rude!

She unloads her cart and looks distractedly at the magazines at the counter while the cashier scans her groceries.

Her cell phone rings again, and she ignores it.

She pays with a card, then picks up the bags and leaves.

I watch through the store window as she loads them into her car, gets in, and drives away.

I quickly leave the store and jog through the rain to get in my own car. Wipers on, headlights off, and keeping a safe distance, I follow along the streets.

Where to now, Kels?

Where the hell are Mikayla and Malcolm?

For days, I've watched my sister's every move. I've followed her from shopping to jogging to watching her sign up for yoga classes at the local studio. I've sat in my car across the street and watched her move about her house. But so far, there's been no sign of her husband or her daughter.

Did she make the whole thing up?

No. I've seen the proof. Malcolm's Facebook profile confirms their marriage, their daughter, their move from Florida to Ellicott City. Though, oddly, that was his last post—announcing his job offer from Saint Bishop's High School. I was overjoyed to learn they were moving to a city so close to where I've been living this whole time.

So where is he?

I see Kelsey come outside through the front door and carry a bag of garbage to the side of the house.

A next-door neighbor walking down the street stops to talk. A man . . . about fifty.

I roll down the car window and listen as closely as I can.

" . . . just moved in . . . family arriving soon . . ."

Arriving soon? Kelsey's come to Ellicott City on her own first? Why? To set up the house before Malcolm arrives? School starts in two days. He's cutting it awfully close.

Weird that Kelsey wouldn't bring Mikayla with her. I'd never be able to leave my daughter like that.

"Jennings?" the neighbor says. "As in Meredith and Walter?"

"My in-laws," she says. "They're away on a mission trip right now."

Walter and Meredith aren't around. That's okay. Probably best to get introduced to Malcolm and Mikayla first . . . then I can meet everyone else.

She waves goodbye to the neighbor and goes back inside. I watch her through the window as she enters the living room moments later, dressed in workout clothes. Yoga pants and a bra top. I watch her stretch, then dance . . . as though no one is watching.

It's time. I'm going to do it. I'm going to talk to my sister face to face for the first time in fifteen years. I took a few days off from monitoring as I took care of a few personal chores—like a haircut. I think I've learned enough. I know her daily routine, where she shops, where she does yoga in the morning . . . her procrastination on unpacking is starting to irritate my obsessive compulsive disorder. If you left your husband and daughter behind to get the home settled before they arrived, then you should get the home settled, Kelsey. Jesus. School started the day before, so Malcolm and Mikayla must be here now.

No matter. I'll do it. She'll appreciate me being there when I get those boxes unpacked in record time. I won't take the duffel bag from the car yet. That would be rude to assume she'll want me to stay with them for a while.

But I know she will invite me to stay. I'm family.

I take a deep breath as I get out of the car and quietly walk across the street. I see her lock her front door, and when she turns around, I'm standing there on the bottom step.

She drops her keys, and a look of fear flashes in her eyes.

I bend to pick up the keys and offer my best reassuring smile, the one that says, *I'm harmless; I'm not here to destroy your life; give me a chance.*

"Hi, Kelsey."

She doesn't answer, her eyes darting right and left . . .

Looking to see if anyone else is around? Or looking for an escape?

I extend the keys toward her, noticing the yoga studio tag and a grocery store membership tag on the key ring, along with several keys. Everything so conveniently in one place. She really should be more careful. If anyone ever steals her keys, they could access information about her based on these memberships. "Here you go."

Her hand shakes as she reaches for them, careful not to touch me. "What are you doing here, Holly? I asked you not to contact me anymore."

"I haven't contacted you on Facebook, but I noticed Malcolm's employment status changed . . . and you were moving so close to where I live, so I had to try to see you."

She frowns. "You live here in Ellicott City?"

"No . . . close by. In the cabin in the woods. The one I told you about in my emails. Before you blocked me." I try to keep my anger and hurt and disappointment from showing. Water under the bridge. Fresh. Start.

"I told you I didn't want anything to do with you."

Kick to the gut delivered. "That's not exactly what you said."

"That's what I meant." Her steely tone cuts straight through me. This isn't the welcome reception I've been hoping for. Her determined, angry stare is just like the one she always wore as a child. I've desperately hoped that she's changed over the years, that she'd be nicer now. Kinder.

"But I know you were just worried about how I could fit back into your life. Here, with Malcolm and Mikayla, with the new house . . ."

Her head snaps up at the mention of her husband and child. "I would like you to leave."

"I don't think you do. Not really," I say gently. I refuse to let her fear deter me. She just needs to realize that I'm here to help. To make her perfect life even better.

"What are you talking about?"

"I've been watching you, and you don't seem happy. I mean, I thought that with everything going so perfectly in your life, you'd be . . . happier. But I know this move must be stressful. Not knowing anyone in town and keeping to yourself . . . but I'm here. I want to help. I want to show you that I can be a part of your life."

She folds her arms across her body. Her voice is cold as she says, "I don't want you anywhere near me."

My jaw clenches, but I force a breath. She doesn't know me anymore. We've spent so much time apart that she's forgotten . . . I'm not the evil one.

"Look, Kelsey, I'm not mad at you. For what happened years ago—you were a child and you were protecting us. I don't blame you for leaving, for moving in with those perfect parents and having a great life, even though it meant taking that opportunity away from me and leaving me behind. I know you had no choice, and I owed you that opportunity. I forgive you."

"*You* forgive *me*?" She touches her forehead, and her eyes blink rapidly.

"Are you okay?" She's pale, and her legs look unsteady.

"No, I'm not okay! I told you to leave me alone. I told you not to contact me, and you just show up out of nowhere!" She grasps at the railing of her porch, and I rush forward to help steady her.

She moves quickly out of reach. "Don't touch me! Leave!"

"I want to help. I just want to show you that I'm different now. Get the chance to be in your life." Why doesn't she understand that? Why doesn't she want that? Sure, we had our issues as kids, but we are adults now. I gave up everything—a normal, safe life—so that she could have a chance at a future. I may have owed her that back then, but now *she* owes *me*. "I want to have a relationship with you again."

"I don't."

"Why not? We're sisters. Twins. We're exactly the same."

"We are nothing alike, and we've never been anything alike. I told you before not to reach out to me. I'm calling the cops."

"For what?"

"You're trespassing, and you've just admitted to stalking me." She reaches for her phone, but I slap it out of her hands.

Her eyes widen when I kick it farther away. It lands among the new leaves on the ground.

I step toward her, my pulse racing. "Stalking you? I'm your sister. I came to see you because I've missed you all these years. I've wondered about you every single day." I corner her near the door.

"Holly, please go." Her voice is a desperate whisper. Gone is the cool, angry woman.

"Are you afraid of me?" Is she serious? Does she think I'm here to hurt her? To take something from her? I'm not the twin who does those things!

"Just go, please," she says.

I'm devastated. Heartbroken. She really doesn't want me. Still. "You really want me to leave?"

"Yes. I really want you to leave."

I sigh, knowing it's futile. I'll never be able to convince her to give our relationship another chance. I'll never prove to her that I just want to be in her life to help, to be a friend . . . family again. I take several steps backward, staring at her troubled, nervous face. My face. We have exactly the same face. Even down to the tiny mole on the right side of our chin. How can that connection—from birth—not mean anything to her? It's never meant anything to her.

She relaxes a little as she moves past me on the stairs and hurries to retrieve her phone, buried among the leaves. She digs through them, hastily . . . desperate to find her lifeline to safety.

Call the police. Told you not to contact me . . .

Who the fuck does she think she is? All of this, everything she has, is because of me. Her existence, her ability to leave her past mistakes behind, is all because of me. And now she wants me to leave? She's going to call the police on me for stalking her?

Anger, disappointment, and years of cumulated hurt spiral together into a tornado of rage within me as I watch her stumble around in the leaves in search of her cell phone. The tree on the lawn is basically bare now, the windstorm the night before having shaken every last leaf from the branches. Several thick ones have cracked off the tree from the lightning.

I pick up the largest, thickest one and move closer, silently, avoiding the leaves so their crunch won't give my presence away.

I'll never get to be in her life. Plan A has failed. On to Plan B.

You asked for this. Remember that.

She locates the cell phone and picks it up. She turns back toward me and gives a surprised little shriek to find me standing so close to her.

I swing the branch, silencing her next hurtful words with a hard blow to the head. She staggers, her eyes wide; then they flutter closed as her legs give way, and she falls to the ground.

I look around, but no one saw. The neighborhood is quiet. No one is watching.

"Sorry, sis," I say as I bend to grab her legs and quickly drag her limp body to her car.

I open my eyes to searing pain on the right side of my head. I'm alone in a cabin, locked in a glass case. I blink, trying to remember the details of what happened.

My sister.

She hit me. Brought me here. Locked me in a glass cage.

But where the hell am I? I struggle to sit up and look around. The inside of the cabin smells like a recent wood fire and mold. It's small and cramped inside, like a hunting or fishing lodge. Stuffed animal heads hang on the wall, and several smaller stuffed creatures sit in various corners. Taxidermy. Gross.

To one side of the room, there's a small two-seater table. The wood is old and splintered—a makeshift homemade item. Simply to serve a purpose. Similarly, two stools sit on either side.

Next to the table is an old cot with worn, dirty-looking sheets. It's unmade but doesn't look like it's been slept in in a long time. It sags in the middle, and I can see the folded frame underneath, as though it's endured the prolonged weight of someone heavy. Obviously not my sister's bed. Whose? The old man who adopted her?

I stand on wobbly legs and move closer to the side of the cage.

To my right, I see stairs leading to a loft. My hands press against the cool glass, and I peer through the dim lighting and see another cot upstairs. This one has newer-looking sheets, and the bed is made.

I back away from the glass and shiver.

Mine are not the only handprints. Hundreds of other hand- and fingerprints make the glass cloudy and difficult to see through.

How many other women have been held captive in here?

The cabin door opens, and I swing toward it. A quick glance outside reveals nothing but trees all around us. There's no sound of traffic or other signs of life. We're deep in the woods.

My sister enters, carrying a bag of groceries, and sets it on the floor while she dead bolts the door.

"Let me out of here!" I say. My vision blurs, and I struggle to stay conscious. I need to convince this lunatic to let me go. Her actions have surprised me. What else is she capable of?

"I just want to talk," she says. "You wouldn't talk to me before."

"So, you think locking me in a cage will make me warm up to the idea?" She always was so stupid. I bet she hasn't thought any of this through. And obviously she's forgotten who she's dealing with.

"You wouldn't listen. I needed to take you away from your life so you might listen."

"What the hell do you want?" I know from her sad emails what she wants. She wants to come barreling into my life, when things are already complicated as shit, and make things worse for me. Fucking things up is the only thing my sister has ever been capable of.

"Just what I've always wanted. To be a family. To have my sister back after all these years apart."

Bullshit. She's here to cash in. Having her around is far too dangerous. I have a lot on the line right now, and I can't let her get in the way. "I don't want that. I want you to leave me alone and let me out of here. I haven't even thought of you since I left that shitty foster home."

"Why do you have to be such a bitch all the time?" she asks. After taking food from a grocery bag and putting it on a plate, she slides it through a small hole in the glass cage.

I slap it onto the floor. "*I'm* a bitch? You hit me over the head—you could have killed me, and then you locked me in here."

She pulls a wooden stool away from the table and sits on it in front of the glass. "Let's start over."

I stare at her. It's like gazing into a mirror. My gut twists at the sight of my own face staring back at me. Same eyes, same nose, same cheekbones, same everything. Her haircut looks fresh, the ends of her hair hitting her shoulders free of split ends. She is seriously fucking crazy. I've always hated her. Hated having a mirror image. I wanted to be unique. One of a kind. I'm convinced our parents hated that there were two of us. That's why they loved neither of us. Twins share a soul, I'd hear my father say all the time.

"I've been looking for you for a long time," she says. "I've been desperate to find you."

"I couldn't give a shit about you."

She flinches at my words. Good. I hope they hurt. She's always been so weak, pathetic. I'm almost impressed by the way she's abducted me. It shows more strength of character than she's ever possessed.

"I can't let you go until you agree to let me be a part of your life. I'm tired of living alone. No family, no friends . . . I want to belong somewhere," she says.

Friends. Family. She thinks she wants those things? Wait until friends and family turn out to be just a huge disappointment. Useless. She has no idea what she's asking for. "You don't belong with me."

"You and I are sisters. I know as kids we didn't get along, but we're adults now. I can be a great aunt to Mikayla . . . I want to meet Malcolm. I can help you. I know you feel overwhelmed. I can see it on your face. I can sense it."

"I don't want or need your help. Mikayla and Malcolm have no idea you exist. I've never told anyone about you. I left my past behind . . . buried with Mom and Dad. I hated being shackled to you all those years, moving from one group home to another. You never would've survived those years if it wasn't for me."

"And yet you left me all alone. You didn't even look back as you drove away with your adoptive family. The ones who wanted the good twin . . . and only the good twin—me."

My eye twitches, and my hands clench at my sides. The good twin. What was so good about her? She had no talent, no drive, no ambition. She was cowardly and refused to stand up for herself. She had mediocre grades and no athletic ability. The family who adopted me deserved a child with more to offer than my sister did. "*I* was the good twin. You've always been nothing but a burden."

She stands abruptly and lets the stool tip over behind her. She stalks across the cabin and goes to my wallet and cell phone sitting on the tiny table. She flicks through the wallet's contents—pictures of Malcolm and Mikayla . . . credit cards . . . local business cards. Then she walks toward me with the phone in her hand. "What's the password?"

"None of your business," I say.

Let's see what you got, Sis. Do you really think you can take me on? I look forward to it.

"Tell me, or I'll shoot you and use your fingerprint to unlock it," she says.

I actually find myself grinning at her strength. For the first time ever, I'm impressed by my sister. I actually believe that she might really do it.

But that's not why I give her the access code.

I do it because I want to watch her fall on her face with whatever she's planning next. Between my phone and the information in my wallet . . . in the house . . . things I've briefly told her and that she's puzzled together on her own, she's armed with just enough to fuck herself if she tries to be me . . . and obviously that's her next course of action.

I just wish I could watch what's about to explode in her face. The exact replica of my face.

She takes the phone, wallet, and house keys and leaves the cabin, slamming the door behind her. I hear the key turn in the lock.

Well, if she expects to waltz in and steal my perfect life, then she's in for a surprise, and when I get out of this box—and I will—she will wish she'd continued to allow me to have her identity.

I grin as I sit on the floor of the glass cage and reach for a carrot stick.

PART THREE

September 13—5:35 p.m.

"Paul . . ." The voice sounds far away, like it's drifting.

I open my eyes, and my sister stands above me, dressed in white. Her long dark hair a stark contrast to pale, nearly transparent skin. Ghostlike skin. I can almost see through her apparition as it stands, peering down at me. She looks concerned . . . unsure . . . as though she's the one seeing things.

She disappears from sight, and I struggle to look around to find her. Kelsey Jennings's kitchen. That's where I am. My eyelids are heavy weights as I try to keep them open. I'm not sure how long I've been lying here. I reach out around me and feel the wet, sticky liquid. Blood. I can smell it. I can feel it leaving through a wound on the right side of my body, trickling down my skin. The room spins, and my eyes close . . . I'm bleeding to death.

"Paul . . . try to wake up. Don't fall asleep." My sister's voice is back. Lower, more hollow, like an echo . . . fading fast.

I'm so tired. I feel as though my body has been drained of life. My limbs feel heavy, and my body throbs.

How much blood have I already lost?

"Come on, Paul. Stay with me. It's not your time to go yet . . ."

I want to let go. My body is already shutting down, and I'm struggling to bring myself back from this heavy pull toward darkness. My eyelids flutter. I see my sister's face.

"Paul, you need to radio for help."

I try to shake my head. Too late. Soon, I'll be where she is. I want that. I'm tired of living in this world with the guilt and the grief and the searching.

"Paul . . . don't give up. You've almost found me. You've almost found the truth."

Her words are like a lightning bolt to my chest, shocking me back to consciousness. A foggy, hazy consciousness. I look around me again, but she's gone.

But I see my radio on the floor a few feet away. I stretch as I try to reach it. I need to call for help.

Pain radiates through my body, and the floor beneath me feels like waves on a turbulent sea. My head swims and my vision blurs, but my fingers touch the radio. I try harder, reaching just a little farther, and finally I grab it.

I struggle to lift it to my face and press the button. "Unit 678 requesting assistance. Officer shot . . . I'm shot . . ."

I hope they've heard me. I hope I've done enough, because darkness closes in around me again and I can't be certain I haven't already died.

A long time later, I hear sirens in the distance drawing nearer. So close. But they are too late. The sirens are a hopeful sound, but I don't think they can save me.

Loud noises. Voices. Louder sirens. People standing above me in the kitchen. Real people, not ghosts . . . I'm not sure if I'm relieved or disappointed.

Don't give up, Paul . . . you've almost found me.

I have no idea what's real and what isn't. But I cling to my sister's voice as I'm lifted off the ground and into the clouds.

September 13—6:08 p.m.

That bitch has left me in here for a week. The disgusting food she brought the first day ran out three days ago, and there's just a little bit of water left. Was she really planning on leaving me in here to die? To starve to death?

How could this be going on so long? I expected this to end that same day she abducted me. Once she assumed my life, only to realize it wasn't what she expected. When there was no Malcolm. No Mikayla. When none of her assumptions were true. Why didn't she return to confront me? To find out what's really going on?

She has to know by now that the life she once thought I have isn't reality.

So, why hasn't she returned?

Being alone in here doesn't bother me. I've learned to channel my thoughts and energy in a productive way, a self-preserving way. For a week now, I've gone over every detail of how I will kill my sister as soon as she comes back.

Trying to find a way out is futile, and unless more time passes and I'm actually going to die from hunger, I don't even want to try to escape. I need the police to find me in danger; it's the only way out of this. I need them to see how insane my sister is. That way, when they find her dead, my self-defense plea won't even be questioned.

I stand and stretch slowly. I walk around the glass box. Staying limber, not letting my muscles seize, will be important when the time comes. I sit in the center, cross my legs with one ankle over each knee, join my forefingers and thumbs together, and close my eyes. I can meditate for hours. It calms my mind, helps me to focus, and keeps the hunger pains at bay.

I'm not sure how long I stay that way, but the sound of the door latch has my heart picking up pace.

She's back.

The wooden door creaks open, but I keep my eyes closed. I won't let her know that her weeklong absence is starting to worry me. I refuse to give her the upper hand at all. If she's back, there's a reason. My guess is that the veil has been shattered. Her perceptions have been destroyed.

I hear the door close and lock and then her footsteps. Determined. Angry.

I almost smile.

She bangs on the glass. I ignore her. I stay in my pretend meditative state. She bangs harder.

Good. Go ahead and break the glass, dumb bitch.

"Wake up!" she screams.

I slowly open my eyes and look at her with all the creepy stillness I can convey.

"You lied to me," she hisses, her hands pressed up against the outside of the glass. Her angry, confused expression just inches from it.

I stay silent.

"Why did you lie?" she demands. She starts pummeling the glass again. Her wild-eyed crazy expression narrows in on me like daggers. "Damn it! Tell me what the hell is going on!"

I finally speak. Quietly. Calmly. "Why don't you tell me? I'm the one who's been locked inside this glass prison in a cabin in the middle of the woods for a week."

"Don't play with me! You lied about everything. You said you were married . . . you said he was starting a teaching job."

"Did I? Or did you piece the pieces together wrong while you were cyberstalking me and my family?"

She paces frantically. Her eyes wild . . . desperate. She looks horrible. Sweatpants, messy hair, makeup streaking down her face. Her bare feet, in an old pair of my flip-flops, look like they've been bleeding. What the hell has she been doing this whole time?

"You ruined everything," she says. "Things should have worked out . . . but you didn't tell me the truth. You said you had a husband, a child . . . the perfect life."

"You assumed all of that." I'm not taking the blame for her weird obsession with me and my life.

"Your husband is dead!" She swings back toward the glass cage, stalks toward it. "What happened to him?"

The accusation is already in her tone. Jesus. She automatically assumes that I had something to do with his death. I did, of course, but that's beside the point. "There was a car accident." I shrug. No sense pretending like I'm upset about the loss of my husband. The one person on the planet who wouldn't fall for my fake remorse or crocodile tears would be my sister. She's seen it far too often. She's stupid and gullible enough, but she also knows me better than anyone. The hazards of sharing a womb. I need to be smarter in how I deal with her. Manipulate her in a different way.

"Did you do it on purpose?"

I barely hear the question. Her voice has lowered, and she has this sickening disappointed look on her face. The same look parents give their children when they've done something wrong. My sister is disappointed in me. She's disappointed that I'm still the same person I always was. Cruel. Soulless. Psychotic. Whatever else they called me. I've learned not to fight against my true nature anymore. I am who I am.

If she's disappointed by that, then fuck her. I never asked her to come back into my life, to enter into this chaotic mess . . . this is all on her.

"Tell me the truth," she says.

"Malcolm presented himself as something he wasn't."

"Rich, you mean?"

"Yes."

"That's all you've ever cared about. Money, fame, success, dancing . . ." She stares angrily. "You're so greedy and manipulative you can't appreciate all the good you have."

"Oh, and I suppose you do. I suppose you still see the world through rose-colored glasses, despite the shit hand you continue to be dealt. No one has ever loved you or cared about you. Yet, here you are still trying to find this wonderful, beautiful life that you think is out there for you. It isn't."

"Well, at least I can make the best of a situation. You're never satisfied with anything!"

"Why should I settle?" She's always been mediocre. I can't expect her to understand drive and ambition.

"What about Mikayla?" She looks pained again. As though having a daughter should have changed me. Made me more maternal, a better person . . .

"What about her?"

"Do you love her at least?"

I look away. Not because I don't know the answer, but because I'm still unsure how to play this game with her. She's surprising me with her strength. Something she's never shown before. "How did you figure everything out—about Malcolm . . . ?"

"After I had the entire state on alert for a missing child . . . your in-laws reappeared with her, safe . . ."

I blink, my mouth gaping. "You called the police?" After kidnapping me and locking me in a glass cage, she thought that was the right thing to do?

"I thought Mikayla had been abducted . . . she wasn't at the day care when I tried to pick her up."

Okay, now I'm confused. "What day care?"

"Paradise Day Care. Fran's business card was in your wallet . . ."

"So you assumed that because of the business card in my wallet, Mikayla would be there. That's on you," I point out. Her fault. Not mine. "I don't even think that woman we met with still works there . . . she was getting ready to retire months ago."

My sister stops pacing and turns to look at me. "Fran's dead."

My eyes widen, and this time I can't stop the small grin from forming. Holy shit! Could my sister really have grown a backbone, gotten some balls since we were kids? Maybe we're more alike than I thought. "You killed an old lady?"

"No!" She pauses. "But I may have killed a cop."

I full on laugh at that. "Wow . . . and here I thought for a moment that you weren't so stupid, after all." I slowly get to my feet and walk toward the glass. I stop just an inch from it. My sister stands less than six inches away, only the sheet of glass between us. I stare into her face—a mirror image of my own—and I start to take back the control. "I'm hungry. Go get me some food, and then I'll figure out how to get you out of the mess you've created. Again."

September 14—2:09 a.m.

I open my eyes, and the blinding light above me forces them closed again. A beeping monitor to my right tells me I'm at the hospital. So, I didn't die on Kelsey Jennings's floor, after all. Or I did, and they somehow brought me back to life. I don't feel pain, which means I'm heavily sedated. An IV drips medication into my hand, and another provides fluids. I try to move, and there it is. The searing pain in my lower-right side. I know I'm lucky to be alive, but I'm nervous about the damage. So far, I can't tell if it was a flesh wound or if I'm paralyzed from the waist down. I try to move my legs, with no luck.

I look around the room, but it's empty. Boring, dull, beige walls surround me. Rough bedsheets that used to be white but are now a light gray from the countless sanitization washings lie over me. It's obviously a surgery-recovery room, as it's barely big enough for the bed and the machines. There are no windows, so there's no way to know if it's still nighttime . . . but I feel like I've been asleep for a long time.

Too long. I need answers. Kelsey Jennings shot me, and I need to know why.

My mind is fuzzy, and the details of the last hours I remember aren't coming back as clear or as quickly as I'd like . . . she reported the child stolen, even though she knew the little girl was with her grandparents . . . why? What was she trying to do?

I shut my eyes tight as a wave of nausea hits. Too much, too soon . . . but I need to figure this out.

I confront her about the truth, and she shoots me. That part makes the least amount of sense. Did she think she'd do time for lying? Was she afraid? Or is there a whole hell of a lot more that she's hiding that she was afraid I'd find out?

I need to talk to the department . . . see if they've located her yet. Questioned her.

I turn my head slowly, from side to side, to look for my things, but besides this thin blue hospital gown and slippers I have on, I don't see any of my personal belongings. No clothes, no gun or badge . . . no cell phone.

I press the buzzer next to my hand for a nurse, and one appears almost immediately. I must be worse off than I thought for that kind of speedy service.

"Detective Ryan . . . welcome back," the young, friendly-looking nurse in rainbow-colored scrubs and dark-rimmed glasses says as she checks my vitals. "How do you feel?"

"Like I was shot. I need to make some phone calls . . . can I have my cell phone?"

She shakes her head. "You need rest. You're still in recovery. We'd like to monitor you for several more hours before moving you into a room on the third floor." She adjusts the pillows under my legs.

"How bad are my injuries?"

"Bad enough that when the morphine starts to wear off, you will be in tremendous pain."

"Wonderful. Maybe we can keep that drip flowing a little longer then, okay?"

She laughs. "I'll see what I can do."

"I've had surgery?"

"Yes. We needed to remove the bullet . . . and repair damage done to your bowel."

Shit.

"Your doctor will come in and see you soon. He'll explain everything to you at that time," she says. "You're lucky. You lost a lot of blood and were barely conscious when they brought you in."

"I'm sure I'll feel lucky once I'm out of here."

She laughs. "That won't be for a while, so take it easy. Enjoy your forced vacation."

"Yeah . . . thanks." I reach for her arm as she goes to leave. "Phone . . . please. As soon as possible." Not knowing what's going on will drive me insane in here. "I just want to make a call to the station for an update."

She hesitates and then gives me a look that says, *You're going to be one of those patients.* "I'll see what I can do about that as well. But for now, rest," she says as she closes the door behind her.

I don't have a choice in the matter. That sneaky little nurse put something in my IV. I can feel my body getting heavy. My eyelids refuse to stay open. Sleep is seconds away, whether I want it or not.

September 14—2:13 a.m.

I sit and stare at my sister, balled up on the wooden floor inside the glass cage. Fast asleep. How she can sleep so soundly, without so much as a blanket, would surprise anyone else. I get it. Rarely were we afforded comfort in those early days after our parents died. It doesn't shock me at all that she can sleep peacefully in the most uncomfortable situations.

What's most annoying is that she seems perfectly fine in captivity. I know she isn't, which means she's planning something. An escape. An attack, no doubt.

I've had her in there for seven days. Thank God she didn't starve to death while I was trying to steal her life. And I really wasn't trying to do that. I never meant for any of this to happen. This isn't what I've planned at all. I came to Ellicott City to find her, be with her, be a family again. She pushed me away, and I panicked.

Once I locked her in there, there wasn't a plan. I was acting on some insane impulse, hoping I'd figure it out. I thought maybe I could pretend to be her for a little while, while she sweated it out in here . . . then, once she came to her senses and realized having me in her life wasn't a bad thing, I'd release her and join her family as "Aunt Holly." We'd never tell anyone about this, and life could be perfect for both of us.

But what happens now? Nothing is as it seems, and my sister is still the hateful person she always was. If I let her go, there's no way she won't make me pay for this. For the first time in our lives, *I'm* the bad one, *I'm* the criminal . . . of course the detective was lying on Kelsey Jennings's floor . . . no one knows who I am. That I even exist.

Could we hide out here forever? Could I simply keep my sister locked away? Grandpa was able to keep his victims from the police for years . . . until Detective Ryan's father discovered one of the burial grounds of bones two miles from here.

And he didn't find his daughter . . . which means he's going to keep searching. Would he make it this far out into the woods? Would he find us?

My hand shakes as I sip my cold tea.

This was all just a big mistake.

None of this was supposed to happen. I just wanted to see my sister, have her accept me, be a part of her life . . .

One that wasn't so perfect after all. Dead husband. Limited access to her daughter. No dancing career. No money from rich in-laws. I wonder why she didn't tell me. Why she didn't reach out to find me when her life was going so wrong. I could have helped. Together, we could have figured things out. For once, I could have been the strong one, the protector . . .

I watch her sleep, and a small part of me feels bad for her. Unlike everyone else, I want to believe that there is a good person in there somewhere. That circumstances made her who she is and not just an intrinsic evil . . .

I'd like to open the cage to give her a blanket and pillow, but I can't trust her yet. She said she would help me figure out a way out of all this . . . but I'm the one who needs to find an escape from the mess I've made. Maybe she'll consider leaving with me. Leaving all this behind. Just the two of us. Start over.

New identities. New lives. New lies.

September 14—3:34 p.m.

When my eyes open again, I know a long time has passed. Daylight shines through the hospital window blinds. I've been moved out of recovery and into a room on the third floor. I'm starting to feel clear-headed and, with it, a lot more pain. I still don't know the extent of the injuries or how long they plan to keep me here . . . or what's going on with Kelsey Jennings. That's the most concerning part. For far too many reasons.

In my drugged-up, foggy state, I was dreaming. About her. Before I learned that she was lying to me in ways I didn't even think I could be lied to. Has she been playing me all along, for a deeper purpose?

Given her latest actions, I think I can safely assume that our affair is over.

With my eyes drifting between open and closed, I hear shuffling near the end of the bed. This time I'm not alone.

"Hey, it's about time you woke up." My father. Good. Someone who can tell me what's going on and possibly get access to my phone.

I focus my blurring vision on him and try to sit higher on the bed, but the effort pulls at my incisions. Lying down it is then. "Hey, Dad. What time is it?"

"Three thirty in the afternoon. You haven't slept this late since you were fourteen," he says in the same disappointed tone he used back then. No doubt he thought I should be back out in the field by now. Surgery was over—what was I waiting for?

I'm with him. Now we just need to convince the nurses. I can't remember what the nurse told me they did surgery for . . .

"What are my injuries?"

"The bullet grazed your intestine and punctured it. Internal bleeding. They did surgery to repair it."

Shit. "Where's Kelsey Jennings?"

"The department is still looking for her . . ." His voice trails off, and he stares at the floor.

There's more. My father's not one to sugarcoat things. I need him to be straight with me now. "What's going on?"

He places a file on my lap. "There's a lot more to this case."

I read the name on the file. Holly Sterling. Who the hell is that?

"Parsons ran the license plate of the car parked in front of the Jenningses' home. It was registered to this woman," he says.

I open the file and see a mug shot of Kelsey . . . a lot younger. Maybe thirteen, but still looking exactly the same.

"We think the woman who shot you is Kelsey Jennings's twin sister. Apparently, Kelsey and Holly are the daughters of the late Max and Jasmine Sterling—Hollywood movie stars." He shrugs as though he's never heard of two of Hollywood's most famous actors turned porn stars.

Actually, he probably hasn't.

"The twin girls were placed in different foster homes as kids." He pauses. "We did a few searches and found that Holly was later adopted by Doug Beinfeld."

It hits me why the name is familiar. "The property developer? The one responsible for all the missing teen girls?"

My father nods. "This Holly woman has had quite the troubled past. Killed her foster parents at a young age. Stabbed them to death. It was in self-defense but still a brutal way to escape their abuse."

Jesus. No wonder Kelsey . . . or Holly . . . is fucked up.

"So, she was impersonating her sister?" Stolen identities happen all the time. Guess it's even easier to do when the person stealing your identity is a mirror image with matching DNA. I stare at the photo.

"Explains why she didn't know about the husband being dead or where the little girl was this whole time," my father says. Forty years on the force and nothing shocks him anymore. There's little he hasn't seen.

"They got guys out looking for her?"

"Yes . . . so take it easy. Get some rest. I'll keep you posted."

"Okay . . ." I don't have a choice. I know they won't release me yet. But when they do, I'll be starting my own search for this Holly Sterling.

My father leaves the room, and I stare at the picture. Juvenile-murder charges. Therapy and anger-management courses that seem to have had no effect . . . somehow narrowly avoided any real jail time.

Malcolm Jennings's accusations about his wife in his divorce file no longer seem so far fetched if Kelsey Jennings is anything like her sister. Troubled youth. Troubled adult.

And if Holly Sterling was adopted by Doug Beinfeld, then she has to know something about the missing teen girls . . . the bodies we found . . . my sister?

I stare at the face in the file folder as anger coils through my chest. This whole time I may have been closer to my sister's abductor, closer to the truth, than I ever could have known.

September 14—9:14 p.m.

The door to the cabin opens, and I'm ready.

I don't know who my sister thought she was fucking with, but she should never have underestimated me. I was the one who got us out of our situation years ago, wasn't I? I was the one who got us away from that boring old smelly great-aunt of ours and the insane lawyers.

She watched me sleep on the floor of this cage—perplexed, guilty, uncertain, unsure . . . at one point, I think she was dumb enough to open the door to give me a blanket.

God, she's so stupid.

Stupid enough not to examine this holding cell before once again leaving me alone all day. A crack low on one of the panels near the lock provided just enough leverage to squeeze my hand through and pick the old, worn, rusty lock with a hairpin I found on the floor.

I could have been home by now or at the police station, reporting my crazy-ass sister for abduction. Watching her ugly ass go to jail, where she belongs.

Instead, I waited. Jail isn't enough. She'll just keep coming back to haunt me. She's already talking crazy. Wants me to run off with her. And go where? I'd rather stay in here and rot alone than spend a life on the run with her. I have a life that I'm trying to rebuild, and my sister has no place in those dreams.

I sit inside the unlocked glass room. I'm missing fingernails, and my hands ache and are covered in blood, but I'm ready for her.

She enters, and I pretend to be sleeping . . .

Her footsteps sound on the stairs, and then I hear drawers opening and closing. A duffel bag zipper. She's packing. She's really planning on running. Where the hell does she think she can go? She's reported false information to the police. She's shot a detective. My in-laws are back, and by now they'll have reported me missing. The department has to be looking for her.

I wait until all the noise stops. The lights in the cabin go off, except for a lamp in her upstairs loft. She's still afraid of the dark.

The creaking of bedsprings finally ceases. I hear deep, heavy breathing. She's asleep.

I get up and strain to see in the dim lighting as I approach the glass wall with the lock. I slowly reach through the crack, the glass once again tearing my flesh as I reach up to unfasten it. I wait. Listening. I can't underestimate my sister this time. She did manage to get me in here, after all.

Silence from upstairs, so I push the door open and slowly step out onto the wooden floor. I look around and see an old, dirty, rusty fire poker and shovel near the wood-burning stove. I slide my feet noiselessly across the floor and take one in each hand. Then I make my way up the stairs to the loft.

A small single bed, a dresser, a night table, and a lamp. Several packed duffel bags sit in the corner. Everything she owns, ready to go. Pathetic. I look around the depressing, dingy space. How the hell did she grow up here? In this? Why didn't she ever leave?

Too late now.

I move closer and stare at her in the bed. Her arms are wrapped around a pillow. Her eyes flutter as though she's dreaming, and her lips move . . . I've always hated having a twin. Twins aren't unique. I've craved being the only one.

I'm finally going to get that.

I consider my weapons and select the shovel. I'll hit her first, knock her out . . . I'm a little rusty in stabbing people. I raise the shovel, but her eyes open. Fear registers in them before she rolls quickly away from my attack.

"How did you . . ." She stumbles, her legs tangling in her bedsheets as she scrambles out of the bed.

"You can't win against me. You never could." I advance toward her, and she looks around the room, frantically. Her face illuminated by the lamp in the otherwise dark cabin looks eerily translucent . . . like the ghost she'll soon be.

There's no weapon for her. No escape. I'm blocking the stairs. She's trapped. "Don't do this. We can leave here together," she says.

"I'm leaving here. You're not," I say, lunging at her midriff with the poker.

She dives out of the way and jumps over the bed. "Put that down. Let's talk . . . just listen to me."

I laugh. "I don't want to talk to you. I've never wanted to talk to you. I hate you. I always have. I never wanted a twin." I move toward her again.

She's quick, though, and grabs the lamp and tears the cord from the wall. "I don't want to hurt you."

I laugh. "Your recent actions suggest otherwise. That tree branch to the head didn't tickle."

"I just wanted to be in your life." Her pleading desperation makes me nauseated.

"You tried to *steal* my life." I jab the poker and get her in the side, slashing through the fabric of the T-shirt she wears.

She gasps as the rusty metal tears her flesh. Blood seeps out, covering the fabric, but it's just a flesh wound. I jab again, but she moves out of the way. She swings the lamp, hitting me in the shoulder. Not hard enough. "You're going to have to do better than that." I lunge at her again and stab her leg.

Pain crosses her expression, then a determined anger.

Finally, she's realizing only one of us is making it out of here tonight.

She drops the lamp to the floor, shattering it; then she leaps over the broken pieces at me. Her body hits mine hard, sending me reeling backward. My foot hits the edge of the top stair, and I teeter off balance. I reach out for her as I fall, and we both tumble down the flight of stairs.

My dancer training is on autopilot, and I curve my head into my chest and protect myself as I roll, hitting the hard splintered wooden stairs one at a time.

At the bottom, I'm quicker on my feet, and I kick her several times before she can stand. In the stomach, in the face, in the ribs.

She grips the edge of the railing and pulls herself away from me and up off the floor. "Stop this. We don't need to do this."

"I do," I say as I lunge at her and take her down to the wooden floor. Punches rain down on her face and head. She protects herself the best way she can, but I'm stronger. My will to survive has always been stronger than hers.

But then, she hikes her hips fast and hard, sending me flying overhead. I crash into the table as she rolls farther away.

I get to my feet, stagger slightly, and pick up one of the wooden stools. I swing, breaking the legs against her body.

She picks up a plate and throws it at me. It hits my face, and I can immediately feel a gash, oozing blood on my forehead. I taste it in my mouth.

I swing the broken stool again, but she dives low, taking me out at the knees. We fall to the ground again, and she rotates my body so that my nose is pressed to the hard floor. Her weight is positioned on my back, and my hips and legs are pinned.

Her hand tangles in my hair, and she yanks my head backward. "Stop this! I don't want to hurt you!"

"Let me up, and I won't stop until I kill you," I hiss, daring her . . . she won't do it. She can't do it. She was always the good twin.

"Don't make me do this . . . ," she pleads.

"Don't be such a fucking wimp!"

She pulls my head back harder, and an arm comes around the front of my neck. She squeezes hard. My air supply is cut off, and I flail to get out of her hold, but I'm stuck.

I can hear her breathing change . . . hear the first sob.

Such a pathetic loser. What the fuck is she crying about?

The room starts to spin, and my head feels light.

"Please . . . please don't make me hurt you. I love you," she says.

"I hate you," I croak as I continue to struggle, expecting her to let go in the last seconds . . .

She doesn't. I gag and grip at her arm, but her hold just tightens even more. With the pressure and pain at my throat, my eyes widen as I panic and struggle to take a shallow breath. She's not stopping. She's not letting go. What the hell? My struggling is useless against her newfound strength and determination.

"I'm sorry," she whispers.

Then, there's no air left.

My hands fall away from her arm, and my legs go limp on the floor.

My eyes flutter shut, and my head falls to the side. Everything goes black.

September 14—9:58 p.m.

I sign the release papers saying I won't sue the hospital if I die from my own stubbornness and then accept my personal belongings from the disapproving nurse. I have to get out of here. I can't lie here while this woman is out there. I want to be the one who finds her.

I don't allow myself to consider the many reasons for that.

My father sneaked in a laptop, and hours of Google searches that day provided all the sordid details about the Sterling twins and their troubled life from the beginning. Twins—one good, one pure evil.

"Need some help?" the nurse asks.

"I got it." If she stays and sees me struggling to get dressed, she might insist on not releasing me. Besides, putting on pants is the least of the tough things on my to-do list tonight.

I remove the hospital gown and see blood appear on the bandages wrapped around my midsection. Perfect—more ripped stitches are a great start. I quickly pull on my T-shirt and wait for the wave of nausea to subside before sliding my legs into my jeans. I sit on the bed for a long moment, the effort taking more strength than it should.

Or maybe it's the deep loathing I've developed for myself. Lying here, thinking of all the things I'd overlooked about that woman, how I'd let my attraction to her cloud my better judgment . . . ignored all the signs that something wasn't right.

The house keys. She didn't know which one unlocked the front door because they weren't her keys. She'd never been inside the house until that day she entered with me.

The pills. She hadn't gotten rid of them because she hadn't known they existed.

The car parked in front of the house. I should have run those plates earlier and dug more deeply. Instead, it fell through the cracks.

If Holly was impersonating her sister all along, then where has the other twin been this whole time? And if everything I know is about the real Kelsey Jennings, the one who was abducted, then who is the woman I've been spending time with? Since her juvenile police file, no other crimes have been reported that involved her, until she shot me, so what's her story, what has her life been since that mug shot was taken?

Do I really want to know?

I stand and tuck my gun and badge into my belt. Then I shove my feet into my running shoes as if they're flip-flops. This will have to do. Bending over is too much of a bitch.

"Do not tell me they released you already?" Faith's voice in the doorway sounds almost like a hallucination . . . but of course my father would have told her about me being here. And of course, she'd come.

She looks amazing as usual in a pair of skinny jeans and a tight-fitting sweater . . . but the look of concern behind her dark-rimmed glasses makes me uneasy. I follow her stare and see the blood seeping through my T-shirt. Shit. "It's not as bad as it looks."

"You're unbelievable," she says.

I force a grin. "Thank you."

She enters the room. "That wasn't a compliment."

"Sounded like one." Keeping the tone light is a challenge. Whatever meds they have me on have my heart racing and palms sweating at her presence. Almost like the emotions I once had for her, the ones I've convinced myself I no longer have, have come tumbling back on a morphine-induced high. I don't like it.

"Sit down," she says.

"Nah . . . I gotta go."

She moves so close that our shoes touch, and the stern look on her face makes me gulp. She gently but firmly places her hands on my chest and forces me to sit on the bed.

"Really . . . they said I'm good to go . . ."

"Shut up, Paul," she says, annoyed. She knows no one's cleared me to leave yet.

Still, she reaches behind my foot and helps it into the running shoe.

"You don't have to . . ."

She glares up at me, and I shut up.

I watch the top of her head. The smooth, silky hair falling into her face as she helps me with the other shoe.

She's so good. Too good. Feelings are making me weak. I sit on my hands to resist touching her. She's only here because I was shot. It's sympathy. Not love.

She stands and looks at me. "Your dad told me you were under investigation at the station."

"His fault." Despite the fact that we solved a dozen old cold case files, Captain Baker is pissed that I got the illegal warrant for my father to search those premises. I have a pending suspension waiting for me . . . which is why I need to get the hell out of here and find Holly Sterling before they might potentially take my badge and gun away for a while. I need to be the one to find her. This woman has messed with me over the last week, and I need to know to what end. Was she simply trying to steal her sister's identity, but she didn't know all the facts? And what is her connection to the cold case files . . . does she know about the abductions? Was she part of that psycho's plan—helping him lure those teenage girls? Does she know where else Doug Beinfeld might have buried more bodies? If she's lived with him all these years, she must know something. She may even know where my sister is. I need to find her and find out everything she knows.

"So, I guess *he's* the hero who solved all of those cold cases then," she says with a grin.

"Guess so." I'll gladly allow my father to accept that honor. He deserves it. He's never given up.

Tears gather in her eyes, and I'm doomed. Faith doesn't cry. Even when we were breaking up, she held it together; she saw sad shit in her daily job as a social worker all the time, and she never broke down . . . never in front of me anyway. She was so strong. Tears now aren't good. "Hey . . . what's up?"

"It's just after all these years . . . those families finally getting closure."

I nod. Yeah, so many other families. Not us. Not my father.

Faith reaches out and touches my arm as a tear slides down her cheek. "I'm sorry you didn't find her, Paul."

Right now, there is someone else I need to find, and time is wasting. I reach for my jacket, but Faith's arms around my ribs—gentle, careful not to hurt me—make me pause. Maybe it would be nice to let the rest of the department deal with it for a few days . . . let Faith play nurse . . .

I hug her quickly, then pull away. I may want to deserve this woman, but Faith deserves better than me. "I have to go . . . thank you for coming by."

She wipes her cheeks and smiles. Beautiful, vibrant, no-expectations Faith is back. "Of course. For the record, I don't think you should be going anyway yet, but I know I'm wasting my breath trying to stop you."

I'm reaching for my cell phone on the table next to the bed just as it rings. My father's number lights the screen. "It's my dad," I say to Faith. "Hey, Dad, I'm just leaving the hospital."

"Good, 'cause I think I found Kelsey Jennings. The real one."

September 14—11:10 p.m.

An hour later, a squad team surrounds a cabin in the woods about two miles from where my father and I discovered the bones of the missing teenage girls. It's dark and raining, and thunder rumbles somewhere in the distance. With my looming suspension, I shouldn't be out here, but this has been my case from the start, so no one is telling me to stand down. This woman tried to kill me, and the real Kelsey Jennings—her sister—could be locked up inside this cabin.

My father was out searching these areas for more bodies when he heard screams and noises coming from this direction. After finding the cabin, he was smart enough to call it in and not to go in alone.

I struggle to breathe as I move along the side of the weather-worn exterior. Each inhale feels like a sharp jab to my side. A quick glance inside my jacket reveals I'm still bleeding as I direct the team around the dark, now-quiet cabin.

I sway slightly off balance, and my father supports my weight, steadying me. "You really shouldn't be out here. We need to get you back to the hospital."

"Soon."

The sound of a door slamming in the wind against the back of the cabin has us approaching that side. Slowly. Cautiously. Guns drawn.

I enter first, my father by my side.

I squint in the dark as I peer around the interior. Dead, lifeless, glowing, creepy animal eyes of stuffed creatures stare back.

I like them better stuffed . . .

Taxidermy. This cabin belongs to Holly's "grandfather" . . . Doug Beinfeld. This could be the place where my sister was held. I take a deep breath, forcing myself to hold it together.

The cabin is practically empty, except for a small table-and-stool set . . . one of them lying in the middle of the floor, legs broken off. An old woodstove—long burned out—is in the corner, and a small, dirty-looking cot is in another corner.

Nothing else, except a glass cage.

With Kelsey Jennings in it. She's lying on her side . . . unmoving. She's not tied up or blindfolded . . . but blood covers the floor beneath her.

"What the hell?" my father says.

This is definitely fucked up.

The team enters and searches quickly. No one else is here. "All clear."

"Head out in teams of two. Search the woods."

"What are we looking for?" Rookie Cop is back. I'm actually happy to have him here. He's been a part of this from the start. I may actually learn his name after this is over.

"A suspect that looks exactly like the victim," I say, moving closer to the box, and I stare inside at the real Kelsey Jennings. She's absolutely identical to her twin. Same hair, same body . . . same face. She stirs and rolls to her back. Her swollen eyes open, and she blinks several times before she realizes she's not alone. She sees me, and I wait for some sign of recognition . . . which is stupid—this isn't the woman I've been spending time with . . . having sex with.

She sits up quickly and looks around, like a terrified caged animal.

"It's okay . . . I'm Detective Ryan . . . we're going to help you. We're going to get you out."

"It's locked," my father says.

We look for keys, but the interior of the cabin is sparse. There's nothing inside except a bed, a desk with an old laptop, a bookshelf, hunting gear and rifles on the wall, and a small kitchen with a microwave and coffee maker.

"We're going to have to break the glass."

Rookie Cop picks up a chair. "Stand back!" he yells.

Kelsey moves away. She sits in the far corner and hugs her knees to her body, bringing her head down to them to protect her eyes.

He swings the chair. The glass is shatterproof, so it takes several more attempts to cause the glass to crack. Several more, and a large enough shard is broken to get her out.

I enter the cage and kneel next to her. "Hey . . . you're okay now." I scan her quickly, but her injuries seem mostly surface.

She trembles on the floor, and I remove my coat and wrap it around her. "Mrs. Jennings? You are Kelsey Jennings, right?"

She nods, staring off in the distance.

"How long have you been in here?" Holly reported Mikayla missing nine days ago . . . but she may have had her sister locked up for longer. We still haven't gotten to the bottom of all this yet. Holly's motive . . . though stealing her sister's identity seems to be a safe bet. But why didn't she know about Malcolm being dead and Mikayla being with her grandparents? Why did she freak out at the day care that day and start this entire investigation in the first place? Had Kelsey Jennings misled her sister, her abductor? By mistake or on purpose? I repeat my question, but she just blinks, her mouth quivers, her eyes stare at me, unrecognizing . . .

"Kelsey?"

She nods. "Who are you?" she whispers.

"I'm Detective Ryan. This is my father, former head detective of the Ellicott City Police Department. Are you hurt?"

She shakes her head, but she's clearly in shock. There's dried blood on her face that's also matted into her blonde hair. She continues to shake violently.

"She's suffered a head injury . . . all of this might be fuzzy for her," I tell my father.

I stay next to her as he radios for an ambulance and a rescue team with a litter to help us get her out of these woods quickly and safely.

I need to keep her talking. Help her refocus. Help her calm down. I rub her arms through my jacket and pull her closer, my own pain numb for the moment, but a familiar scent reaches my nose—Kelsey's scent . . . no, Holly's scent—I hold my breath as best as I can. "Do you know who did this to you? Who put you in here?"

She nods, turning to look at me. Her voice is hoarse and wobbly. "My sister, Holly."

"Your twin sister?"

"Yes."

Fantastic. It's confirmed. There's two of them.

September 14—11:56 p.m.

Pain from my bullet wound and recent surgery grips my right side and radiates through my entire body as I comb through the wet overgrowth of the woods. The fog is heavy and fills my lungs, making it difficult to breathe. Flashlights illuminate the darkness as the team searches every inch of the Beinfeld property, which extends all the way to the river running from Bowie to Ellicott City.

There's nothing out here for miles. Holly Sterling could be anywhere. Hiding. Running. Kelsey Jennings has finally calmed enough to recount the details of her attack and her abduction. According to her, her sister left her for dead hours ago. By now, she could be out of these woods and fleeing Maryland.

I see my father about twenty feet away, trudging slowly along with the rest of us. He's no longer an active detective, but he won't give up the search until we do. Who knows if we'd ever have found this cabin or the abducted woman if he hadn't been out here, forever on his quest to find answers. I certainly didn't link the two crimes together.

I can't think about the fact that I've been intimate with this stranger, who might have been the last person to see my sister alive, the last one who could have helped Julia—helped all the victims—without my anger causing my blood pressure to rise to unhealthy levels. Did she recognize my sister in the picture in my wallet? Did she even then keep her secrets about the crime to herself?

What would I have done if she'd told me?

Moments pass torturously slow . . . until I see her.

Knees to her chest, hands covering her ears, she sits on the ground with her back to a tree, humming wildly. The unfamiliar melody sounds panicked and chaotic as I get closer. I holster my gun. She's unarmed.

Unhinged.

Her frightened, wild gaze is terrifying when it lands on me.

Almost as though she doesn't recognize me. As though she has no idea who I am or where she is. Her face is beaten as well . . . she's as bruised and bloodied as the woman in the glass cage is.

Must have been one hell of a battle.

I stare at her, feeling as though I'm seeing double. Despite their injuries, her blonde hair, blue eyes, and facial structure are a mirror image of the woman we found inside the cabin. I've never seen two people so exactly alike. No wonder she believed she could convince everyone that she was the real Kelsey Jennings. How far was she willing to take the con? Would she have let her sister die in the cabin? According to her record and the psychiatric report in her juvenile file, she had no problem with murder if she thought it was justified.

She stands and immediately starts running.

Toward me. Not away.

Is she really that crazy to assume that I'll help her? Why? Because we've been physical. She shot me. And she had a woman in a glass cage.

"Oh, thank God . . . help me! Please!"

I draw my gun. "Stop right there!"

"Are you a cop? Oh my God—thank God." She keeps running toward me on fragile legs.

What the hell? Is the darkness preventing her from seeing that it's me? "Holly Sterling, you are under arrest. Stop where you are."

Her expression clouds, then takes on a frantic look. "No! No . . . I'm not Holly. I'm Kelsey Jennings. I've been held hostage for days . . . over a week." She winces and rubs her head.

A matching bruise to the one the woman in the cage had on her head. What the fuck is happening here?

She steps toward me.

I raise the gun higher, but I see her torn, dirty clothing. "Holly, it's me, Detective Ryan. I know who you are now."

"No! I'm telling you, I'm not Holly. Holly is back at the cabin . . . she might be dead. She tried to kill me. We fought. I didn't mean to hurt her, but I had to get away. I'm Kelsey Jennings. My sister abducted me about a week ago." She struggles to speak calmly, clearly.

A shadow of a doubt has me lowering the gun slightly. "You're saying you were held captive?"

"Yes! Help me! It's my deranged sister, Holly. She found me . . . she hit me in the head and locked me away . . . she was trying to steal my identity. She mentioned my daughter, who is supposed to be with her grandparents overseas . . . is Mikayla okay?" She starts to cry and moves closer.

What the hell is going on? There's zero recognition on her face when she looks at me. "Ma'am, please stay where you are."

"Please help me. Just tell me if my daughter is okay. She's still with her grandparents, right? Please . . . just tell me. She didn't hurt my daughter, did she? Holly is crazy . . ."

I'm starting to think we all are. "Mikayla Jennings is fine." I'll give her that much, at least, but I refuse to assume this woman is the mother.

I stare at her. Those eyes, those fucking familiar eyes. But I got the same prickly sense in the cabin looking at the other woman. So identical. Both insane if both are acting . . .

"Oh, thank God," she says again.

For a woman who was supposedly kidnapped and abused, she's giving a lot of credit up above. I stopped believing in a higher power fifteen years ago.

"Please, you have to believe me. I'm not Holly. I'm Kelsey."

"Why would Holly release you? We found *her* in the glass cage."

"She's crazy! She's trying to steal my life! She let me go, we fought, and then I guess she must have gotten in there to make it look like she was me. You have to believe me, please."

She stumbles, falls forward, and seemingly loses consciousness when she hits the ground at my feet.

"Paul!" My father's voice is the only concrete, logical thing I can grab onto. My own injury and loss of blood make my own legs weak. I'm confused and disoriented as the woods around me start to spin.

Next, I'm falling to the ground next to whoever this woman really is.

September 15—4:00 a.m.

"It's like looking at the same woman."

I turn to my father. "That's why they're called twins, Dad," I mutter. I've been trying to get him to stop talking for ten minutes now. He's convinced he can smooth things over with Captain Baker, but he's only making things worse.

I was facing a suspension, and I hadn't been cleared by our doctors to resume working. I shouldn't have been out there tonight.

"So, both women are claiming to be Kelsey Jennings?" Captain Baker looks annoyed that we are all too stupid to tell two people apart. He paces behind his desk at the station, his coffee-stained shirt missing a button around the midsection.

"Yes, sir. We're holding both right now for further questioning." The women are sitting in separate cells, both claiming to be the victim. And both are crazy convincing about it. Though in completely different ways. One is freaking out, demanding a lawyer, and demanding to be released. The other is cooperating. Calm and patient.

I'm not sure which reaction is the most genuine.

"Well, it's obvious that the one in the glass cage was the prisoner," Captain Baker says.

You would think so. "Not entirely. This woman, Holly Sterling, the victim's identical twin, has been impersonating her sister. She's convinced herself that she's Kelsey, and neither woman seems to know who

I am . . . despite spending the last week and a half on the missing-child case . . ."

My father sends me a sidelong look, which I ignore. I'll never admit how close I got to this woman. Will she keep her mouth shut about it once we figure out which one she is? Captain Baker will have my badge if he learns I've had relations with the impersonating woman. My career is on thin ice already. I'm not sure I'm ready to find out which woman is telling the truth.

"The wild goose chase case, you mean?" Captain Baker is seriously annoyed. His retirement is in sight. This is the last shit show he wants to deal with before he leaves.

"Yes, sir."

Captain Baker shakes his balding head. His comb-over shifting. "DNA is not helpful?"

"No, sir. They match almost as though they are the same person."

He eyes me as he sits on the edge of his desk. "You spent time with this impersonator—you can't tell them apart?"

Both have the same piercing eyes, tortured souls. Both are equally tempting . . . my body reacts physically to them both, which is complete bullshit, knowing what I know now. These women are manipulative and dangerous. What the hell is wrong with me? "No, sir."

"This is crazy." He stands and paces. "Can we order a lie detector test on them both?"

"We can, but I'm not sure how accurate it will be . . . Holly Sterling successfully fooled the department therapist during her psych evaluation . . . and the twins' parents were actors."

My father clears his throat, and Captain Baker raises an eyebrow. "My mother was an Olympic gold medalist for gymnastics—do you see me capable of performing on the parallel bars?"

"No, sir." Okay, so it was a dumb thing to assume the twins may have inherited their parents' talents. But if he actually took a look at them himself, talked to them, he might be a little less quick to assess this situation.

"Go! Order the tests," he says. "We need to start somewhere."

"Yes, sir." My father and I stand as Parsons knocks on the door.

"What?" Captain Baker asks sharply.

"Hey, um . . . have we fingerprinted the women yet?" she asks.

Captain Baker looks at me.

"No. Not yet."

"Identical twins have different prints, and we have Holly Sterling's in her file, from her juvenile offenses, so we just need a confirmed match and then we'd know which one she is," Parsons says, the clearheaded genius she is.

Captain Baker stares at me in disbelief. "Why the fuck are you still sitting there?"

September 15—7:09 a.m.

"I'm not Holly Sterling." The woman I found in the forest looks better now. She's been cared for by medical and has eaten. She's in clean clothes—prison scrubs with the Ellicott City PD logo on them, but at least they're clean.

She seems clear minded and determined now. If she is the real Kelsey Jennings, I expect a lawsuit once all this is over.

"Well, then, you have nothing to worry about, do you?" I study her. She gives zero indication—words or body language—that she's even seen me before our encounter in the woods. No recognition. No remorse or guilt. No memory whatsoever of us being together.

She's either a fantastic actress or the real Kelsey Jennings.

Unfortunately, the next woman acts the exact same way.

"I'm not the one who should be behind bars," she says immediately as we take her out of her holding cell.

I sigh. "That's what the other one said."

"She is not me! How stupid are you people? I was the one in the goddamn cage when you found me."

"The other woman claims you put yourself in there after she escaped the cage." I can hear myself. I know this is insane.

What I'm trying to determine is which reaction is the most credible—the calm, collected nature of the first woman or this erratic, angry temper of the second. How would the innocent act when wrongfully accused?

"And you can't figure this out? I know my daughter is back from overseas with her grandparents . . . Holly told me. Let my daughter see us. She will know who her mother is."

"We don't think that's a good idea."

"Who's we?" Her tone is icy and so is her skin as I take her hand to do the printing.

"Meredith and Walter Jennings agree that it will be too confusing for the child to see two of you."

She whips her hand back. "There's only one of me!"

Wow . . . is the Kelsey I was intimate with capable of this theatric nature? Is everything an act with her? The tears and desperation the first day at the day care . . . the lust and sexual attraction in her bed . . . her sister's bed. Pretending not to know me . . . at all.

This has all been a mind fuck, and I can't seem to focus on the case without thinking about how this has all affected me . . . affects me still.

"You'd want to put her through that?" I ask, more for a reaction than anything. Either way, it's not happening. An old parable from the Bible about a ruler suggesting cutting a baby in half to see which woman would protest to prove which one is the mother flashes in my mind. So far, this is the only thing tipping me toward the other "Kelsey."

But then this one sobs and shakes her head. "No. Of course not. But I haven't seen her in days. I just want to know she's okay."

"She's fine. She contracted a virus in the country they'd been visiting, so they returned home immediately. The Jenningses say she's feeling much better." I tell her only what I told the first one.

She nods as I hand her a tissue to wipe the ink from her fingers. "Good . . . I'm glad she's okay."

I watch her hands, all destroyed and damaged from her fight for survival against her twin. What kind of crazy relationship do these women have? Their stories about what happened line up exactly. The months of Facebook harassment, the stalking, the abduction . . . every detail matches, except they both claim to be the victim in the story.

"Sit tight a little longer. We'll submit these prints to the lab, and we'll know soon enough which one of you is Kelsey Jennings."

Her face clouds. "Wait. That's what this is? You're trying to identify us by our prints?"

"You're twins. It's really the only way to tell you both apart."

She grips my forearm. New desperation and fear on her face. "No! That won't work!"

My heart races, and my skin crawls beneath her touch. I uncurl her fingers from my arm. I don't want her touching me. "Identical twins have different prints. It will work."

She shakes her head.

Here we go. Here comes the truth.

"It may tell you who the real Kelsey is, but it will be wrong."

"You're making no sense."

"Holly and I switched places before . . . as kids. The prints will lead to you setting the wrong woman free."

My fucking brain hurts, and I'm so done with the *Parent Trap* garbage these women are pulling. I slam my hand onto the desk when she continues her rant.

She stops talking but doesn't flinch.

"I'm done with the bullshit. One of you shot me. One of you kidnapped the other and tried to kill her." One of you fucked me and used me in whatever twisted game you're trying to play. "One of you is going to prison, and since neither of you will tell the truth, the prints will decide your fate."

I leave the room, ignoring her desperate pleas once more as she's led back to her cell. I can't get this shit solved and these women out of my life fast enough.

September 15—11:23 a.m.

Fingerprints. My way out of this.

I watch my sister sitting in her cell next to mine. Once again she's in a cage, awaiting her fate. She's freaking out and crying. She actually looks sincere.

I just need to be a better actress than she is.

I stare at her. I know the truth now, so even if a part of me feels bad for what I've done, I need to be the one getting out of here.

I gave her a way out years ago when we switched places at the foster home. Gave her every opportunity to turn her life around, to leave her past behind. Live a fantastic life. Do better. Be better. And she squandered it.

Killing her husband in a car accident, giving up custody of her baby girl—what the hell was she thinking? All for money and her obsession with a dancing career that just wasn't meant to be . . . I want to scream at her through the bars. I want to reach across and pull her hair, shake her, make her finally smarten up.

She has a beautiful, perfect daughter. She doesn't even have enough love for her own child to try to turn things around. She doesn't deserve Mikayla. She can't take care of her anyway.

I've always given my sister the benefit of the doubt. When everyone else thought she was insane, psychotic, dangerous, I chose to believe that she was a troubled, damaged kid trying to survive horrific circumstances who just needed love and guidance to see that she could let her guard down and accept good things into her life. I believed she killed those foster parents to save us.

Now, I believe what everyone else said about her.

They say twins share a soul. I think in our case, I got the full one and my sister got none.

This will be better for everyone. A few months from now, I'll prove that I can care for Mikayla, and I'll get custody back. We will be a family, and that little girl will get the mother she deserves. One who wouldn't throw it all away. One who knows how special a mother's love really is. I'll make amends with the Jenningses. Let them know I no longer want their money . . . this experience will have "changed" me. Apologize to them for all the hurt my sister—all the hurt I—caused. Repent for her sins. Now, my sins.

I shouldn't have to do it. I should be able to walk away from this and be myself. Let them get to know me and love me for me. I could adopt Mikayla as Aunt Kelsey . . . I guess that might be a little confusing for her, though, and we need to do what's best for her. Always.

I see Detective Ryan watching us, so I can't get mad or upset. I need to be calm and calculated. Show no sign that I know him, despite the fact that I do know him—so well. I feel bad for shooting him. I'm glad he didn't die. I just needed to find the truth, and I knew I couldn't trust him. Right now, he's desperate for a sign to tell him which one I am. Does he want me to be the good one? The one who walks free?

In time, I'll find him again. As this new, innocent victim who is piecing her life back together. Of course, I'll have to wear the stains of my sister's sins . . . I hate her a little for that. I'm a good person. I shouldn't have to live forever tarnished by her actions, but if that's what it takes to make things right, I'll have to live with it.

I like Detective Ryan. He's smart. He's caring. Most of all, he can't resist me. And while he may believe I'm someone else, he will fall for this version of me just as easily. At my core, I'm the same, and he won't be able to resist the magnetic pull that drew him to me in the first place.

His eyes on me now are scrutinizing. Such a good man. Tortured by his inability to figure this out. It's not his fault, I want to tell him. My sister and I have mastered this switch.

The young woman they call Parsons appears, and she speaks to Detective Ryan.

In the next cell, my sister jumps up and stands next to the door. I stare at her. She knows how this is going to go. There's terror in her expression and desperation in her voice as she pleads for them to listen to her.

But fingerprints don't lie like we do.

It's my cage that Detective Ryan opens.

September 15—1:23 p.m.

In one room, Kelsey Jennings . . . the *real* Kelsey Jennings—mother and widow—sits with her in-laws. Her little girl, Mikayla, sits on her lap, and tears of happiness stream down the woman's face. She's dressed in clean clothes, and all her personal belongings have been returned to her. She's being released. She looks happy and relieved . . . and still shows no sign of knowing me at all.

In the room across the hall, Holly Sterling sits in handcuffs, waiting to be taken into custody. She's screaming and irate and insists that we are making a mistake. Threats of lawsuits spew from her mouth. She's demanding to see her in-laws, her daughter . . . a lawyer. I wait for her to realize the game is over, to give up the act and show any sign that she knows me.

We've questioned her about Doug Beinfeld and the missing teens— the bodies we found . . . the ones we haven't—but she denies knowing anything about it. She claims she wasn't the one in that cabin in the woods for all those years, the one who could have ended the torture and abuse of those innocent victims.

I crave for one of them to look at me with some recognition. Otherwise, with both women denying any knowledge of those past abductions, I'll never get the truth about what happened to my sister. Though if this Holly woman is as insane as her file suggests, maybe she's convinced herself that she is really her sister . . . she's been able to put on a convincing show before.

From the hallway, I look back and forth between the two rooms. Two physically identical women. So very different on the inside.

Has this always been the balance between these twins? One good. One evil. One deserving of love, freedom, a second chance. The other . . . what? What does Holly deserve?

Fortunately it isn't up to me to decide.

It's time to end this nightmare case. I knock once on the open door and enter the room with the family reunion.

Tears of joy stream down this Kelsey's face as she receives support from her father-in-law. "Oh my God . . . I'm so happy to see you," she tells her daughter.

"Mommy crying?" the little girl asks.

"I just missed you, sweetheart . . ." Kelsey smooths her daughter's hair. Hair exactly like hers. The little girl looks like a miniature version of her mother and her aunt. Unfortunately, I fear, she may have inherited some of her aunt's genetics as well.

Kelsey glances at her mother-in-law. "Are you all okay?"

The relationship may be strained, but there's concern on the older woman's face. The couple was shocked to learn about Holly. They never knew Kelsey had a twin. Seems she wanted to leave every aspect about her tumultuous upbringing in the past . . . I feel a slight pang of sympathy for Holly. Is it really a crime to have wanted her sister back? I know how that feels, and it's clouding my emotions right now. Making me see something in the crazy woman that isn't really there.

"We're fine, dear," Meredith tells her daughter-in-law. "It's been a terrifying forty-eight hours. Are you hurt?"

"No . . . I'm okay." Kelsey hugs her daughter tight again, and her gaze meets mine above the little girl's head.

An irrational irritation courses through me.

I want to believe Kelsey . . . Holly. All my instincts were right about her, yet I want to somehow be wrong. I wanted the case to be a simple parental abduction. Malcolm Jennings would be the villain in the story. The little girl would be okay.

No one could have predicted this going as it has.

"You are all free to leave whenever you're ready," I say. "I apologize again for the holdup. I trust that you all understand that we needed to be sure . . . for your family's continued safety."

Walter Jennings steps forward and shakes my hand. He's different today from how he was the first time we met. He understands now that I was only doing my job before, trying to make sure his granddaughter was safe. "We do. Sorry for the inconvenience our family caused the department. We'll be sure to make a donation in the coming year."

Money. They have lots of it.

But the man looks like he wishes this had ended differently . . . with both women behind bars maybe? While he must be relieved that the "psychotic" twin with the history of murdering people is in custody, maybe he thinks his daughter-in-law isn't exactly innocent either.

Their family problems are not my concern.

"I'm sure the department will appreciate that." I nod politely to his wife and turn to walk away, but Kelsey calls out to me.

I turn back.

"Thank you," she says.

I simply nod. She's not welcome. Saving her has cost me more than I'll admit. I walk away and out of the room. I don't pause as I pass Holly's holding cell.

Regardless of whatever other twisted truths have emerged in this case, at least one of these women belongs behind bars . . .

March 4—9:00 a.m.

Six months later . . .

I hug Mikayla tight at the door of Paradise Day Care. It's the best one in town. My sister was right. And since our little incident, they've stepped up their security—a better drop-off and pick-up process, with signing in and out, more security cameras . . . Ms. Bennett is happy to have us. It's helped restore their image in the community. They didn't lose a child. It was all just a misunderstanding.

I breathe in the soft, baby powdery scent, and I'm reluctant to let go. I've only seen her twice a week and every other weekend for the last six months as we work things out—the Jenningses and I. I've made the house a home . . . replacing a lot of Holly's things with new stuff. Things I like. Furniture that makes sense with a toddler in the house. I've learned Mikayla's routine, and I've picked up this parenting thing quickly. All children need is love. That's all anyone needs. And for the first time in my life, I'm getting it in return. I'm a natural mother—caring, nurturing, attentive, patient. Even the Jenningses seem to have seen the change in me.

If they're questioning whether I'm really their daughter-in-law, they haven't voiced their suspicions . . . they didn't spend a lot of time with my sister before, so now they might even be questioning whether she/I was as bad as Malcolm claimed. Guess they've realized that, either way, I'm the better twin.

Mikayla's smiling, happy face when she looks at me is validation that I've done the right thing. My sister could never be the mother to Mikayla that I will be.

Holly's been calling me from prison. I see the number lighting up on the cell phone, and I send the call straight to voice mail. She pleads for me to come see her. She says we need to talk. But I'm over that now. I tried to be in her life, be a sister to her, and she pushed me away every time. She rejected me.

Now she'll know what that feels like.

"I'll be back in a few hours, okay, sweetheart?" I tell Mikayla, kissing her cheek again quickly before Rebecca takes her into the playroom with the other kids.

Today is the day. The custody hearing is set for ten a.m.

Malcolm's parents are not contesting my parenting application. Over the past six months, I've made an amazing recovery. The clearance letter from my therapist, along with the statement from Malcolm's parents saying that I've become a new person since the incident, are enough to make everything okay again.

I stand and wave as Jacqueline leads Mikayla inside the day care toward the playroom. I sign her in for the day and scrawl my signature on the parent-authorization line.

Kelsey Sterling.

Once again, I get to be me.

March 4—10:45 a.m.

I shouldn't be here. The case was solved months ago, and this issue of custody is none of my business. Meredith and Walter Jennings requested a full statement of what happened from the department—that's the only reason I even knew this was scheduled for this morning.

Truth is, I haven't been able to let go. I haven't seen Kelsey Jennings in six months, except for every waking moment in my thoughts and in my troubled dreams at night. My gut still thinks there's more to this story. I'm not sure this has ended as neatly wrapped as we've made it appear.

So, here I am in the back of the courtroom, trying to duck out unnoticed as the judge gives his final judgment.

Kelsey Sterling—she's gone back to her original last name—will once again have full custody of her daughter, Mikayla.

I'm happy for her. I think.

As I've stared at the back of her head for the last hour in the courtroom, my thoughts and emotions have spiraled. Why can't I let this go? Let *her* go? It was a casual affair that never should have happened. And she's not even the woman I was intimate with.

It was a stupid misguided mistake that could have cost me my job.

Funny that Holly Sterling hasn't tried to do just that. She's been behind bars for six months, still claiming she's been wrongfully accused. No one is listening. By now, I'd think she would have changed her story.

Admit to being Holly and then try to sabotage my life by outing the affair . . .

Maybe she really doesn't know that part of the story, but entertaining that thought opens this case up again, and that's not something I'm eager to do. Unfortunately, she was sentenced to only fifteen years for the abduction of her sister and attempted murder of a police officer, so my gut tells me I may be dealing with this family again in the future.

I jog down the courthouse steps and head for my car. The spring day is bright and sunny. I wish it were dark and raining.

"Hey, Detective Ryan!"

I should keep walking. Pretend I don't hear her. Looking into the eyes, so eerily familiar, is too much of a mind fuck. But I stop as I feel her hand on my back. I have no other choice. My spine tingles at her touch as though I'm paralyzed, frozen to the spot. I turn slowly. "Hi . . . Mrs. Jennings . . ." She's dressed in a light-gray suit, with a white blouse underneath and two-inch heels. Practical, sensible court clothes, and still my body reacts the same way it did when she was in revealing yoga clothing. Her hair is pulled back away from her face in a high ponytail, and her makeup, clean and natural, subtly covers the remaining scars from the attack. Her magnetic pull is stronger than ever.

"I'm not Mrs. Jennings anymore, as of today," she says softly.

That's right. "Sorry, Ms. Sterling."

"That's okay." Her voice is thick, hoarse. She was emotional in the courtroom as she apologized for her past mistakes, her past failings as a parent, and recounted how the events of six months ago had changed her. The temptation to comfort her is overwhelming. "Please, call me Kelsey," she says.

That's difficult. I've already known one Kelsey. I don't need to get friendly with an exact replica of another.

I clear my throat. "So, things worked out in there . . . congratulations."

She smiles. So sincere. So real. No trace of the twisted, broken woman I knew . . . so maybe it really isn't her.

Jesus. This back-and-forth will drive me to the brink of insanity. Holly is in jail. I need to believe and accept that. Stop looking for signs that the woman I can't stop craving, can't stop thinking about, is standing in front of me. A free woman.

"Thank you. It's been a challenging few months . . . year, really, but I'm ready to move forward."

I nod. "Well, good luck." I turn to walk away.

"Wait . . . I wanted to give you this." She extends a small wooden jewelry box toward me. It's old, and the corner is broken off. An engraved bird and initials—H. B. on the lid.

I refuse to take it. "What is it?"

"I found it among my things at the house. It's not mine. Holly must have had it . . . please."

I take the box and open the lid. Inside is my sister's necklace. My hand shakes, and I nearly drop it. I haven't seen this necklace in fifteen years. Looking at it now, I can see it around her neck. I remember the day my parents gave it to her. It's the first real sign that she was out there in those woods as well . . . that Holly may have known, may have seen her, may have been able to prevent her death.

Too many emotions are wrapped up in a simple piece of jewelry.

"It was engraved to another girl . . . so I assume it might be from one of the victims . . . Holly's adoptive father's victims." She sounds sad, remorseful, as though even those horrific tragedies were somehow her fault, connected to her by the unfortunate family connection.

"My sister. This belonged to my sister." I'm not sure why I say it. Probably to explain my reaction to it.

Sympathy fills her expression. So kind. So unlike the Kelsey I once started to foolishly fall for. "I'm sorry. So, so sorry . . ."

I nod and swallow the lump in my throat.

"I assume it means . . ." Her voice trails off.

That my sister was one of Holly's "grandpa's" victims and that the woman behind bars was an accessory to the murders. "Yes, I assume it does." I close the box quickly. "Thank you. I'll submit this for evidence." Evidence that Julia was in those woods, perhaps in that cabin, tortured, used, abused by the man Holly was living with. Trapped inside that glass cage.

Did Holly know the whole time who I was? Did she know that she may have been able to save my sister? I told her about Julia. I explained the damage her disappearance had caused my family. She knew that my father and I were still searching . . . she could have ended all that. She could have given me peace. The anger coursing through my veins should be enough to extinguish the longing and desire I have for the woman, but it isn't.

I turn to walk away, but Kelsey says my name again. I pause.

"If you ever want to talk . . . I mean, I just know what it feels like to lose family . . . lose a sister, in a different way," she says. "To feel lost and hopeless, as though somehow it's my fault that I couldn't save her."

The kindness, the understanding, in her voice does something to my insides. They twist and coil. She looks just like the other one, but this one isn't crazy, just a little damaged.

You like the damaged ones, don't you, Detective?

I should just walk away from her. Nothing good can come of continuing to know this woman. Yet, I hesitate. "Yeah . . . I mean, if you're free sometime . . . maybe I can buy you a coffee, and we can talk?" I hold up the box. "A thank-you for this."

"I'd like that," she says.

"Great." I start to walk backward toward my car with a wave.

She smiles, and all I see is her sister. And maybe that's enough. Maybe my mind, my body, my feelings can be tricked into believing this woman—the good twin—is the one I want.

My forced smile falls from my lips as the detective walks away. Seems that even though I have my identity back, the only way I'll ever get the things I want is by pretending to be my sister.

It doesn't matter, though. I've given Paul at least some of the closure he was looking for. And also evidence. Evidence that my sister was involved in those missing cases for all those lost girls . . . so now I can rest easy. I won't have to worry about her getting out of jail too soon and ruining the quiet, peaceful life I've found, the one I deserve.

My perfect life. Finally.

ACKNOWLEDGMENTS

Thank you to my amazing agent, Jill Marsal—your support and encouragement mean everything. Thank you to my wonderful editors, Jessica Tribble, Charlotte Herscher, and Bill Siever, who always make my books stronger with their insightful feedback, and to the entire team at Thomas & Mercer Publishing. A big thank-you to Detective Ryan Ferry of the Edmonton Police Department and Mark Hogan at Canada Border Services Agency for all the research help. All mistakes in procedures are my own. As always, this book wouldn't have been possible without the support of my husband and son, who are my biggest cheerleaders and can find food and clean clothing for themselves anytime . . . but especially when I'm on deadline. And thank you, readers, for giving me the opportunity to continue doing what I love.

ABOUT THE AUTHOR

Photo © 2018 PhotoJunkies

J.M. Winchester is the dark alter ego of an author who usually writes happily ever afters. Her fascination with the workings of an evil mind compelled her to start writing psychological thrillers, and *All the Lovely Pieces* is her debut novel in this genre. Originally from the east coast of Canada, she now lives in Alberta with her husband and son. She is a member of Romance Writers of America, International Thriller Writers, and the Film and Video Arts Society of Alberta. More information can be found on her website at www.authorjmwinchester.com.